LETHAL S

Buffalo hunter Billy Ring found himself looking down the business end of a dozen rifles as he entered the Mormon camp. He wisely remained in the saddle, scanning the faces of the company with his crooked eyes until he spotted Gordon Hawkes—at whom he stabbed an accusing finger.

"You!" Ring roared. "I've come to kill you, you son of a bitch! You kilt my brother last summer, and I swore vengeance over his grave. I knew one day we'd meet again. I've been checking everyone who passes this way, and when I heard that someone fittin' Gordon Hawkes's description had shown up at the fort today, I come out to have myself a look. That's you, no question. The man who killed my brother Charley. I'll have your balls for breakfast."

"Name the time and the place, Ring," Hawkes answered.

"The mouth of Laramie Creek. Dawn tomorrow. Be there, or I'll track you down, even if I have to follow you straight down into hell."

MOUNTAIN MASSACRE

Jason Manning

A SIGNET BOOK

SIGNET
Published by New American Library, a division of
Penguin Putnam Inc., 375 Hudson Street,
New York, New York 10014, U.S.A.
Penguin Books Ltd, 27 Wrights Lane,
London W8 5TZ, England
Penguin Books Australia Ltd, Ringwood,
Victoria, Australia
Penguin Books Canada Ltd, 10 Alcorn Avenue,
Toronto, Ontario, Canada M4V 3B2
Penguin Books (N.Z.) Ltd, 182–190 Wairau Road,
Auckland 10, New Zealand

Penguin Books Ltd, Registered Offices:
Harmondsworth, Middlesex, England

First published by Signet, an imprint of New American Library,
a division of Penguin Putnam Inc.

First Printing, June 1999
10 9 8 7 6 5 4 3 2 1

Printed in the United States of America

PART ONE

Chapter 1

As he always did when he was about to leave his mountain sanctuary, Gordon Hawkes rose before the sun, slipping out of the cabin with no more sound than a ghost might have made, leaving his wife and young son undisturbed in their slumbers. He walked to the corral where his horse, a dun mountain mustang still shaggy with its winter coat, nickered a soft recognition, while its two companions, the mules, eyed him warily. Saddling the mustang quickly, Hawkes secured to the hull his Plains rifle, cocooned in a fringed buckskin sheath, and looped his cartridge pouch and possibles bag over the horn. The long winter was over, the snow beginning to melt beneath the onslaught of the spring sun, yet the nights remained cold, and his breath clouded as he gave the cinch one last hard tug. He fit a moccasined foot into a stirrup, and hoisted himself into the saddle. With one final look at the darkened cabin, he turned into the evergreens that rimmed the sloping meadow.

Finding the familiar trail, he began to ascend the steep, wooded mountain shoulder. Now and then he could see the valley below as the trees thinned at rocky outcroppings. The soft gold of the morning sun touched the snow-capped peaks opposite, even as night shadows clung stubbornly to the lowlands. Hawkes knew that before long Eliza would be rising, stirring up the embers of last night's fire, adding kindling and a log or two. She would not be alarmed by his absence. She would know, based on past experience, what he was up to, for today they would leave the valley for the first time in many months, and though he seldom discussed his anxieties, she was well aware of his reluctance to venture forth into the world.

And why shouldn't he be reluctant? Gordon Hawkes had received more than his fair share of misery at the hands of his fellow man. At least that was his conviction. Born the son of a poor Irish potato farmer, he had watched his father die, slowly wasting away from ship fever during the voyage to America. Tom Hawkes had grand dreams of a new beginning in the new land, but he'd found only a watery grave instead, hundreds of miles from the promised land that had so beguiled him.

His father's wretched death had been only the beginning for Hawkes. It had been a long and difficult journey from that sad day until more than a year later when he had first set eyes on the Shining Mountains, and many more months of betrayal, disillusionment, and danger until he had finally found his refuge—Eliza Hancock, the frail, yellow-haired daughter of a Methodist missionary slain by Indians.

But Eliza was only part of his sanctuary. This valley, where they had lived in relative peace for eight years, was the rest of it. Here they had given birth to Cameron, now seven years of age. Hawkes smiled as he imagined Cameron's excitement as he woke to the day he had longed for all those long winter months—the day he went with his father and mother to Fort Bridger. This was the outpost the famous mountain man and Indian fighter, Jim Bridger, "Old Gabe" as his friends called him, had built on Black's Fork of the Green River, in Shoshone country down near the Uinta range, hard by the Oregon Trail. More and more emigrants were rolling west these days, and while, like most mountain men, Bridger didn't have much good to say about emigrants, he was wise enough to know that the fur trade was dying and there was a future in catering to the needs of the pioneers. His post, complete with blacksmith forge and stocked to the rafters with provisions, was meant to provide supplies and repairs to the emigrant families. It was also a favorite gathering place of that fast vanishing breed, the mountain man.

Fort Bridger was a good ten-day journey south of this valley, but it was the nearest source for the few supplies Hawkes needed—powder and shot, some coffee and sugar, and a little tobacco for his pipe. Eliza and Cameron looked forward to the annual visit for other reasons. Unlike Hawkes, they missed the company of others. Now and then someone would drop in on them, an acquaintance from the days when Hawkes had been associated with the Rocky Mountain Fur Company, or an occasional party of Absaroka Crow braves, passing through and stopping by to visit their white brother. For the most part, though, they lived in complete isolation. And that suited Hawkes.

But was it fair to Eliza, and especially to Cameron? Hawkes felt a little guilty as he rode ever higher up the mountain trail astride his sure-footed dun. If Cameron wasn't up by now he soon would be, itching to go, impatient for his father's return. Cameron needed to be with other children, and there were always children at Fort Bridger. A few lived there year-round now, and there were many more passing through, the offspring of trappers or traders and their Indian wives, or emigrants bound for points west.

The only other opportunity for Cameron to associate with children his own age was on the rare occasions that Hawkes called on the Absaroka Crows. In late autumn, as the gold and russet leaves of the hardwoods began to fall, an Absaroka band made its winter camp a few days' hard riding north of this valley, at the southern limits of Crow country, and every now and again Hawkes would go see them. If he did not they would come looking for him sooner or later. They called him White Crow, and by now every band in the tribe knew who he was and what he had done. Hawkes had saved the lives of a chief's wife and son, and while he'd had a bit of trouble with the tribe later on, thanks to his refusal to participate in a raid on a defenseless Blackfoot village, he remained their brother, and would until the day he died. No Crow would raise a hand in anger against him. So when Hawkes visited he brought Cameron and Eliza along, and Cameron played with the Indian boys. It was good experience for him, thought Hawkes, who assumed that his son would make these mountains his home when he was old enough to decide for himself the course his life would take. After all, a mountain man's life was the only one worth living.

At last Hawkes reached his destination, a high shelf of land at the timberline, where he could stand on a rocky, windswept ledge and view the length and breadth of his valley thousands of feet below, or gaze beyond he nearest peaks to the east and see the majestic sweep of the mountains, jagged and blue and snow-capped, extending as far as the human eye could see. Dismounting, Hawkes took the precaution of removing the sheathed Plains rifle from the saddle, ground-hitched the mustang, and went to stand at the brink of the ledge; ordinarily, the horse remained close by, but Hawkes wasn't one to make mistakes like leaving the dun in possession of the rifle. A .41 caliber percussion pistol and a Bowie knife adorned the wide leather belt at his waist, but Hawkes relied on his long gun. Grizzlies and other bears roamed these high slopes. He'd been confronted by the great beasts on more than one occasion, and he had a healthy respect for them. Survival in the high country meant avoiding those greenhorn errors in judgment. As Old Gabe was fond of saying, hell was chock full of greenhorns.

He stood there for a long while, a tall and slender man, a man of scars and sinew, his sandy hair and beard already flecked with gray though he was only in his twenty-sixth year. The beard made him look older, and so did the creases on his weathered brow, and the piercing squint of his sun-faded eyes. From top to bottom he was garbed in buckskin, blackened in places from long use, from his moccasins to the "half-breeds" that covered the lower part of his leggins, to his fringed hunting shirt. Over it all he wore a long buckskin coat lined with fur. Eliza had made it for him. She had become as handy as any Indian woman when it came to working with quill and hide. On his head was a broad-brimmed beaver hat with a low crown.

The wind whispered its seductive song to him as he gazed upon the world he had made his own, watching the night shadows retreat at last as the sunlight flooded the valley floor. He did not feel as though he had conquered this land in any fashion, but rather that he and the land had come to a mutual understanding, and unlike many of the people who populated his past, the land would not betray his trust so long as he did not betray the land. These mountains did not embrace everyone. The bleached bones and unmarked graves of those who had not measured up to its demands were many. He was one of the few who had measured up. He had earned the privilege to call these mountains his home. In return, he honored the mountains, while they sustained him.

More than that, they protected him. They were his refuge precisely because they resisted the encroachment of civilization, which was made up in the vast majority of people who lacked the traits required to survive in the high country. And it was, after all, civilization that Hawkes spurned. This wasn't just because of the murder charge that still, he assumed, hung over his head. Ten years ago he had been falsely accused of the murder of a Louisiana planter. He had killed several men who had thought to collect the bounty placed on his head. But even without the murder charge, even without the threat it posed, he would not have left the mountains, his harborage.

Even going so far afield as Fort Bridger was cause for concern. He didn't like the emigrants. Not because they were bad people—because most of them weren't—but because they brought civilization with them. It lurked like an unseen contagion in their wagons as well as in their dreams, ready to spread across this land and change it in ways Hawkes knew he would not like. They were coming with the idea that they could tame the land, and if for no other reason than that, Hawkes would have set his heart against them. There was more to his distrust of them, though, something intensely personal, something rooted in his past, in all the times that society had chewed him up and spit him out. He wanted nothing to do with society, even the primitive society of a remote frontier outpost like Old Gabe's place. But he had to go. Not just for powder and shot and some Ol' Virginny tobacco, but more important, for Eliza and Cameron.

He had to go—and yet he lingered on the high ledge, soaking in the serenity and beauty of the majestic panorama before him, letting it calm his troubled soul and give him strength. He felt the warmth of the sun between his shoulder blades as it cleared the high reaches behind him. He breathed deep the clean crisp air redolent with the fragrance of the sturdy conifers. From somewhere far off came the rampant cry of an eagle. Each time he came here it was the same—the same sounds, the same smells, the same sights. But of course that was what he valued most, what brought him back, the unchanging nature of the mountains. He always knew what to expect. The same could not be said when it came to dealing with people.

But his thoughts continued to stray to Eliza and Cameron, and his guilt grew more burdensome. He was being selfish, indulging his fears, while they waited. Finally, reluctantly, he turned away from the ledge and went to the mustang, tied his rifle to the saddle, and mounted up.

Arriving at the cabin, Hawkes saw that the two mules had been made ready, one with an old Absaroka "squaw" saddle, the other with a sawbuck pack saddle laden with provisions necessary for the journey and the pack of plews he was set on trading, all lashed down under hides with a diamond-hitched rope. It was a very good job, he noted with approval. Both Eliza and Cameron were adept in mountain ways. Both could pack a mule, set a trap, skin a deer, shoot a rifle, read sign, and do all the myriad things a body had to know how to do in order to live in the high country.

Cameron busted out of the cabin as Hawkes rode in, great expectations illuminating his innocent face. Laying eyes on his son—Eliza said Cameron was his father's spitting image—never failed to fill Hawkes with wonder and gratitude. It filled him, too, with a fierce determination to protect his son from the cruel disillusionment he himself had known in younger years.

"Are we going now, Pa?" asked Cameron hopefully. "Are we?"

"You bet." Dismounting, Hawkes tousled his boy's sandy hair as Eliza emerged from the cabin, smiling knowingly and forgivingly at him. As always when he saw her, Hawkes wondered why he had been so blessed.

"Run inside and fetch your hat and coat, Cam," she

said. When their son had gone, she stepped closer to her husband and put her arms around him, laying her head against his chest. This, Hawkes thought, was his greatest refuge, here in the arms of the woman he loved, and who loved him without reservation.

"We don't have to go," said Eliza, "if you'd rather not."

"No. We'll go."

"I'd just as not go, actually," she said earnestly, and he held her at arm's length, searching her eyes, and seeing that she was deeply troubled.

"What's wrong, Eliza?"

"It's nothing, really."

"Tell me straight out."

She shrugged, expressing the inconsequence of what she was about to confess. "I had a bad dream, that's all." Seeing that this was not enough to satisfy him, she added, "It was about you, Gordon."

"Well, I should hope so," he joked, but his feeble attempt at levity fell flat.

"You were being chased by bad men, and they shot you, and then there was this . . . this angel who came to you and . . . and she took you away . . ." She shook her head fiercely, curling a stray tendril of pale yellow hair behind an ear. "Like I said, it was just a silly dream."

Cameron came bolting out of the cabin again. "I'm ready!" he declared. "Let's get a move on! I can't wait to get to the fort, can you, Ma?"

She smiled gently at his enthusiasm. "No, I can't wait, either, Cam." She glanced at Hawkes, and he nodded, for they both knew not going would break their son's heart, and so they put aside their fears for Cameron's sake. Hawkes helped them aboard the saddle mule and then led the way astride the shaggy mountain mustang. Leading the pack mule, they left the valley's protection behind.

Chapter 2

Fort Bridger had been built in the summer of 1842, in the valley of Black's Fork, astride the route the emigrant wagons would take as they rolled out of South Pass. Old Gabe had partnered up with Louis Vasquez, and since both of them were savvy businessmen who could tell the way the wind was blowing, they'd foreseen the end of the fur trade and appreciated the wisdom of branching out. The post consisted of four log cabins with dirt roofs and dirt floors, encompassed by an eight-foot palisade, rising up from the valley's long grass hard by the river, which was running high and handsome when Gordon Hawkes arrived. The valley was flanked by wooded foothills, and the craggy mountain peaks still heavy with snow soared beyond.

Down from the high country came Hawkes and his family, and after many long days of travel Hawkes was almost as happy as Eliza and Cameron to see the smoke from the outpost's chimneys. It had rained on them for several days straight, and only now were the skies clearing, the clouds chasing their afternoon shadows across the heavy wet spring grass that brushed the belly of the mustang and the mules. Bridger and his wife and a couple of dogs ventured out of the gate to meet them. As Hawkes emerged from the cottonwoods that lined the swollen river, the dogs bounded forward, barking up a storm, but with a single piercing whistle Old Gabe summoned them back.

"Howdy, hoss," said Bridger as Hawkes drew near. "Glad to see you're still above snakes. Eliza, you're as purty as ever. And who might this young feller be? Is that you, Cameron? By God, you done growed a good foot since I seen you last. Step down, you all, and make yourselves at home."

As he swung stiffly out of the saddle to clasp Old Gabe's proffered hand, Hawkes nodded in the direction of the fort. "Looks pretty quiet around here."

Bridger nodded. He was a slight and wiry man—Hawkes towered over him. But only in that sense did he out-measure Old Gabe. Bridger had been in the mountains for a quarter of a century; he had come up the Missouri with Ashley and Henry and the rest of the Rocky Mountain Fur Company back in '22. As trapper, pathfinder, and Indian fighter he had no peer, with the possible exception of Kit Carson and Tom "Broken Hand" Fitzpatrick. Bridger was an expert tracker and crack shot. No one questioned his courage or intelligence, and his memory was a true wonder. He knew the mountain country like the back of his hand. He also knew about a dozen Indian dialects, as well as Spanish and the French of the *couriers de bois*. His weathered face was always clean-shaven; he said it was on account of his wife, the daughter of a Flathead chief, preferred it that way.

"The Snakes done lit out a fortnight ago. And we ain't seen the first wagon yet this season. But they'll be along right soon. You can bet on that. The only visitors we got right now would be Dane Gilmartin and his partner. As usual, they're at each other's throats. Vasquez is inside with 'em, just to make sure they don't kill each other. Come on, Gordon—I know Vasquez will be right pleased to see you again."

"He and I do go back a ways," said Hawkes, but

he didn't give much thought at the moment to a reunion with Louis Vasquez, glancing instead, and with some concern, at Cameron. In the past they had arrived at Fort Bridger before the Snakes—or the Shoshones, as they were better known by some—left the valley. Usually their lodges stood beneath the cottonwoods along Black's Fork, and there would be plenty of Indian children for Cameron to run with. But this time they had managed to get here at the worst possible moment from Cameron's point of view, after the Snakes had departed and before the first emigrant wagon train had made an appearance. Bridger had a daughter, but Mary Ann was off at the Whitman Mission School in Oregon. Old Gabe had wanted to make dead certain she could read and write—which was more than he could do—and he had entrusted her "book-larnin' " to his friend Marcus Whitman, sending her up the trail last year with a wagon train. On their last visit there had been the offspring of a couple of trappers and their squaws at the post, as well. But both families had moved on, Bridger said.

Though he tried gamely to disguise his disappointment, Cameron failed in the endeavor, and Hawkes looked from him to Eliza and then to the mountains from whence they had come, and drew a long breath. "Well," he said, "reckon we might linger here a spell, if that suits you, Old Gabe. No reason to hurry back home, I guess."

"I calculate you'll see wagons rollin' in here within a fortnight," predicted Bridger, with a wink at Cameron. "You know by now I ain't never wrong about such things, boy."

They entered the stockade. Bridger's forge occupied one of the cabins. There he repaired wagon wheels and shoed horses for the emigrants. As a lad, he had been apprenticed to a St. Louis blacksmith, so he knew his trade well. He was a fair hand at carpentry, too. Another cabin housed the trading post, while the other two served as residences for the Bridgers and Louis Vasquez and his wife.

A high-sided wagon filled to the brim with bundles of plews stood in front of the trading post. The mules had been removed from their traces and let out to graze in the tall grass along with Bridger's sizable herd of livestock—horses, mules, and even a few cows, many of them acquired from emigrants as payment for services rendered. Hawkes recognized the wagon as the property of Dane Gilmartin and Red Renshaw. They were Indian traders who by all accounts did pretty well for themselves, trading beads and blankets and assorted foofaraw for the skins their Ute, Crow, and Shoshone customers could harvest. Not just beaver pelts, either, but bear and buffalo and fox and mink and otter, too. Ever since Eastern dudes had started up wearing silk hats in lieu of headgear made of beaver fur, the value of "brown gold" had diminished. Every other year or so, Gilmartin and his partner would take their "plunder" east to St. Louis and sell it, returning with more cheap trade goods and a little hard money besides.

As they neared the trading post, Hawkes could hear voices from within raised in anger. Gilmartin and Renshaw were quarreling again. They never seemed to do much else, and it made a person wonder why they'd floated their sticks together all these years. But as Bridger and Hawkes passed through the door, followed by Eliza, Cameron, Mrs. Bridger, and one of Bridger's hounds, the repartee, generously seasoned with colorful profanity, came to an abrupt stop. The two traders were bellied up to a counter, a jug of corn liquor between them. Vasquez stood behind the counter, arms folded, acting as referee. The grizzled oldtimer's expression, one of resignation and amusement as he watched Gilmartin and Renshaw indulge in their verbal fencing, switched in a flash to one of surprise and delight as he recognized Hawkes and his family. He came around the counter in a big hurry, startling the bickering Indian traders into silence, for they weren't used to seeing him move that quickly.

"Well, lookee here!" exclaimed Vasquez, clasping Hawkes's hand in both of his and grinning from ear to ear. "How'd you winter up yonder?"

"No trouble to speak of."

"How could he get into trouble, with the whole Crow nation looking out for him?" asked Gilmartin. Smiling, he came forward and shook hands with Hawkes. A young man, broad in the shoulders and long in the leg, with curly brown hair and a devil-take-all attitude, Gilmartin turned his attention to Eliza, who was just then recovering from a bear hug administered by Vasquez. "And how fares the prettiest woman west of the Mississippi? I swear, Eliza, you're nicer to look at than a mountain sunrise."

Eliza smiled tolerantly. "I'm well, Mr. Gilmartin, thank you."

"Call me Gil. All my friends do. And we *are* friends, aren't we? How many times have I come calling on you folks over the years?"

"I declare, Gil," said Vasquez, who now had Cameron hoisted playfully on one shoulder, "you're lucky Gordon ain't the jealous kind, the way you always make eyes at his woman."

"Eliza has never given me cause to be jealous," remarked Hawkes.

"Well, if she ever decides to, I hope she'll think of me," said Gilmartin.

Hawkes smiled bleakly. He had known Gilmartin for years, but wasn't sure what to make of him. Over at the counter Renshaw drawled, "Pay Gil no mind. He's had too much pop skull, and we all know he can't hold his liquor worth a damn." A burly, square-jawed man, Renshaw glanced sheepishly at Eliza and swept a woolen cap off his head, exposing greasy, carrot-colored locks. "Beg pardon, ma'am. Ain't like me to cuss in the presence of a lady."

"Who are you trying to fool, Red?" asked Gilmartin dryly. "Everybody knows you've got the manners of a ruttin' hog."

Renshaw glowered darkly. "One of these days, boy, you'll push me an inch too far."

Gilmartin laughed at him, and Renshaw's scowl grew darker still. Like Gilmartin, he'd had more than his share of hundred-proof nerve medicine, and he was feeling more ornery than usual.

"Keep the peace, now, boys," advised Bridger, "or I'll keep it for you. We got women present. How 'bout a drink, Gordon?" He circled behind the counter and produced another jug. "Taos Lightning. Turley sent me a heap of it last year."

"Don't mind if I do."

Vasquez announced that he and Cameron were going out to tend to the mules and the dun mustang, and Eliza told Hawkes she was of a mind to pay Mrs. Vasquez a visit. Hawkes laid his Plains rifle on the countertop of whipsawed planks, shouldered the jug, and took a swig. The whiskey burned like liquid flame in his throat. Simon Turley had moved from Missouri to New Mexico in 1830, establishing a distillery and trading post at Arroyo Hondo near Taos, and his tanglefoot was justifiably famous throughout the frontier. Hawkes took another drink and felt the tension of the long trail seep out of his bones.

"I've got some plews," he told Bridger. "Enough to buy a few necessaries—and a few drinks."

Bridger nodded. He accepted whatever Hawkes brought in and gave top dollar without dickering. "That there jug's on me," he said, leaning his elbow on the counter. "I swear, hoss, I wish sometimes I was wearin' your moccasins. These walls close in on me sometimes. I get right weary of messin' with those westerin' greenhorn folk."

"It's a wonder any of 'em get this far," said Renshaw, his voice edgy with contempt. "They don't know beans about how to live out here. How come they're driftin' out here in the first place? We'd all be a long sight better off if they just stayed put where they are."

"They're coming for the same reasons we did," said Gilmartin. "To make a new start and a better life."

"Well, they'll ruin our lives," groused Renshaw. "Purty soon we'll be knee deep in farmers. Then what are we gonna do?"

"We've had some shinin' times," said Bridger pensively, "but times change, and so must we. That's why I'm here. I do the best I can for the folks who pass this way. Lord, Gordon, you ought to see some of the maps those people rely on. It's a wonder half of them don't wind up in Timbuktu. I try to set 'em straight, fix up their wagons, and provide 'em with whatever they need to get the rest of the way to where they're going."

Hawkes was well aware that Old Gabe's knowledge of the mountains, from the great falls of the Missouri River to the pueblos of Taos, was far superior to the information contained on any map. Bridger was particularly contemptuous of the cartographic creations of celebrated pathfinders like John C. Fremont.

"I would have thought your little trip into the Milk River country would have cured your wanderlust, Ol' Gabe," said Hawkes.

Bridger grinned. "I'm older than dirt, it's true—but I still got enough vinegar left in my veins for an adventure or two."

His eyes lost their focus, then, as he remembered the Milk River expedition of two years back. He and thirty men had ventured north into Blackfoot country, lured by rumors of prime beaver there. The rumors turned out to be false. After a handful of scrapes with the Blackfeet, Bridger and his discouraged band showed up at Fort Union, just west of where the Missouri and the Yellowstone rivers met. Hawkes knew Fort Union; coming west with the Rocky Mountain Fur Company, he had met Kenneth McKenzie there. McKenzie was the so-called King of the Missouri, and one of the leaders of the RMFC's opposition, the American Fur Company. A few days shy of Christmas 1844, a large Sioux war party had hit the fort, running off some stock and killing one man. The cowardice of his crew when confronted by the fierce Sioux warriors had disgusted Bridger, and he'd returned home as quickly as possible.

"So what *are* we gonna do when this country fills up with plowpushers?" asked Renshaw a second time. Once he got his teeth into a topic that piqued his interest, he generally worried it to death.

"You they'll probably hang right off," said Gilmartin cheerfully. "One look and they'll know you're a no-account troublemaker that ain't fit to be around civilized folks."

Renshaw snorted. "I got no use for 'em," he growled, helping himself to the jug. "That's why I'm the one who carries our plews to St. Louis. You and Gordon here are a lot alike in one respect—you want nothing to do with people."

Vasquez and Cameron came in with the furs Hawkes had brought for trade. As he rifled through them, Bridger kept throwing glances at Hawkes, which Hawkes studiously ignored. Finally Old Gabe spoke his mind, pitching his voice low so the others couldn't overhear.

"What will *you* do when the land begins to fill up, hoss?"

Hawkes knew perfectly well why Bridger was posing

that question. Old Gabe was one of the few men Hawkes had trusted sufficiently to tell of the murder charge that haunted his past. Bridger had seen that all this talk about the flood of westering emigrants bothered Hawkes, and he could figure out why that was so: with the emigrants came the law. Hawkes wasn't the old mountain man who was wanted for some kind of misdeed back East. Bridger *knew* Gordon Hawkes was innocent because Hawkes had told him so, and the man didn't lie. He was as honest as a looking glass.

"I don't know," replied Hawkes. "Reckon it'll be a while before I have to worry about that."

Chapter 3

The next few days at Fort Bridger were idle ones for Gordon Hawkes. Gilmartin set out for St. Louis in the wagon, and Red Renshaw left the very next day, bound for the mountains. Hawkes envied him, but tried to make the best of his prolonged visit to the outpost. After a few short days he was ready to return to the high country, yet he lingered for Cameron's sake, and Eliza's.

He enjoyed hearing Old Gabe and Louis Vasquez relate their many adventures, even though he had heard the stories many times before. The two mountain men-turned-traders loved to tell tales, and quite often they embellished their narratives to the point that even hearing an old story could turn out to be a new experience. For his part, Hawkes didn't care to dredge up old memories, so he had few tales to add to the mix.

His wife and Mrs. Vasquez, a white woman from back East, got along well. They sat on the handsome chairs Mrs. Vasquez had brought from Philadelphia, and they drank buttermilk while talking about their experiences. Sometimes they read the Bible together. Occasionally Mrs. Bridger would join them. The Flathead princess knew some English, and she was a pleasure to have about because of her unflagging good cheer.

As for Cameron, both Vasquez and Bridger went

to great lengths to keep him occupied, but the way his son kept a vigilant lookout for the emigrant wagons convinced Hawkes that it was necessary to stay on a while longer. The mountains would have to wait. Fort Bridger was about as remote an outpost as one could ask for; still, Hawkes felt vulnerable. It wasn't just that he had a price on his head. That any emigrant who showed up at the fort would know him for the man who was wanted for a killing in far off Louisiana a decade earlier was highly unlikely. But it just seemed to Hawkes as though every time he got anywhere near a bunch of people he came to grief, sooner or later.

The days were sunny and warm—the rains had moved on, and the air was rich with the heady fragrances of spring. The snow-capped peaks of the Uinta range to the north, blue in the distance, beckoned to him. He spent an inordinate amount of time sitting on a stump in front of the trading post, gazing at the mountains. He also spent a good deal of time joining his son in keeping an eye peeled for the first emigrant wagon to roll in from the South Pass.

Bridger had predicted the first wagon train would show up within a fortnight, and he was dead on, as usual. On the sixth day following the arrival of Hawkes and his family, fifteen prairie schooners trundled into view, their Osnaburg tops stretched over hickory bows resembling from a distance the sails of a ship on a grassy sea. Most of them were pulled by teams of oxen. Though slower than mules, oxen were a sensible choice for the overland trek. They were half as costly as mules, thrived on grass and needed no grain, and were more durable and predictable than knobheads.

The crack of the eighteen-foot bullwhips brandished by drivers walking on the left side of the lumbering teams made Hawkes wince. The sound reminded him of the cat-o-nines the captain of the *Penelope*—the ship that had carried him from Dublin to New York harbor—had used on him with entirely too much relish. It was funny, he mused, how something so long past could bother him still. The scars left on his back by Captain Warren's cat-o-nines had disappeared long ago. But there were other scars, invisible ones, that remained.

These were the first emigrants Hawkes had seen. Old Gabe had told him that a small party had come west in '41, some reaching Oregon, the rest making it to California, but they'd been forced to abandon their wagons along the way. Two years later, Marcus Whitman and Jesse Applegate had guided more than a thousand pioneers from Independence, Missouri, to Oregon's Pacific coast, and this time the emigrants got their wagons through. In the years since, thousands more had braved the Oregon Trail—facing sandstorms and deluges, burning hot winds, occasionally hostile Indians, rattlesnakes and quicksand, overloaded wagons breaking down, and a long list of other calamities. They left their dead in lonesome graves that were often violated by scavenging wolves or Indians looking for loot.

Still they forged on, undeterred by the hardships of the two-thousand-mile journey. Hawkes had made that trip, and he knew how arduous it could be. The grim determination of these pioneers was something he both admired and feared—feared because he knew as sure as he was standing there, watching those wagons roll closer, that these people would fundamentally change his world.

Hawkes stayed in the background as Bridger and Vasquez went out to greet the travelers. An excited Cameron tagged along. The wagons pulled up along the south palisade and some of the men gathered to talk to Old Gabe and his partner. Lingering near the gate, Hawkes watched his son succumb to overpowering curiosity and wander off down the line of wagons, where the women and children were. As for the men who spoke to Bridger, they were of stern stock, sturdy farmers clad in mule ear boots, stroud trousers, flannel or linsey-woolsey shirts, broad-brimmed hats, all of them burned by the sun and the wind. They were plain men, in both their speaking and their pursuits. For all their toughness, the journey across the prairie and the plains had taken its toll on them. Hawkes could tell as much by their expressions and the weary way in which they moved. He could tell, too, by the condition of the wagons and the oxen teams, and the looks of the women and kids in their stained, dusty gingham and homespun.

They had come from western Kentucky, infected with the highly contagious "Oregon Fever" and encouraged by the passage of the Preemption Law in '42, the means by which the federal government hoped to entice a mass westward migration in order to secure the nation's claim on the far side of the continent. Before leaving their homes these people had created an "Oregon Society," pledging to make the trek west together and to stand by one another come what may.

And much had come their way after departure from the "jumping-off" point of Independence in the first days of April, after the prairie had turned green. Heavy spring rains made the rivers swell and turned every low place into a muddy morass that slowed the wagons considerably. Countless times they'd been forced to unload a bogged-down "land canoe," free it from the muck and mire, and then reload. Sometimes the wind blasting across the plains managed to rip the covers off the wagons. The days could be searing hot, the sun a blazing demon, and the nights frightfully cold, the stars glittering like specks of frost.

As they followed the serpentine Platte River the land became more broken and difficult. The early spring storms were gone, but here the country was arid, and the shortage of potable water became a concern, then a crisis. They knew about the threat of cholera—the dreaded killer that had already claimed many more lives along the route than Indians had, and they took the precaution of boiling all the water they found, which hadn't been much. For their campfires they used buffalo chips, because the trail took them across the heart of the northern herd's range. Since the dung burned well enough when dry, they always kept a supply in a "possum belly" slung beneath the wagon. No one had been lost to disease or mishap, though a few were having trouble with their eyes on account of wind-driven dust and the sun's relentless glare.

Nor had they met with any trouble from hostile Indians. There had been occasional sign, and once a small party of mounted warriors was spotted, a few days to the east of South Pass, but they kept their distance. The emigrants had heard horror stories about the depredations of the red savages who ruled the plains, how they swept in on wagon trains, butchering and scalping men, carrying off women to a fate worse than death—or at the very least running off the stock. But nothing like that had befallen this particular band of pioneers.

Much of the pork they'd carried out of Independence ten weeks ago had turned rancid, and they'd had poor luck hunting along the way, so Old Gabe asked Hawkes if he would mind riding out to bag some game. Hawkes didn't mind at all. The presence of the emigrants made him nervous, and he wanted to steer clear of them as much as possible. He chided himself for being so skittish, but there was no helping it. Riding out along the river, he killed a pair of mule deer and then took his own sweet time going back. It felt fine just getting away from the fort for a while.

That evening there was a great feast. One of the farmers broke out a fiddle, while another produced a mouth organ, and the hoedown began. Vasquez regaled the visitors with outrageous tall tales, and was given rapt attention by his wide-eyed audience. Cameron had quickly made friends among the emigrant children, and Eliza had done likewise with the women, who were cheered somewhat by evidence that a female of their own race, and with roots not unlike their own, had managed to survive in this forbidding wild country. The sheer magnitude of the Great Plains had affected them profoundly. These folks and their ancestors had conquered the eastern woodlands with relative ease. But the country west of the Mississippi was something else again. This land humbled them with its primeval power. It was as though they were reconciled to the fact that the West could destroy them almost at whim. This was a bountiful land, full of promise, but survival out here, much less prospering, would not come cheaply.

In a matter of days the emigrants were eager to be on their way. A difficult trail lay in front of them—across the rugged Rockies—but Oregon's siren song was irresistible, and Jim Bridger had given them reliable information about what lay ahead. The trail from his outpost to Fort Hall by way of Soda Springs was a fairly easy one, with abundant grass this time of year and plenty of good water. There were mountains, but the crossings were not that difficult until one got beyond Fort Hall, where the trail would head west along the Snake River.

Bridger and Vasquez worked long hours repairing some of the prairie schooners, and Hawkes lent a hand as best he could, though he was far from being an expert at blacksmithing. His motives were mixed—the two men were his friends, he didn't like to be idle, and he wanted to do what he could to facilitate the departure of the emigrants. He was ready to go home. He'd traded his plews for powder and shot, tobacco and coffee, and a bolt of calico cloth for Eliza. She had it in mind to make a new dress, though Hawkes couldn't fathom why, since she wore buckskin pretty much year round. But in eight years of marriage he had learned that it was often impossible for a man to figure out a woman's way of thinking. Men just weren't usually smart enough to do that.

There had been enough left over in the trade to pick up a McGuffey's primer and a reader, books left at the outpost last season by an emigrant family. Eliza was determined to work harder at Cameron's book learning, even though he was a supremely reluctant student. He much preferred to learn the woodcraft that his father could pass on to him. But Hawkes backed Eliza all the way. His own mother had been adamant about his education, even though his father had begrudged the time it took Hawkes away from the work that needed doing around the farm. At the time, Hawkes hadn't fully appreciated the value of book learning, himself. But he did now.

After Bridger and the wagon train captain settled accounts—a sure sign that the pioneers would be leaving at first light on the morrow—Old Gabe searched out Hawkes, who sat on a stump smoking his pipe and watching the wind make the cottonwoods dance.

"Got a letter here for you, hoss."

Hawkes took the folded vellum, noting the brown wax seal and his name written in a precise, sweeping hand above it.

"How did you come by this, Gabe?"

"That feller I just been dickerin' with. He give it to me. Said he almost forgot he had it. Said a lawyer from Independence gave it to him the day before they set out. The lawyer said it was on account of them being the first bunch out this season. Told him to give it to me, figurin' I knew where to find you. Ain't you gonna open it?"

Hawkes was turning the letter over and over in his hands. "I don't guess I ever got one of these before. A lawyer, you say?"

Bridger nodded. "Reckon it has something to do with that bad business down Louisiana way?"

"I've got a hunch I might be better off not opening this."

"Well, I got some things need doin'." Bridger turned and walked away, giving Hawkes some privacy.

Some time later, Eliza came into the post after saying her farewells to the emigrant women, and found Bridger at his forge. The sun was setting, and she wanted to know if Old Gabe knew her husband's whereabouts. "Seen him outside the gate a while back," he told her, and added nothing about the letter. At the gate Eliza saw a small pile of burned tobacco at the base of the stump, where Hawkes had knocked out his pipe. Looking across at the trees a hundred yards away, she saw him at the river's bank, and went out to join him. When he looked around, hearing her approach, she could tell immediately that something was wrong.

"I'll have to be leaving you for a spell," he said flatly, and handed her the letter, its seal now broken. Eliza noticed that her hands were trembling just a little as she opened it. The bleak tone of her husband's voice filled her with an ill-defined dread.

To Gordon Hawkes, Esq.

Dear Sir,

It is my solemn and unpleasant duty to inform you that your mother, Mary Hawkes, passed on to her heavenly reward August last. A gentleman by the name of William Drummond Stewart has forwarded to me a package which he claims contains personal effects that your mother wished you to possess. Considering the nature of the item now in my charge, I cannot in good conscience entrust its safekeeping to strangers. Therefore I write this letter in the hope that it may find you. I shall hold the package until you see fit to claim it, for I am bound by my responsibilities to all those concerned in this matter to vouchsafe that it is delivered safely into your hands.

Your Servant,
Ira Taggett, Attorney at Law
Independence, Missouri
January 22, 1848

Eliza read the letter twice. Then, not knowing what to say, she folded it carefully and returned it to her husband.

"She's been gone pretty near a year," he said, gazing at the surface of the river, which seemed to have captured and held the last quicksilver light of day. "Nearly a whole damn year and I didn't know."

Eliza put her arms around him. For a while she just held him and finally, reluctantly, let go and stepped away.

"I'm going back," she said. "I suppose you want to be alone for a spell."

As she turned, Hawkes said, "You're not going to try to talk me out of this?"

Eliza was relieved that the shadows of night had deepened here beneath the trees, so that he could not see the worry on her face. "You'll do what you have to," she replied softly, without rancor or resentment. "That's why I love you."

She left him there alone, and he stood a long while beside Black's Fork as the last shreds of daylight seeped out of the western sky, and he was still there a few hours later when the moon rose to cast the distant snowy peaks in a cold blue light. Finally he walked back to the outpost. Vasquez was sitting on the stump outside the gate, whittling on a stick by a lantern's mustard-yellow light, accompanied by one of Bridger's old hounds. By now the hound was accustomed to having Hawkes around, and its tail thumped lethargically on the ground. Moths made a clinking sound as they hurled themselves against the lantern's scorched chimney.

"Eliza tells me you're goin' east," said Vasquez, keeping his attention on the stick he was shaving with a razor-sharp Green River knife which had known so many whetstones over the years that the blade was half gone.

"Got no choice in the matter. My ma's dead. She's left me something. I'm bound to go and get it."

"Why don't you just send for it?"

"Won't work."

"Well now, I reckon it's occurred to you that a big town like Independence ain't exactly the safest place for a feller with a price on his head. Might even be that this is some kind of trap, laid out all nice and neat."

"Doesn't matter. I've got to go. I owe it to her. I ran off and left her alone after my pa died. She was sick and broke and I just ran off."

"You never told me about that."

"It's not something I'm proud of."

"Still, I'd wager you had good reason for what you done."

"She wanted me to go back to Ireland with her. I wasn't going back. Whatever the reasons, I abandoned her, and now I owe her this, at least."

Vasquez nodded. "What about your wife and son, Gordon? What happens to them if you don't come back?"

"I'll come back."

The old mountain man stopped whittling, sheathed the knife, and tossed the stick away. The hound lifted its head, watched the stick sail into the darkness, and decided it wasn't worth the effort to go investigate. With a sigh it laid its massive head down and went back to sleep.

"You might could catch up with Gilmartin," said Vasquez. "A man would do well to have company on a trek like that."

"That's what I was thinking."

"Eliza and the boy are welcome here for as long as they want to stay. And if they want to go home I'll see to it that the Crows know about that. They'll keep an eye on things for you, I reckon."

"They will, yes. I'm obliged to you."

Vasquez stood up stiffly and ruefully patted his paunch. "I'd trail along with you, Gordon, but I'm too old and fat to be of much use. Now Gilmartin, he'll stand by you through thick and thin. I'd share a jug of tanglefoot with you, 'cept I calculate you'd be wantin' to spend what time you got left with Eliza and Cameron." He stuck out his hand. "Keep your powder dry, partner."

Hawkes clasped his old friend's hand. He didn't need to ask Vasquez—or Bridger, either, for that matter—to look out for his family if for some reason he failed to return. They would do it without question, for they and Hawkes belonged to a close-knit brotherhood that usually took care of its own.

Eliza and Cameron were in their beds of blankets and furs on the floor of the trading post. A dying fire in the stone hearth gave off some heat and a little light—sufficient enough for Hawkes to gaze for a spell at his sleeping boy's face. For a moment he wavered in his resolve to go to Independence. That was the last place he wanted to go, and he was cognizant of the risks, even acknowledged that Vasquez could be right about it being a trap. But none of that mattered. He'd been plagued by an abiding guilt for ten years now. He was certain his mother was dead—how else would the attorney have known her name if Captain Stewart hadn't been in touch with him? It was entirely plausible that his mother would entrust the performance of her last request to Stewart, for she knew that her son had gone west with the adventure-seeking Scotsman. Consumed by a widow's grief and an addiction to opium, Mary Hawkes had arranged to bound her son to serve the sadistic Captain Warren, skipper of the brig *Penelope*, as a cabin boy. Warren's cruelty had driven his previous cabin boy to suicide, and Hawkes had escaped the villain with Stewart's assistance. It was a matter of survival, yet no matter how justified his actions, the fact remained that he had turned his back on his mother, leaving her to fend for herself in a world short on mercy.

Much as he hated to leave his family—and the mountains—he had no choice but to acquire the package it was his mother's dying wish that he have.

As he lay down beside Eliza, she stirred in her sleep and draped an arm across his chest. He lay there, very still so as not to disturb her further, treasuring the touch and warmth of her body and dreading the long separation that would come with the approaching dawn.

Chapter 4

Several weeks out of Fort Bridger, on the trail of Gilmartin's wagon, Hawkes woke to the sound of distant gunfire. A High Plains dawn painted the sky with bloody strokes as he scattered last night's banked fire and threw his saddle on the dun mustang. This was the day he was counting on catching up with the fur trader, for the sign informed him that Gilmartin was only hours ahead. Hawkes had made good time, reaching Fort Laramie in two weeks, traveling through South Pass and along the Sweetwater, then along the North Platte, with the distinctive spire of the landmark Chimney Rock to the south. Gilmartin was making good time, too—better than Hawkes had expected. The shooting could mean that Gilmartin was in trouble, so Hawkes made haste, and was on the move in a matter of minutes.

A mile or so due east he came to a dry creek bed that for all its twists and turns seemed to be pointed in the direction he wanted to go. Guiding his horse down the sandy cutbank, Hawkes moved on at a more cautious clip, for the shooting was being done right up ahead, the shots spaced out, now almost methodical, and accompanied by a kind of rolling thunder. Rounding a bend in the creek bed, he saw Gilmartin's high-sided wagon—and the fur trader himself belly down at the rim of the embankment, peering over at something to the east. Hawkes startled him, and in turning too quickly, Gilmartin disturbed the rust-colored sand so that it crumbled beneath his weight, and he tumbled to the bottom, cursing vigorously and clutching his Lancaster percussion rifle as though his life depended on it.

"What kind of trouble have you stepped in now, Gil?" asked Hawkes pleasantly as he stepped down, tying his horse to the back of the wagon and drawing his Plains rifle from its buckskin sheath.

Gilmartin nodded toward the rim. "Come on up and see for yourself."

Together they climbed the bank. Shedding his hat, Hawkes took a look over the top and saw a broad sweep of buffalo grass, stretching a good mile up to a rocky backbone. Between here and there lay at least thirty buffalo, dead or dying. To the south, a cloud of pale dust bleached the blue out of the morning sky—a sizable herd of shaggies on the move. Hawkes could spy a dozen or so stragglers, mostly females trailing calves. A shot rang out, then another, from the rocks yonder. The sun was in his eyes, and Hawkes couldn't see the powder smoke, but he knew that was where the shooters were located.

"Never seen the likes of this before," muttered Gilmartin. "Who are they, Gordon, and what are they doing all this killing for?"

"Sit tight and keep your eyes peeled."

The shooting soon stopped. A short while later, a pair of wagons pulled by six-mule teams appeared from behind the rocks, swinging out onto the killing ground. Several buckskin-clad riders came down out of the rocks and fanned out; they were checking the buffalo carcasses, and once or twice a gun boomed as a dying shaggy was finished off. The riders then congregated at the wagons. Hawkes counted seven men—three on horseback and four in the wagons. All but one of them stepped down and went to work on the carcasses, skinning and butchering.

"How come they killed so many, do you reckon?" asked Gilmartin.

Hawkes shook his head. "They must be out of Fort Laramie."

Gilmartin anxiously scanned the horizon. "I'll tell you one thing certain. If any Indians happen along they sure as hell won't be too happy with this. I saw tracks yesterday. Hunting party, I figure, since there weren't any women or children. Arapaho, probably."

Hawkes nodded. "I saw them too. Could be Cheyenne."

"That's why I camped down here in this dry crik. You can see a campfire ten miles out here at night."

Hawkes smiled. "You're as dumb as a post, Gil. This creek runs into the Platte, most likely. If a storm came to the north or west you'd be up to your topknot in a flood."

"At least I'd still *have* my topknot—which I couldn't guarantee were I to meet up with Arapaho dog soldiers."

"They were Cheyenne, probably. Come on. Let's introduce ourselves to those gents."

"Maybe we ought to just swing around them."

"They'll be here all day with that many kills, and they'll see your dust when you move that wagon. You want to sit here until the sun goes down?"

Gilmartin was peering at a few buzzards who had already gathered, soaring high and graceful above the killing ground. "No, I don't reckon so," he answered, thinking about hostile Indians crawling around in the dark.

Hawkes slid down the bank, retrieved his horse, and found a place where he could lead the mustang up the dry bed's sandy flank. Then he and Gilmartin walked out to meet the buffalo runners. Hawkes wanted the dun along just in case he and Gil had to leave in a hurry.

They were spotted by the man who had remained mounted. He rode out to intercept them, a brawny character, bearded and long-haired, with teeth yellowed by long tobacco use, and a crooked eye that made it seem as though he were looking right at you and past you at the same time. He wore a buckskin shirt trimmed with fur and breeches tucked into moose hide boots, and even though he kept downwind, Hawkes could smell him when he got near enough. He carried a .704 caliber British-made rifle that could deliver a big punch at long distances, if you could figure out some way to shoot accurately with it. A belted knife and pistol completed his armament.

"Name's Billy Ring," he said, baring his yellow teeth in a wolfish grin that Gilmartin had to assume was meant to be friendly. "Them yonder's my crew. Who might you be?"

Gilmartin introduced himself. "Carryin' some fur down the trail to Missouri. This feller here is . . ."

"Henry Gordon," said Hawkes.

"Where's your furs?" asked Ring, looking around.

"A dry crik back a ways," said Gilmartin. "I was camped there last night. Woke up to your shooting."

"We hunt 'em where we find 'em. Sorry if we disturbed your sleep. I'm out of Fort Laramie. Me and the boys have took to runnin' shaggies on account of all the wagon trains comin' up trail. Those folks take to buffalo meat something fierce once they've sunk their teeth into a good hump steak. Then we sell the hides for up to twelve bits apiece. The shaggies ain't had time to fatten up much, but them wagons won't wait."

"Had any quarrel with Indians?" asked Gilmartin.

"Not yet. Don't care if I do. A man's got to make a livin' somehow. Besides, we're the first that I know of to make a go of this business. Must be millions of shaggies out here—the Injuns can spare a few."

Despite this assertion, Hawkes figured the day would soon come when Ring and his crew tangled with Indians, for the buffalo was the source of life for the Plains tribes, and he didn't think this kind of slaughter would sit well with them. Apart from the meat that fed them year-round, the Indians used the buffalo hides for shelter—a dozen or so would be used in a teepee—and for shields, cradles, leggings, dresses, quivers, and medicine bags. Sinew was used for bow-strings and thread for sewing, along with an awl fashioned from a bone splinter. The best sinew came from the backbone and the tendon beneath the shoulder blade. Buffalo robes were used for bedding and winter garb, while painted robes and buffalo horns were essential for certain ceremonial occasions. The brains were needed for tanning hides, the bladder for pouches, the lining of the stomach as a water container. Large bones were sometimes fashioned into weapons. There wasn't any part of the buffalo that the Indian did not put to good use. Even the scrotum was sometimes used for rattles.

"You're welcome to some coffee—or something stronger if you've got a hankerin'," said Ring.

Gilmartin glanced at Hawkes. He did not want to linger here. It wasn't a smart move, for a couple of reasons. For one, the killing had attracted buzzards, and a congregation of buzzards might attract the attention of any Indians who happened to be nearby, and Gilmartin knew for a fact that an Arapaho—or Cheyenne—hunting party was on the prowl in the immediate vicinity. For another thing, he didn't trust Billy Ring or his hunters, mostly on account of Ring's immediate curiosity about his furs. It seemed to him that Ring was the type of man always on the lookout for an easy profit, and one who lacked compunction in how he went about acquiring it. But Hawkes didn't look worried at all, and Gilmartin conceded to himself that he might be getting all worked up for no good reason. Besides, it wouldn't be polite to turn down Bill Ring's invite, and he didn't want any trouble with this character.

So they made for the wagon, and along the way they got a close look at Ring's crew going about their business. The skinners used Wilson knives with big curved blades to slit the hide down the inside of the legs and then along the belly from tail to neck. Then the hide was pulled back, the men cutting it away from the flesh little by little, and when there was enough loose hide to bunch up, a rope was put around it. With the other end of the rope secured to a saddlehorn, one of the riders mounted up, backed up his pony, and pulled the hide the rest of the way off the carcass, while the skinner cut with his knife to facilitate matters. Once the hide was off it was staked out, fur side down, and salted. After a day or so in the dry air and hot sun, it would be added to the pile on one of the wagons with the hair side up.

The bitter scent of blood was strong in the air. In the butchering, Ring's crew took only the best cuts—the "fleece" that lay along the spine, the side ribs, the "boss," and the big hump. The buffalo runners saved the tongue and the liver for themselves, both considered High Plains delicacies. A Mexican cook built a fire with buffalo chips, put hump ribs on a spit, and cooked up a kettle of belly fat for drinking. The liver was eaten raw, seasoned with gunpowder. Bones were cracked open for their marrow. The meat earmarked for consumption by the emigrants who passed through Fort Laramie on their way up the Oregon Trail was wrapped in hides and loaded into the second wagon.

When they reached the camp, Ring offered them some of the coffee the Mexican had put on the fire to boil. The "something stronger" he had mentioned turned out to be a jug of snakehead whiskey. Gilmartin declined, as did Hawkes. "It's a tad early in the day for me," said the latter, who accepted instead a tin cup filled with the Mexican's thick brew. Ring just laughed and took a snort from the jug. "Ain't all that bad. Pure alcohol, colored with some coffee, a little pepper, and a drop or two of snake venom or strychnine to give it a kick. Beats that black slime you're drinkin'." Ring took another long pull, drinking the liquor like water.

Ring's brother, Charley, came over to the wagon for a closer look at the two strangers. He was younger than Billy, of slighter build and with gaunt features. His mouth was disfigured with sores that oozed pus. Hawkes knew the signs—Charley Ring had a bad case of syphilis. He carried a Kentucky caplock rifle and, by the looks of it, a chip on his shoulder the size of a boulder. He was a taciturn and unsmiling sort.

"Charley and I do most of the shootin'," explained Billy Ring, "and I'm the first to admit that my kid brother is a better marksman than me. He can do a whole lot of damage with that old caplock of his. You see, the secret to shootin' shaggies is you don't want to kill 'em right off. You put your lead about a hand's width back of the shoulder. That way you're likely to hit the vitals. The beast'll run around for a spell before it drops. A shaggy don't scare when he hears a gunshot—but iffen it hears a shot and a critter drops right off, they'll all take to runnin'. And you drop the cows first, 'cause a calf will stand right there till you shoot it, too." Ring had been eyeing Hawkes's Plains rifle, and now he said, "That's a right handsome hair-saver, friend. Tailor-made for shootin' buffs, wouldn't you say so, Charley?"

Charley Ring didn't say anything at all.

Hawkes finished the bitter coffee, thanked Ring for the hospitality, and said it was time to be moving on.

"No need to rush off," said Billy Ring. "You're welcome to stay for a spell. Hell, I'd admire the company. The Mex don't speak a lick of English and, as you can see, Charley is about as talky as a stump. Them skinners I just hired on at Fort Laramie, and to be honest, they're just prairie scum."

"No thanks," said Gilmartin. He'd had enough of Billy Ring and his outfit. "We'll be going."

On the way back to the dry creek bed he cast a couple of over-the-shoulder looks and then muttered, "That feller Ring's one to talk about prairie scum. I got a bad feeling in the pit of my stomach, Gordon. Reckon they'll try for my plews?"

"We'll find out quick enough."

They put the killing ground behind them, and Hawkes rode alongside the wagon in silence for about five miles before speaking again, informing Gilmartin that he intended to circle back and see if they were being followed.

"Watch yourself," advised the trader. "Those Ring brothers have to be damn fine shots to put a ball behind a buffalo's shoulder at five or six hundred yards." He shook his head. "That Charley looked plumb loco to me. What do you think? It was like he'd skin you and eat your liver just for fun."

Hawkes smiled grimly. "Don't go getting spooked, Gil."

"I ain't spooked. Just cautious. I'm telling you, Billy and Charley Ring are crazy sons of bitches, and they're not to be trusted."

Hawkes had spotted an outcropping of rock south of the trail, about a mile back. Returning to it, he tied the mustang's reins to a heavy stone and climbed up into the rocks to settle down with the Plains rifle. From his vantage point he had a clear view from horizon to horizon. To the north and east and south stretched the rolling plains. Not far north lay the upper fork of the Platte River. Folks said of the Platte that it was too muddy to drink and too wet to plow. It was not much of a river, but the emigrant trail followed it from Missouri clear out to the mountains. Far off to his left, Hawks could see the hazy outline of the heights where Scott's Bluff and Chimney Rock were located. In that direction, but closer, he could see a splotch of black in the blue sky—the flock of turkey vultures marking the buffalo killing ground. The plains that stretched out before him, often crossed by herds of buffalo, were claimed by no one tribe, though many came here—the Cheyennes, the Utes, the Snakes, the Pawnees, and even his old friends, the Crow. Here they hunted, raided, and traded. Lately, though, the warlike and numerous Sioux from the north had been very active in these parts, or so his Absaroka brothers had told him. The Sioux wanted to rule supreme over the High Plains. They would be the ones who would give the westering pioneers the most trouble in the future, mused Hawkes.

Whatever else he thought about Billy Ring and his buffalo runners, Hawkes had to concede that they had a lot of hard bark on them. To slaughter shaggies in this country, at this time of year, when the Indians had departed their winter camps and were ranging far afield, was a flirtation with disaster. Truly these were men who would go to any length and take any chance for profit. Did that include murder and thievery? Was Gilmartin right about them, or just paranoid? That was what Hawkes intended to find out.

Inside of an hour he saw them, two riders in the distance, hardly more than dark specks silhouetted for a moment on the skyline, but he had a good idea who they were—Billy Ring and his brother, on the trail of Gilmartin's plews. They'd left the rest of the crew at work at the killing ground. They didn't need help, for they were the kind of men who killed from ambush. And perhaps they did not care to share the loot they intended to collect.

The trail would bring them to within a half mile of the rocks, and Hawkes considered shooting them from his vantage point. But what if he failed to stop them? Dying here would be of no help to Gilmartin. He decided against such a rash course of action. Returning to the dun, he rode east at a gallop to intercept the wagon. Applying himself to the problem at hand, he'd built a scheme by the time he reached Gilmartin.

"I take it they're on their way," said Gilmartin, disgusted.

"They are." Hawkes glanced at the midday sun. "Reckon it's time we stopped and brewed some coffee."

"Have you lost your mind?"

"We've got to deal with them sooner or later, Gil. They'll hit us before we can get too far. I'd rather it be in daylight, so we can see them."

"And they can see us."

"They'll just think they see us."

Gilmartin was dubious. "What are you planning?"

"Stop those mules and I'll show you."

Gilmartin climbed the ribbons, bringing the wagon to a halt. Using buffalo chips from the possum belly under the wagon, he built a fire as Hawkes instructed. Meanwhile Hawkes stripped the saddle off the dun and hitched the horse to the wagon. Setting the saddle on end near the fire, he draped Gilmartin's blanket coat over it and put the fur trader's hat on top. Rolling out his blankets, he wrapped the plew of a cinnamon bear in one of them and laid his hat at one end. As Gilmartin studied the setup, Hawkes scanned the surrounding terrain.

"You honestly think this'll fool them?" asked Gilmartin skeptically.

"They won't get in too close. Way I see it, they'll take their shots from that high ground yonder. Come on, we've got to get set west of that point."

The fur trader grabbed his .50 caliber Lancaster percussion rifle, shooting pouch, and powder horn, and followed after Hawkes. They jogged west over the high ground Hawkes had mentioned, then veered south. About a hundred yards off the tracks Gilmartin's wagon had made, they came upon an old buffalo wallow. Hawkes took another look around, sizing up the lay of the land, and nodded his satisfaction. "This will do," he said. "They'll come past here and, if my guess is right, set up on that rise over there. If we're lucky we'll be able to come in close behind them."

"We could pick them off from here, Gordon."

"Don't want any killing unless there's no other choice."

"There won't be," predicted Gilmartin. "Not with those two."

They settled down at the edge of the wallow to wait. Hawkes checked the load in his Plains rifle.

"You still using those paper cartridges, aren't you?" said Gilmartin. His voice was edgy with nerves, and he wanted to break the tension. "Most mountain men wouldn't be caught dead with those things."

"I use them when I have them. Saves time, and sometimes seconds count. Keep your eyes skinned, Gil. They'll be along shortly."

A quarter of an hour passed before they saw the two riders in the distance. The horsemen were sticking to the tracks of the wagon, and that brought them plenty close for Hawkes to see that they were in fact the Ring brothers, just as he had suspected. Their attention was riveted to the telltale smoke from Gilmartin's fire up ahead, and they passed by the buffalo wallow without an inkling they were being watched. Dismounting, they ground-hitched their ponies and climbed the low rise, right where Hawkes had expected them to be. From the crest they could look down into the mock camp. This was the moment of truth. Would the ruse work? The answer was soon in coming. Billy and Charley Ring were not ones for a lot of time-consuming soul searches or second thoughts. They divvied up their targets, brought their rifles to bear, took aim, and fired. The gunshots rolled across the plains. As he reloaded, Billy Ring got up on one knee to take a better look down at the camp. His more impetuous brother jumped to his feet and started down the slope. He was sure of his shot and confident that there was no danger in showing himself. Older and wiser, Billy called him back. Like a wily loafer wolf, Billy Ring seemed to have a sixth sense for danger.

"Let's go," said Hawkes, and left the buffalo wallow at a dead run.

They got to within fifty yards of the hidehunters before Billy looked back over his shoulder and spotted them. Hawkes stopped, brought the Plains rifle to his shoulder, and drew a bead.

"Don't go getting yourself killed, Ring," he said.

The buffalo runner froze, calculating whether he could bring his rifle around and get a shot off—and realizing in the next instant that he would be eating dirt forever if he made a fool play like that.

"Neat trick, hoss," he said, with a humorless grin. "Couldn't have done better myself."

Hawkes started up the slope, keeping his rifle to his shoulder and his finger on the trigger, hearing Gilmartin advancing behind him and to his right. "Shed those long guns, boys."

"No!" shouted Charley. "We can take 'em, Billy! We can!"

"Don't try nothin'," advised Billy.

But Charley was working himself into a frenzy, mad that someone had put one over on him. Moving sideways along the rim, he put some space between himself and his brother.

"Don't do it, you damned fool," rasped Billy.

"Shit!" snapped Gilmartin. "He's going to . . ."

Charley brought his caplock rifle around and Billy roared something that Hawkes couldn't make out because his Plains rifle boomed, kicking hard against his shoulder. Through a veil of powder smoke he saw Charley jackknife, performing a wobbly pirouette, and crumble. Gilmartin wisely held his fire, putting his sights on Billy Ring. Ring threw his weapon away. Standing, he raised his hands. One look and he knew Charley was dead.

"You sons of bitches murdered my brother," he said.

"That's rich," muttered Gilmartin, "comin' from a bushwhacker who rode all this way to backshoot us."

"It was his choice," said Hawkes. He forced himself to take a long look at Charley Ring's corpse. It gave him a hollow feeling inside knowing he'd snuffed out a life, even one as worthless as Charley's. He'd been forced to kill men before, but that didn't make the deed any easier to live with.

"We'd better finish this," Gilmartin told him. "Wouldn't do to leave this one above snakes."

"I can't shoot down an unarmed man," replied Hawkes curtly. "You want it done, you do it yourself."

"I will, because it needs doing." But Gilmartin didn't pull the trigger.

"You can't do it either," said Hawkes. "And I'm glad of that." He gave Billy a long, hard look. "I'll bury your brother. You better get. Leave the horses."

"So you're horse thieves on top of everything else," sneered Ring. "Leavin' a man afoot out here's the same as killin' him. You just lack the guts to do it the right way."

"I'll set the ponies loose up trail. It's not that far of a walk back to your crew." Hawkes picked up Billy's British-made long gun and discharged it into the sky, then passed it to its owner. "You can take that with you—but don't load up where I can see you."

"I'll bury my own, thank you very much," said Ring. "Meanwhile, you two can go straight to hell."

He set to the task with his knife, digging a shallow grave on the high ground. Laying Charley's corpse in the hole, he covered it up with dirt. There weren't enough rocks to be found to stack on the grave, and Hawkes knew that if wolves or coyotes happened by they would likely dig Charley up. Indians might, too, if just out of curiosity.

Billy Ring removed his battered hat. "Reckon I need to say a few words," he muttered. "Ashes to ashes, dust to dust." He raised his eyes and fixed his gaze on Hawkes. "And an eye for an eye. That's what the Good Book says. We'll have a reckoning, you and me. I'll see you in the ground before I die. I'll cut you open and roast your heart over my cook fire, so help me."

"Get moving," said Hawkes.

Billy Ring took up his rifle and walked west without once looking back.

"Big mistake, letting him live," said Gilmartin.

"Won't be the first mistake I ever made, or the last."

"Might just be the last." Gilmartin headed for camp. Hawkes retrieved the horses of the buffalo runners. Accustomed to gunfire, they'd stood their ground. Back in camp, Hawkes saddled the dun and noticed that one of the Ring brothers had put a bullet hole clean through the hull. Riding back to the rise where Charley was buried, he looked for Billy Ring. The buffalo runner was still walking west. Down below, Gilmartin was whipping up his mules. With one final look at the grave, Hawkes rode on.

Chapter 5

Hawkes and Gilmartin met a number of wagon trains in the five weeks it took them to cover the seven hundred miles from Fort Laramie to Independence. One of the largest trains was also one of the last they saw prior to reaching their destination. It consisted of seventy wagons, one hundred and thirty men, and nearly two hundred women and children. Hawkes and his companion approached their night camp one long day's journey southeast of Fort Leavenworth. They were welcomed by a tall, well-dressed man wearing a white Panama hat. His name was Owl Russell, and he had recently been elected captain of the caravan.

"We've heard rumors that the Kansa Indians are on the rampage up ahead," said Russell. "Have you met with any trouble from hostiles?"

"Mr. Russell, just about everything is hostile from here on," said Hawkes.

"Pay my friend no mind," said Gilmartin. "We've had no problems with Indians. Treat them with respect if you meet with any and you'll fare well."

"That was Colonel Kearny's advice," said Russell. "I contacted him at Fort Leavenworth and asked him for protection."

Hawkes was scanning the wagons as folks gathered around to see the westerners and hear what they had to say. He noticed that *California* was painted on some of the prairie schooners, and *Oregon* or *54 40* on others.

"You've got over a hundred men here," he said. "That's enough to handle most Indian raiding parties. Assuming you all plan to stick together."

"We shall, at least to South Pass. As you can see, some of us are bound for California. Take George and Jacob Donner, for instance."

Two sturdy farmers, both in their sixties but strong and fit, stepped forward and shook hands with Hawkes and Gilmartin. They were prosperous men with big families, and they had come from Springfield, Illinois, with James Frazier Reed, in a company that numbered thirty-two emigrants, all from around the Sangamon River. The prosperity Reed and the Donners enjoyed was evident from the quality and quantity of their belongings. Each man had not one but three wagons. Reed even had a land canoe decked out with beds and a stove, and a chest filled with fine wines. Hawkes had no way of knowing that George Donner's schoolteacher wife even had thousands of dollars' worth of banknotes sewn into a quilt. They did not fit the emigrant mold Hawkes had come to know. Unlike most of their fellow travelers, they were not seeking a new life because the old one lacked promise.

"I am told there is no winter in California," said Jacob Donner. "I'm tired of winters on the Sangamon. They are bitter and my bones are too old to tolerate them any longer. I want to live out the remainder of my days someplace where the snow doesn't pile up to the windowsills of my home."

"And California's a place where children can live a life of ease and culture," added Jacob's brother, George. "My wife intends to start a school for young ladies there."

"I've never been to California," said Hawkes, "but I wish you all the luck. You'll need it, to get across the Sierra Nevada. Those are hard mountains. Jim Bridger can tell you the best way to go. But you must get across the high country before winter sets in, or you'll have to wait till the following spring."

He and Gilmartin gratefully accepted the offer of a meal, consuming the beans, pork, and bread placed before them and washing it down with the best coffee Hawkes had tasted since leaving home. The leaders of the company sat around the fire with them, asking for details about the trail that lay before them, while some of the children lurked in the background, gawking at these two living, breathing examples of the legendary "fringe people" who lived in the western wilderness.

One of the men who came to sit at the fire was Lillburn Boggs, and it was he who posed a question that surprised Hawkes, not least for the venom in the man's voice as he asked it.

"Have you seen any murderous scum calling themselves Mormons on the trail?"

"Mormons?" queried Hawkes. "Who are they?"

"They are vermin, take my word. Must be ten thousand of them, maybe more, loose on the frontier, armed to the teeth and bent on destroying good, decent Christian folk by fire and sword."

Hawkes and Gilmartin exchanged a mystified glance at one another. "I've not seen nor heard of such," confessed Hawkes.

"If you are Missouri-bound, watch yourselves. They are brigands, my friends, ruthless cutthroats. Worst of all, they've incited Indians to attack our settlements. I don't know why the president won't act. I've written him countless letters, urging him to send the regular army in force to expel the Mormons. Or, better yet, exterminate them."

Owl Russell's smile was tight. "Mr. Boggs used to be the governor of Missouri, gentlemen. Six or seven years ago he sent his state militia to drive the Mormons out of the state. It was Mr. Boggs here who issued the famous Extermination Order. Mormon homes were burned, their livestock slaughtered, and many lives were taken."

"Nothing was done to them that had not already been committed *by* them!" snapped Boggs, bristling. "I will tell you exactly the kind of people they are. They sent one of their angels to assassinate me."

"Angels?" asked Gilmartin.

"Mormon assassins. They call themselves the Sons of Dan. One of them came to my home in the dark of night and shot me in the back. Then he fled to Illinois, beyond the reach of justice. There is a nest of them in Illinois at a place called Nauvoo. The Illinois assembly has tolerated the Mormons in return for Mormon money and votes. But I am happy to say that the patience of the good people of Illinois has run out. They have risen up and driven the Mormon devils out of Illinois, just as we have done, more or less, in Missouri."

Boggs left the campfire a few minutes later, still brooding angrily. Jacob Donner watched him go, shaking his head. "A most powerful hate burns inside that man."

"Is he leaving Missouri on account of the Mormons?" asked Gilmartin.

"That's not what I've heard," replied Owl Russell. "His crusade against the Mormons doesn't sit well with everybody. A lot of folks would just as soon live and let live. Boggs is bound for California because he knows we're going to take that country away from Mexico. The political future of a man who plays a role in that little melodrama will be bright. Very bright indeed."

"He's married to Daniel Boone's granddaughter, by the way," offered Jacob Donner.

"Are the Mormons as bad as he makes them out to be?" asked Hawkes.

"I'll tell you what I know about them and then you can make up your own mind," said Russell.

It turned out he knew a lot. The Mormon leader, Joseph Smith, president of the Church of Jesus Christ of Latter-day Saints, known to his followers as The Prophet, had been murdered by a mob of black-face ruffians in a Carthage, Illinois, jail back in the summer of '44. It was Smith who claimed God had spoken to him during his youthful wanderings through the woodlands of upstate New York. Later, an angel visited Smith and directed him to golden tablets containing God's directives to His chosen people. Smith and his followers moved to Ohio, where they built their first temple. But some shady dealings in the bank business forced Smith to dust out of Ohio in a hurry. He took his flock to Independence, but they were driven out, as they were from their next Missouri communities, to which they had affixed the odd names of Far West and Adam-ondi-Ahman. They settled in Illinois, on the banks of the Mississippi River, in a town called Nauvoo. But now, said Russell, they were being forced out of Illinois and were heading west in a mass exodus, searching for the New Jerusalem.

"The mobbers in Illinois call it a 'wolf hunt,' " he told Hawkes. "That's when they get together and set out to burn a few Mormon homes and leave a few Mormons bruised and bloody—sometimes even dead. It got so bad that the new leader of the Saints, as they call themselves—a man named Brigham Young—decided their only hope was to pull up stakes and move. That's why Boggs asked if you'd seen or heard of Mormons on the trail. I understand that more like fifteen or twenty thousand of them are on the move somewhere to the north."

"But why do so many folks have it in for these people?" asked Hawkes.

"Because they're different. Peculiar in their ways. They believe themselves to be the saved, the chosen few, the only true state of Israel. They say they'll one day dominate the world. They call non-Mormons Gentiles. If you're not one of them, you're no better than a heathen. To their way of thinking, the church and state are one, so they make their own laws. They practice polygamy, for instance, and that doesn't sit well with a lot of people. The priesthood rules the Mormon community. Everybody works for the good of the whole. It's been likened to a beehive. Twenty thousand members working together to achieve a common goal—well, you can imagine what they've been able to accomplish. In five short years they built Nauvoo into a thriving city and they control all the trade, land, and banking in the whole region. They prospered like you wouldn't believe. Naturally, their Gentile neighbors were envious of their success. In this country, it seems that if you're different, you're in for trouble—but if you're different and prosperous, you're done for."

"Sounds to me like you admire them," remarked Jacob Donner.

"I admire their thrift and energy," answered Russell. "They are a hard working people. Sure, they've got some strange ways about them. And a hard-nose Yankee trader's got nothing on a Mormon when it comes to business. But they don't deserve the treatment that has been doled out to them. I hope the West is big enough for them, so that they can find a place where they will be left in peace to live their lives as they see fit. What Boggs did when he was governor doesn't sit well with me, Mr. Donner. I knew some Mormons who lived in Clay County. Boggs and his butcher-boy Missouri Pukes killed some of them and drove the rest clean out of the state. It's a stinking business."

The conversation moved on to other topics, but Hawkes continued to dwell on the plight of the Mormons. Was Lillburn Boggs right about them? Were they demons in the guise of men? Or were they being unjustly persecuted? Though born in Scotland, Hawkes had grown up among the Irish, and he knew that the Irish were generally treated badly when they immigrated to America. He'd seen evidence of that ten years ago during his brief stay in New York City. NO IRISH NEED APPLY signs were often seen in storefront windows and on factory gates even then, and by all accounts it was much worse now, as more and more of Ireland's poor fled economic strife in their famine-ridden homeland. Many found their lot little improved in America. Irishmen were lucky to find work building canals or post roads or eastern railroad lines. The only positions open to Irish women were as low-paid domestic workers. The southerners had their slaves—northerners had the Irish to do their menial work. But too many of the Irish immigrants found no work at all. They lived in filthy slums like New York's Five Points—if you could call that living. They begged or thieved in the streets. Some of the women sold their bodies for the price of a hot meal. Those men unable to support their families turned to crime, or drowned their sorrows in cheap whiskey in bucket-of-blood grog shops.

Naturally, these ruminations brought Hawkes around to thinking about his mother, for it was to that harsh environment that he had condemned her, alone and ailing, when he'd jumped ship in New York's harbor. It didn't matter now that in her opium-addicted state she had tried to indenture him into the service of the cruel Captain Warren, master of the *Penelope,* that cursed ship on which Hawkes had watched his father die, and had nearly died himself. What had Mary Hawkes been forced to do in order to survive? How had she managed to return home to Ireland? Had the intervening years been ones of toil and sorrow for her? Had she known even a fleeting happiness? Hawkes doubted it. He cursed himself for a coward and worse. His father's death had left to him a solemn duty to provide for his mother. Instead, he had shirked that responsibility and run away. Now her tragic life was over, her burdens lifted, and he was left with his own burden of guilt that would weigh upon him until the day he died.

He wanted to repay the kindness of the emigrants in Owl Russell's company, so he slipped out of the sleeping camp an hour before dawn in search of game. But game was hard to find along this trail, and he was forced to range far afield before finding what he sought. When he returned to camp with a white-tail deer across the front of his saddle, the sun was two hours high and Gilmartin was as restless as a tumbleweed, past the point of being ready to move on. The emigrants had already left camp. Hawkes told the fur trader to start for Independence. He would catch up by midday. Riding hard, he found the wagon train. The emigrants were grateful for his donation to the food supply. Fresh meat was always welcome on the trail. They gave him a sack of corn pone and salt pork in exchange. He wished them luck with mixed emotions, admiring their grit but resenting their designs on the wild country he called home.

Rejoining Gilmartin, he pressed on to Independence, nearing the town by nightfall. They camped a few miles from the outskirts.

"Independence has boomed since you passed this way some years back," said Gilmartin as they hunkered down around the campfire. "Last time I was here I got a fair price for my furs—as good as any I'd get in St. Louis. I know the town well. Tomorrow, when I go in, you'd better stay here."

"I don't think so. It'll be safe enough, I reckon. We've met hundreds of folks on the trail and nobody has looked twice at me. And I'm bound to get my mother's package."

"Don't be a fool, Gordon. I'll get it for you. I'll tell that lawyer feller that I'm you. If he's playing it straight he won't know the difference. Give me that letter. I figure I know enough about you and where you come from to pull this off."

"Why would you take such a chance for me?"

"Let's just say I owe you. Without you being along, I calculate Billy Ring and his brother would have put me under." Gilmartin flashed his ne'er-do-well grin. "Besides, Eliza would be awful mad at me if I let anything happen to you. I want to stay on her good side, seeing as how I'm going to win her over one of these days."

"I'm obliged, Gil, but I can't let you do this. It's too risky."

"You just said it wasn't. But if it is, my plan makes sense. If it sours, I'll just tell them that I'm *not* you. That I got hold of the letter by hook or crook and figured I'd try to collect the package on the chance it contained something of value. You know me. I can talk myself out of any scrape. Use your head for something besides a hat rack, hoss. Think about your family."

It was consideration for Eliza and Cameron that led Hawkes to agree, albeit reluctantly. He didn't cotton to anyone taking big risks on his account. But Gilmartin was a slick talker and sharper than a Sioux scalping knife. He had gotten out of a lot of trouble in his time with his hide intact, and with no help from anyone.

The next morning, Gilmartin was on the move early, giving Hawkes assurances that he would be back by sundown. When he was gone, Hawkes settled down by the campfire and brooded over his coffee, gazing into the flames. The prospect of an entire day with nothing to do but wait was an encumbrance to him. He didn't know how to sit idle that long. And he just couldn't shed the feeling that things would not go smoothly for Gilmartin in Independence.

Chapter 6

Less than an hour after leaving camp, Gilmartin was rolling into Independence, a booming frontier town and the terminus of both the Oregon and Santa Fe Trails. It was trade from the latter that had gotten Independence started, for after 1822, when Captain William Becknell returned from New Mexico with the exciting news that the young republic of Mexico had lifted the old Spanish ban on foreign trade, Missouri traders jumped at the chance to deliver all manner of goods to a commodity-starved Santa Fe. The traders came back with silver, furs, and Mexican mules. For a while, Franklin had rivaled Independence as a jumping-off point for these outfits. But Franklin had been largely destroyed by the rampaging Missouri River. Six miles away from the unpredictable river, Independence was safe from the Big Muddy's whimsy, but its citizens had financed a nice macadam road to connect the town with the river commerce. These days, the outfitting of emigrant trains bound for Oregon or California contributed just as much to the town's prosperity as the Santa Fe trade.

Gilmartin was in high spirits as he maneuvered his wagon through the wide muddy streets. Unlike his partner Red Renshaw and his friend Gordon Hawkes, he appreciated the amenities that only a town like Independence could provide a man. The mountain life suited him well enough, but there were some things you just couldn't have in the high country—a bath in a big copper tub with perfumed water so hot it made your skin turn crayfish-red; or an oyster and champagne dinner at the restaurant over by Smallwood Noland's famous hotel, which could accommodate four hundred guests; or a visit to one of the ubiquitous "watering holes" where a fellow could quench his thirst with Napoleon brandy or honest-to-God Scotch Whisky. All of which Gilmartin had every intention of doing—just as soon as he sold his furs and took care of the little errand for Hawkes.

The streets were full of characters from all walks of life—trappers and traders in buckskin, bullwhackers with their high boots and coiled blacksnake whips, emigrants in their homespun and gingham hustling to get a late start up the trail, Indians in their paint and blankets, Mexicans in their sombreros and concho-studded pantaloons, freighters, soldiers, merchants, peddlers, and women—proper ladies as well as fallen angels. Near Robert Weston's blacksmith shop, a man wearing a beaver hat and a pilot cloth cape hailed Gilmartin and braved the street's red clay muck to look over the wagon's cargo.

"I'll give you three hundred for the lot, hard money."

This was as good a price as Gilmartin had hoped to get. But he shook his head. "I'll take the offer only if I can't get a better one down the street."

"Four hundred, then."

"My pa told me never to take the first offer in a business deal."

The man smiled. "That's the final offer, not the first."

"In that case I better take it."

In short order Gilmartin's wagon was empty and he had a sack of gold eagles under his shirt, as well as directions for finding the office of Ira Taggett, attorney-at-law. Arriving in Courthouse Square, he spotted the lawyer's shingle and stopped the wagon across the way, watching the place for a spell and seeing nothing out of the ordinary. His performance well-rehearsed in his mind, he crossed the square carrying his rifle, and strolled into the lawyer's office like a man without a care in the world.

A pale, gangly young man wearing eyeglasses was toiling at a cluttered desk in a small front room, his quill pen scratching furiously on the heavy paper in front of him.

"Morning," said Gilmartin. "I'm here to see Mr. Taggett. Name's Hawkes. Gordon Hawkes."

The clerk peered at Gilmartin over the top of his see-betters like Gilmartin was something that had been tracked into the office on the bottom of a boot.

"Mr. Taggett is expecting me," said Gilmartin, putting a stern edge to his voice as he produced the letter. "Give him this and be quick about it."

Resentful, the clerk got up from his stool, took the letter, and disappeared through a door in the back.

Gilmartin moved to a window and scanned the courthouse square. All was as it had been before—nothing out of the ordinary. He relaxed a little. Maybe all these precautions were unnecessary.

The door behind him opened and a man in a gray frock coat emerged. He was tall, narrow-shouldered and balding, with bushy brows jutting over piercing green eyes and a thick mustache sheltering a terse mouth. The letter was clutched in a hand that Gilmartin figured had never been fitted around an ax handle or gun barrel.

"So you are Gordon Hawkes."

Gilmartin smiled and nodded. "Come for my mother's package. I know you must be a very busy man, Mr. Taggett, so if you'll just hand it over I'll be on my way."

Taggett's smile was unctuous. "I fear it is not as simple as that, sir. Captain Stewart charged me with a solemn duty and I must be certain that the item in question does not fall into the wrong hands. No offense meant, of course. I'm sure you appreciate my position."

"No offense taken, but I haven't got all day."

"This won't take long, I assure you. Merely a few queries. Your mother's name, of course, was Mary Hawkes. And what was your father's name?"

"Thomas." Gordon Hawkes had once spoken of his father and luckily, Gilmartin had a steel-trap memory.

"And from what part of Ireland did you come?"

Gilmartin blinked. Hawkes had never talked about *that.* "Near Dublin," he replied, because Dublin was the only Irish place name that came to mind in an instant.

"Yes, fine," said Taggett. "And how did you happen to become associated with Captain William Stewart?"

"My father died in the sea passage over. I came west with Captain Stewart. You got a letter from him, didn't you? He must have told you all about me."

"Indeed, that letter is the only source of information about you that I possess."

"Let me save us both some time, Mr. Taggett. I went with Robert Campbell and the Rocky Mountain Fur Company. Lived among the Absaroka Crows for a spell. Married the prettiest gal west of St. Louis. Her name's Eliza. She and I live in the mountains, free as the air. And I'm kind of in a hurry to get back to her, if you don't mind."

"Certainly. Just one or two more questions."

"Listen here, Mr. Taggett." Gilmartin stood his rifle against the nearest wall, planted his knuckles on the clerk's desk, and leaned forward. "I am Gordon

Hawkes. I'll swear to it on the Good Book. Just give me what I came here for and—"

A commotion in the back room interrupted him. The sound of a door opening and shutting on stiff hinges, a gruff whisper, boot heels beating an urgent tattoo on the floor. Taggett backed away, hooded eyes riveted on Gilmartin, whose hand dropped to the pistol in his belt. He half-turned toward his rifle just as two men barged out of the room from whence Taggett had issued a few moments before. One of them carried a big dragoon pistol, the other a blunderbuss. The flared barrel of the latter was two inches in diameter but it looked a whole lot bigger from Gilmartin's perspective. At such close range the blunderbuss could cut him in half.

"That's him!" shouted Taggett. "That's Gordon Hawkes! Seize him!"

Gilmartin whipped the cap-and-ball pistol out of his belt as the two rough-looking customers leveled their weapons at him. It flashed through Gilmartin's mind that Taggett's clerk must have slipped out the back way to fetch these men, who had been waiting somewhere nearby. Meanwhile Taggett had kept him occupied with questions. He'd walked into the trap, nice as you please.

"Hold on, boys," he rasped. "Lay those guns aside or suffer the consequences."

"Careful, Dolan," one of the men muttered to his companion. "He's killed a dozen men from what I've heard."

"A dozen!" Gilmartin snorted. "Closer to a hundred. So back off."

"Don't let him get away!" exclaimed Taggett.

"He can only shoot one of us, Cooley," reasoned the man named Dolan.

"Which one of you is ready to meet his Maker?" asked Gilmartin. He watched their eyes, for it was a good bet that he would be able to see who would pull his trigger first. In the next instant he knew that neither man was ready to die, and he pressed his advantage. "Now, I've got no quarrel with you," he said, pleasantly surprised by his own calm delivery, under the circumstances. "So I'm just going to walk out this door and we can all live to fight another day. Deal?"

He took another step backwards. The door was just behind him now and a little to the right. Dolan and Cooley didn't lower their weapons but they didn't shoot, either, and Gilmartin thought for one fleeting and astonished moment that he was actually going to bluff his way out of this scrape with his hide intact.

Then, as he reached back and opened the door something pushed hard against it and the door swung into him, knocking him off balance. He began to turn, catching a brief glimpse of a man cut from the same cloth as Dolan and Cooley—only bigger, much bigger—and then the barrel of the man's pistol came down hard on Gilmartin's head and he blacked out.

Dolan lowered his horse pistol and drew breath. "Good work, Geller."

Geller was huge. His bulk filled the doorway as he stood there above Gilmartin's body, his murky brown eyes dispassionately surveying his handiwork.

"Splendid," said Taggett, his balding head glistening with sweat. "Outstanding. You fellows have each earned your thousand dollars."

"He's still alive," remarked Geller, his voice flat, without emotion. He put his pistol away somewhere beneath the folds of a soiled and tattered black greatcoat. Kneeling, he performed a deft search of Gilmartin's person and found the pouch of gold coins, which he slipped into the pocket of his coat.

"Here now!" exclaimed Cooley, starting toward

Geller. "What have you got there? We're all in this together, remember?"

Geller stood up and fastened his dead gaze on Cooley. "You want it? Come and get it."

Dolan took a long look at Geller and said, "Don't press your luck, Cooley."

"That sack is full of hard money," protested Cooley. "I heard it jingle. We deserve our share."

"Now, gentlemen," said Taggett nervously. "Let's not do anything rash."

"He'll kill you," Dolan told Cooley. "So just forget it. You're getting a thousand dollars out of the reward for Hawkes and that's more money than you've seen in your whole miserable lifetime. So forget it." He turned to the lawyer. "You're sure this is him? This is Gordon Hawkes, certain?"

"I'm absolutely convinced."

"Well, it's about damn time. We've been hanging around here plenty long enough. I got tired of waiting for him to show a long time ago."

"I paid for your keep and kept you in whiskey money," replied Taggett. "I'm out of pocket a good sum."

Dolan snorted. "You're not out much of anything. You're getting the rest of the bounty. That's seven thousand dollars."

"Hardly seems right," complained Cooley, who was feeling more cheated by the minute. "We took the big chance. Hawkes was a hair from killin' one or t'other of us, Dolan."

"We had an agreement," said Taggett sternly, glancing warily at Geller, because it was Geller that he feared most. He could handle Dolan and Cooley, but the big brooding man in black was a cold-blooded killer by all accounts. Geller had worked with John Murrell, the notorious Reverend Devil who had been responsible for countless heinous crimes up and down the Mississippi River before his capture and imprisonment. Since then Geller had made his bad reputation worse in the rougher sections of Independence, a cutthroat of the first order involved in a number of nefarious enterprises. Taggett had heard that if you needed someone to do a rough or bloody job, then Geller was your man. The fact that he had not been convicted of any crime was a direct consequence of the dread which the local underworld harbored for him. No one interested in his own survival would testify against Geller.

Dolan was the one who had enlisted Geller in this business. Taggett had defended Dolan and his partner, Cooley, after they'd been accused of stealing a team of mules, and he'd gotten the two petty criminals off. After determining that he would need some help capturing a dangerous fugitive like Hawkes, Taggett had signed up Dolan and Cooley. He didn't trust the city marshal, a man who would keep the reward for himself. Later, Taggett had begun to wonder if Dolan and Cooley were sufficiently tough to handle a desperado like Hawkes—after all, rumor had it that Hawkes had killed many men, had lived among the wild Indians, and was a right bloodthirsty character. It was then that he'd told Dolan to find a third man, and Dolan had approached Geller. Taggett didn't like having Geller involved. He could keep Dolan and Cooley in line, but no one could handle Geller. Still, he was too afraid of Geller to try to cut him out of the deal once he was in.

"We made an agreement like he said," Dolan told Cooley. "We'll stick to it." He turned back to Taggett. "Now what do we do?"

"Simple. One of you find the city marshal and bring him here. We turn Hawkes over to the authorities as soon as the marshal has witnessed my claim for the reward. When we receive the money you'll get your share."

"Fetch the marshal, Cooley," said Dolan.

"Marshal won't like it, us bein' involved," predicted Cooley apprehensively. He had a strong aversion to any sort of association, no matter how brief or benign, with an officer of the law.

"Doesn't matter if he likes it or not," said Taggett. "You haven't done anything wrong. This man is a cold-blooded murderer and you have assisted in bringing him to justice."

Cooley mulled this over, chuckling. "You sayin' I done the community a service? Hell, I ain't never been on the right side of the law before. Feels funny."

As the door closed behind Cooley, Dolan noted, "He's coming to."

Groaning, Gilmartin rolled over. His eyes fluttered open. He managed to focus on Geller's face, then sat up and propped himself against the wall. Dolan played it safe and confiscated Gilmartin's rifle. Gilmartin gingerly felt the back of his skull.

"I guess I owe you for this," he told Geller.

Geller just looked at him the way a man might look at an insect while trying to decide if he wants to make the effort to step on it.

"You've got a hard head, mister," said Dolan. "I've seen Geller hit a man so that the brains dropped right out of his skull."

"I haven't got any brains," replied Gilmartin. "If I had, I wouldn't be here."

"If it's any consolation, Hawkes, your friend Captain Stewart *did* send me a package from your mother," said Taggett. "That much was true."

"Looks like he made a mistake trusting you."

"I suppose I came highly recommended. Only modesty prevents me from telling you how well-known I am in Missouri."

"You made a mistake, too. Because I'm not Gordon Hawkes."

Taggett just smiled. He went into his office and returned with a package under his arm. This he placed on the floor and kicked it over to Gilmartin, who put his hand on it. He could tell that it was a wooden box, about a foot in length and width and half as deep, wrapped in heavy brown paper torn in places and wrapped with stout hemp twist.

"Thanks," he said, "but it doesn't really belong to me."

"You're a cool customer for one on his way to the gallows," observed Dolan.

Gilmartin shrugged. "You've got the wrong man, I tell you. Reckon it's the reward you're after. Well, you won't get a bounty for turning me in. My name's Dane Gilmartin. I didn't come from Ireland. I've never even been to Louisiana. I've only killed one man in my whole life and that was an Arapaho Dog Soldier. It was self-defense."

Dolan glanced at Taggett, a shadow of doubt cast across his rough, unshaven features. "Are you sure this is Hawkes? The only paper out on him is ten years old . . ."

"It's him. I never mentioned Louisiana. If he isn't Hawkes how did he know the murder was committed there?"

"I know because I've heard all about Gordon Hawkes," said Gilmartin. "He was something of a legend in the crowd I'm usually seen with."

"Was," said Dolan. "You said was."

"He died last year. That's why Jim Bridger gave me the letter those wagon folks gave him. I'm taking care of his wife and son, you see. That's why I came for the package. Reckon it belongs to them by right."

Taggett shook his head, lips curled. "You've got a

limber mind, Hawkes, I'll grant you that. But you can't lie your way out of this."

"Yeah," said Dolan. "He could talk a beaver right out of its plew." He wasn't as certain as Taggett about the truth. But if the lawyer was sure that he would be able to convince others, the reward would be paid. That was the important thing. It didn't matter to Dolan if the man they hanged was really Hawkes or not, guilty or innocent. He wasn't one to let scruples stand in the way of one thousand dollars.

Dolan's mention of a plew reminded Gilmartin of the business that had brought him to Independence in the first place. He felt for the money pouch. His calm demeanor slipped. "Which one of you thievin' bastards took my poke?"

"That would be me," said Geller, his voice deep and rumbling like the growl of a grizzly.

"Guess I'll be killing my second man pretty soon."

Geller glanced at Taggett. "If that reward is dead or alive I'd as soon blow his candle out right now and be done with it."

"I will not abide cold-blooded murder," said Taggett, offended. "Do you think I am no better than *he* is?"

Geller shrugged his indifference, just as Dolan moved suddenly to the front window, having heard something that piqued his interest. "Hey, Taggett. Come over here."

"That's *Mr.* Taggett to you," sniffed the lawyer as he joined Dolan at the window.

"Whose wagon is that?" asked Dolan.

Taggett shook his head. The wagon looked like it had been down one too many rough trails, and the mules in the hitch didn't look much better. A dun mustang wearing a saddle was tied to the wagon's gate. The lawyer saw no one near the wagon.

"I could swear that warn't there a minute ago," said Dolan dubiously. "I think I'd better have a look around."

Before Taggett could say yea or nay, Dolan was out the door.

As he emerged onto the boardwalk, Dolan saw someone out of the corner of his eye. He swung around, crouching, bringing the dragoon pistol in his hand to bear.

Hawkes had been standing at the corner of the building, checking the street and the alley that ran alongside Taggett's office. When Dolan came out, Hawkes turned, saw the horse pistol, and fired the Plains rifle at hip level. The ball struck Dolan squarely in the chest, the impact at such close range lifting him off his feet and hurling him backward. The dragoon pistol discharged, shattering the office window.

Drawing a pistol from his belt, Hawkes charged through the door, hitting it with his shoulder. Wood splintered as the door cracked back on its hinges. The first thing Hawkes noticed was Taggett slumping against the clerk's desk, clutching his arm with bloodstained fingers—Dolan's errant bullet had grazed him. In the next instant, Gilmartin was shouting a warning and Hawkes realized there was a very large man crouched in the corner of the room, drawing a pistol from the folds of a tattered greatcoat.

As Hawkes brought his own weapon around, Geller changed his mind and let the pistol drop.

"Can you walk?" Hawkes asked Gilmartin.

"Walk? Hell, I can run."

"The wagon is outside. Get to it." Covering Geller, Hawkes helped an unsteady Gilmartin to his feet, who had the package under his arm.

"This is what you came for," he said. "But why

the hell are you here? I told you I could handle things."

"Yeah, I see. Get going."

Gilmartin looked at Geller. "That one's got my money."

"Hand it over," Hawkes told Geller.

Geller produced the pouch and tossed it. Gilmartin caught it and turned to the door. Remembering Taggett, he smiled coldly at the lawyer. "I told you I wasn't Gordon Hawkes. Reckon now you know I was telling the truth."

"You talk too much Gil," said Hawkes.

As Gilmartin staggered out, Hawkes sized Geller up and said, "I ought to kill you right now. I can see that in your face."

"But you won't."

"No. Don't make the mistake of coming after me."

"I don't make mistakes," said Geller.

Hawkes backed out into the street, helped Gilmartin into the wagon, and climbed up alongside him. Handing the fur trader his pistol, he gathered up the ribbons and put the mules into motion while Gilmartin kept an eye on Taggett's office. People were running in the street—the gunfire had stirred up Courthouse Square. But no one tried to stop them.

As soon as the wagon pulled away Geller picked up his pistol.

"Get after them," hissed Taggett through teeth clenched in pain. "For God's sake don't let them get away."

"They won't get away," said Geller.

He raised the pistol and shot Taggett in the face.

When Cooley and the city marshal showed up a minute later, Geller informed them that Gordon Hawkes had killed the lawyer and Dolan and made good his escape. Then he melted into the gathering crowd of gawkers, leaving Cooley to stand stricken over the body of his friend Dolan. Geller didn't care about Dolan, or Cooley either. He didn't invite Cooley to come along. He wanted the whole reward to himself. All he had to do was steal a horse and he'd be on his way to collecting it.

Chapter 7

A few miles out of town they quit the road. Heading into the brush meant leaving the wagon behind. Gilmartin shrugged off the loss. He was just pleased to be alive, and he had his money. Riding one of the mules and leading the other, he followed Hawkes for about two hours through broken country. It was the longest two hours of his life because his head hurt like the dickens, and going about bareback on a knobhead wasn't helping matters any. Finally Hawkes called a halt on a wooded ridge so they could watch their back trail for a spell. It was important to know if they were being followed and by how many.

"You figure us to have the law on our heels?" asked Gilmartin. He was content to let Hawkes do the looking; he slumped down on the ground with his back to a tree and laid his head back, eyes closed.

"Wouldn't surprise me. How are you doing?"

"Feels like somebody's carving up my brain with a dull knife." Gilmartin opened his eyes and frowned at Hawkes. "Why did you come in after me?"

"Just a feeling."

"Well, I was handling the situation okay."

Hawkes had to laugh. "Yeah, I could tell as soon as I walked in. When I got there it took me some time to find Taggett's office, and when I did I saw two men sneaking around back. While I was watching them I guess I missed the big one, though."

"Geller. He came in the front way. He's the bastard who cracked my skull."

"I figured it was a trap, sure enough. Saw your wagon across the square so I knew you were inside."

"Aren't you going to open up that package, after all the trouble we gone to to get it?"

Hawkes glanced at the package, secured behind his saddle. After a moment's hesitation he retrieved it, unsheathed his Bowie knife, and cut off the wrappings. Prying the wooden box open with the point of the blade, he removed the contents.

"What is it?" asked Gilmartin. Hawkes had his back to him and he couldn't see.

"My mother's Bible. I remember her reading to me out of this book, just about every night in front of the fireplace back home."

Though Hawkes was doing his best to conceal it, Gilmartin could tell that he was deeply moved. "Anything else?"

"No. This is it."

"No letter?"

"Nothing. I guess this is the only possession of any value she had when she died."

"Well what do you know." Gilmartin was puzzled. He couldn't fathom why folks had gone to so much trouble sending a Bible halfway around the world. And he and Hawkes had sure gone to a lot more trouble to get it. But he wasn't about to say anything, since clearly the worn, leather-bound book meant a lot to his friend.

Hawkes folded the wrapping paper around the Bible and put it away in his possibles bag. He returned to watching the country south of the ridge. Gilmartin dozed off, only to be roughly shaken awake.

"I thought for a minute there that you were dead," said Hawkes, kneeling in front of the fur trader. "You look like hell warmed over, Gil."

"Thank you very much for the compliment."

"Maybe we ought to have a doctor take a look at you."

"I'm fit as a fiddle. Seen anybody?"

"Nope. But we won't take chances. We'll stay off the main trail and keep riding north along the Platte. Swing west in a couple of days."

"Let's get started." The prospect of long days on the move, straddling a mule's bony backbone, was not a pleasant one, but Gilmartin didn't want to leave Hawkes with the impression that he was a weakling. He got up, then swayed precariously as the world began to tilt and spin around him. Hawkes gave him a hand to the mule.

They made ten miles across rough terrain before nightfall. In a fireless camp deep within a thicket, Gilmartin turned down an offer of cornpone and salt pork from Hawkes. He was too sick to his stomach to eat a bite, and too weak even to fight the mosquitoes that feasted on his blood all night.

The next day they made fair time, always heading north, even though Gilmartin wasn't feeling much better. Toward midday they came to a burned-out cabin on the banks of a creek. Wisps of smoke still curled from the blackened timbers piled around a stone chimney. The day was warm and humid, and Gilmartin settled in the shade of a sycamore while Hawkes read sign.

"Whatever happened," he told Gilmartin, "it happened yesterday. Four men rode in from the north. They headed back the way they came, this time with a wagon, another horseman, and a couple of cows."

"Who burned the cabin, and why?" wondered Gilmartin.

Hawkes was gazing south, back along their trail. "I think we're being followed."

"You've seen something?" asked Gilmartin, alarmed.

Hawkes shook his head.

"Another hunch," said Gilmartin with a grimace. His companion's hunches always seemed to prove out. He hoped it wasn't Geller who was tracking them. A posse was preferable to Geller.

"What I can't figure," Gilmartin said, looking at the cultivated field on the other side of the creek, where green young sprouts of corn pushed up through the rows of rich black earth, "is why somebody would go to all the trouble of plowing and planting—and then pull out."

"Maybe they didn't have a choice."

"I got a hunch, too. I think we've got trouble up ahead as well as behind us."

They rode on. Two hours later, Gilmartin's hunch turned out to be true, and they got answers to some of their questions. A band of riders had paused in a meadow strewn with wildflowers. Some of the men turned their guns on Hawkes and Gilmartin as the latter cleared the tree line. Hawkes could see there was nothing to do but brave it out. As they rode closer he could see two dead men draped over horses and a third man lying on the ground, his head propped up on his saddle. Yet another wore a bloody makeshift bandage on his arm. They'd been in a shooting scrape, and Hawkes could almost smell the fear and the blood and the gunsmoke on them.

A man stepped forward, a rifle cradled in his arms, suspicious gimlet eyes peering out from the brim of his hat. "Who you be?" he grated.

"Fur traders," said Gilmartin. "Sold our plews in St. Louis. Now we're going home. What happened here?"

The man spat a stream of yellow tobacco juice. "Mormon filth, that's what. We drove most of 'em out of Missouri some years back. Still a few families left, though. Now they're all headed west. Called a gatherin' up in Nauvoo. Some Danite avengers rode down here to collect those of their kind what stayed in Missouri. We heard about it and come to hurry 'em along. Ran into an ambush about ten miles north of here. Two kilt, and a third about to be." He nodded at the man on the ground. "Gut shot. Worst way to die, slow and painful like. This is about as far as he'll go."

"Passed a burned-out homestead back a ways," remarked Hawkes.

"That be our handiwork," said the man, and he sounded satisfied. "Good bottomland that somebody'll want. But won't nobody live under the same roof as Mormon vermin."

The dying man coughed up blood, his body rigid with pain. He suddenly went limp as one final breath rattled in his throat.

"He's done for," said one of the others.

"Put him on his horse and we'll carry him home to his family," said the first man, turning his attention back to Hawkes and Gilmartin. "If you value your hide, you won't go further north."

"Thanks for the advice. Come on, Gil."

As they left the field, Gilmartin took a glance back. "Missouri Pukes," he said. "Thought they'd have some fun and got more than they bargained for. Maybe we ought to turn west, Gordon."

"They'll be looking for us along the Missouri River. Whoever those boys tangled with has probably moved on."

As the day perished, bleeding into the western sky, their route along a stony creek took them through a narrowing passage between bare bluffs rimmed with rock outcroppings. They were still on the tracks made by the Mormons and their Missourian pursuers, and Hawkes surmised this was where the ambush had occurred. It looked to be prime spot for that kind of thing. There was no good reason for the ambushers to have lingered, but he kept his eye on the high slopes just the same, and when he saw the flash of sunlight up in the rocks he got over his surprise in a hurry and shouted a warning just as a gunshot echoed through the gulch and Gilmartin's mule went down in the shallows of the creek. Cursing a blue streak, Gilmartin got clear and scrambled for the cover of some nearby elm trees, dragging his second mule along. Hawkes dismounted, laid his Plains rifle across the bow of his saddle, then aimed and fired, sending lead into the rocks where he had seen the flash. Then he led the dun mustang into the trees, following in Gilmartin's footsteps.

"That's just fine," said Gilmartin, disgusted, backed up to the sheltering trunk of an old elm. "First my wagon and now one of my mules. I'm just starting to feel better and some damned fool takes a shot at me. Guess you were wrong this time."

"Guess so," acknowledged Hawkes, reloading. "Sorry, Gil."

"Hell, that's okay. I'm just glad to know you can make a mistake. I was beginning to wonder if you were even human."

A ball whistled into the trees, clipping a low-lying branch and thumping into the ground behind them. Another gunshot rolled like slow thunder down the draw.

"He's got us pinned down," observed Gilmartin. "What do we do now?"

"Wait for dark. Won't be long coming."

"Then what?"

"I'll go up there." Hawkes smiled grimly. "Least I can do to make up for my mistake."

Gilmartin sighed. "I'll have to go with you. Can't let you do that all by your lonesome." A while later he spoke up again. "I must say, hoss, this sure has been an exciting trip. Beginning to see why you don't come out this way too often. If I ever get back to the high country, reckon I might just stay there. It's a heap safer."

Before long the night shadows had gathered. When the last thread of daylight had unraveled from the star-scattered sky, Hawkes said it was time. It wouldn't do to wait until moonrise. Leaving the mule and horse in the elms, they went across the creek at a dead run, finding cover in some rocks at the base of the bluff. Since the two long shots Hawkes had not seen or heard from the bushwhacker, but he figured him to be there still.

"Work your way up a bit and take a shot or two," he told Gilmartin. "Try to draw his fire. I'll go up in that direction and come around behind him."

Gilmartin nodded and started up. Hawkes did, too, angling off to one side, moving quickly but carefully, not wanting to betray his progress with a careless step. When by his calculations he was as high as the rocks where he'd seen the sun flash on metal, he changed course. At that moment Gilmartin fired his first shot. There was no answering fire. Hawkes climbed higher. When Gilmartin fired again, he dropped down. Scanning the steep slope below and to his right, he saw muzzle flash as the ambusher replied. The man hadn't moved. Hawkes started down the slope. Gilmartin's third shot screamed off rock, too close for comfort, and when the ambusher rose up from his place of concealment to answer back, Hawkes saw the movement in the gloomy night and drew a bead.

"Put that long gun down real slow," he said, his voice pitched low and calm, his voice hard as tempered steel.

The man put the rifle down and sagged back against a rock.

"No more shooting, Gil," Hawkes called down the slope, edging closer to his prey.

"Well," said the ambusher, "the Prophet himself told me that no bullet could end my life. Why don't you put one right between my eyes and prove him right or wrong? I must confess, I've been a little curious."

"I'd rather not, if you don't mind. Got any more weapons?"

"An Allen pepperbox pistol and an Arkansas Toothpick."

"Throw 'em away."

The man took the weapons from his belt and tossed them aside. Hawkes ventured closer to retrieve the rifle, a .50 caliber Northwest percussion, with a 48-inch barrel. Gilmartin came clambering up the incline in a hurry. When he arrived, he sank down on one of the rocks, hissing through clenched teeth.

"Damn. My head feels like it's going to split open like a ripe melon. Who do we have here, Gordon?"

"Don't know. Stand up, friend."

"Can't stand up. One of you Pukes hit me in the leg. Knocked me down and I broke the other leg below the knee. Best I can do right now is sit up high enough to shoot over these rocks."

"You got us wrong," said Hawkes. "We're not with those boys you shot to pieces earlier. We met them a ways back. They're going home."

"How many did I get?"

"Three."

"Good."

"A bullet and a broke leg explains why he's still up here," said Gilmartin. "Where's your horse, mister?"

"Other side of the hill."

"You figured to sit up here till hell freezes?"

"My fate rests in the Lord's hands."

"I say we just leave him here and ride on," Gilmartin told Hawkes.

Hawkes took a long look at the bushwhacker. From what he could see in the dark, the man had a lanky frame and a mane of unruly hair grown long past his shoulders, framing a gaunt face pale in the starlight.

"I reckon not," said Hawkes.

"What do we owe him? He was trying to kill us a little while ago, remember? You know what he is—one of those Mormon killers like what tried to murder Lillburn Boggs."

"One of the few times I missed my shot," said the ambusher. "Another was today when I killed your mule by mistake."

"You? You're the one who tried to assassinate the governor of Missouri?"

"He ordered the extermination of my people."

Gilmartin let out a low whistle. "Come on, Gordon. I think I've had about all the excitement I can stand for one day."

"We'll make camp down by the creek," decided Hawkes, passing his Plains rifle and the Northwest gun to Gilmartin. He extended a hand to the Mormon. "I'll help you along."

"I need no help from the likes of you."

"We're not leaving you up here, mister. I want you where I can see you."

The Mormon assassin hesitated, then clasped the proffered hand. Hawkes hauled him upright. The man could put some weight on the leg carrying the bullet, but none at all on the other. It was no easy task for Hawkes, getting him down the slope.

Gilmartin descended ahead of them. "I can't wait to find out what'll come our way tomorrow," he muttered.

Chapter 8

"My name is John Bonham," he said, sitting across the campfire from Hawkes and Gilmartin as a cool night wind rustled through the uppermost branches of the elms that grew along the gurgling creek. He wore a Kossuth hat and a gray duck duster, and his trousers were tucked into Wellington boots adorned with spurs. The firelight accentuated his gaunt cheeks and prominent cheekbones—and the piercing blue eyes beneath a stern brow. A prominent scar slanted across his forehead, splitting his right eyebrow and angling above the cheek; the lobe of the ear on that side was missing. It was clear evidence that Bonham had been in one hell of a knife fight long ago. He had declined all that Hawkes offered him to eat or drink with the exception of cornpone; he was not in the habit of eating the flesh of animals, or using tobacco, or drinking strong spirits.

"I am one of the Sons of Dan," he told them. "I have been chosen to defend the Church against its enemies. I am the instrument of the Lord's vengeance on those who seek to destroy the Chosen."

He went on to tell them that Brigham Young and the Quorum of the Twelve Apostles—the leaders of the Saints—had sent several parties south into Missouri to gather up all the faithful who yet remained in the state, so that they could join the westward trek to the New Jerusalem.

"New Jerusalem?" queried Gilmartin. "Where is that, exactly?"

"We will know when we find it, the land God has set aside for Israel. His kingdom on earth."

"I thought all Mormons had been driven out of Missouri years ago," said Hawkes.

Bonham nodded. "Most of us were. I was among those who settled ten years ago near Independence. But we were driven away from there and tried again at Far West. We began to build our temple. There were ill omens from the start. For example, a lightning bolt struck our flag in the town square. The Missouri Pukes began to raid our farms and ambush our settlers. Then Boggs sent his militia against us. We fought them at Crooked River and drove them back. A few days later they struck at us again at Haun's Mill, killing women and children, shooting them down without mercy.

"Three thousand of the Missouri militia marched on Far West. Many of our leaders were captured, including the Prophet and his brother, Hyrum Smith. They would have been shot had Colonel Doniphan not intervened. He is one of the few Gentiles who has dealt fairly with us. Warrants were issued on those of us who fought at Crooked River, orders given to shoot us on sight. But most of us escaped. In the months to come nearly all the Saints who had lived in Davies and Caldwell counties moved away, some to Iowa, most across the Mississippi to Nauvoo. I returned later, with the Prophet's blessing, to wreak vengeance on that devil, Boggs."

"We met him some days back," remarked Gilmartin. "He's headed for California."

Bonham was silent for the moment, digesting this information. "God willing," he said softly, "I will be given an opportunity to avenge the deaths of the women and children whose blood stains his hands."

Gilmartin lifted an eyebrow at Hawkes, who said, "You folks are bound up in those Old Testament ways, aren't you? Eye for an eye, tooth for a tooth."

"Yeah," said Gilmartin dryly, "him and Billy Ring are two peas from the same pod."

"So the burned-out homestead we saw this morning belonged to Mormons," said Hawkes.

"Lyman Thomas and his family. He sent word to the Twelve Apostles that he wanted to join us in our journey to New Jerusalem. I and three others came to fetch him. We had gone but a few miles when we saw the smoke behind us, and we knew the cabin was aflame. I waited here while the others moved on, as I was certain the men who had burned the Thomas home would follow."

"Sounds like if you get caught here in Missouri they'll kill you for certain."

Bonham's smile was warm as winter. "Death holds no fear for me. I would gladly die in the service of the Church." His voice was a husky whisper as he gazed into the fire. "You see, my wife and child were murdered at Haun's Mill. I have other wives now, and yet . . ."

"Wives? How many wives do you have, exactly?" asked Gilmartin.

"Two."

"Two wives. Maybe there's something to this Mormon religion after all, Gordon."

Bonham glared at him. Gilmartin's tone was heavy with sarcasm, and the Danite avenger was not amused.

"Shut up, Gil," said Hawkes.

"Hell, Gordon, it just doesn't seem right. I know Injuns do the same, but it don't suit white people."

"You are unacquainted with the Bible, then, I take it," said Bonham.

"I'm just saying it's small wonder other folks have turned against you," said Gilmartin. "You make your own laws. You have your own army. From what I've heard you even have your own president in Brigham Young."

"They hate us because we prosper where they fail," replied Bonham. "They hate us here in Missouri because we are abolitionists. But most of all they hate us because we are God's chosen people, and it is written that at the time of the Resurrection we will rule the earth."

Shaking his head, Gilmartin stood up. "You see? It's that kind of talk that gets people riled." He looked at Hawkes, who was busy building a smoke in his pipe, and then left the camp, walking down to the creek to watch low clouds scudding in from the west and to let his temper cool.

"So what's to be done with me?" Bonham asked Hawkes. "You know, they've posted a sizable reward for my capture in Missouri."

"Wouldn't do me much good to try and collect, because there's a bounty on my head, too. Ten thousand dollars, last I heard. I'm wanted for the murder of a man in Louisiana."

Bonham said nothing more. He lay down, tilted his hat over his eyes, and in spite of the pain he was in, he went to sleep.

Later, Gilmartin returned to sit on his heels by the fire. "Storm rolling in," he said. "Should make us harder to track." He glanced at Bonham. "What are we going to do with him, Gordon?"

"Take him with us. Leave him in the care of his people."

"I was afraid you were going to say that. You realize, of course, what will happen to us if we're caught in Missouri with a Mormon assassin."

"Then we'll just have to keep from getting caught, I guess."

"But what do you care? You'll hang anyway if they catch us."

Hawkes puffed on his pipe. "You don't have to buy into this, Gil. Make your own trail if you want. You've already stuck your neck out for me as it is, and I thank you for it. No need to stay with me from here on."

Chagrined, Gilmartin said, "Didn't mean it that way. Just that this Mormon business makes me as jumpy as a green-broke pony."

"One thing you might think about—I doubt if a pack of Missouri vigilantes will hound us once we hook up with the Saints."

"You're probably right as rain on that count." Gilmartin peered uneasily into the darkness. "I got an itch between my shoulder blades, hoss. Like somebody's drawing a bead on me right this minute. You still got that feeling we're being followed?"

"I still do." Hawkes knocked out the pipe bowl and stretched out in his blanket, hand resting on the Plains rifle that lay beside him. "Good night, Gil."

" 'Night." Gilmartin stood there for a while, listening to the sounds of evening, the crickets and the frogs and the song of the creek and the wind in the trees. He kicked dirt over the fire and felt a little less like a target as the camp was plunged into darkness. Sitting with his back to an elm tree, rifle across his knees, he eventually dozed off. But he slept fitfully, waking every now and then to make sure he was still alive.

Early the next morning Hawkes rode around to the other side of the bluff and found Bonham's horse, a handsome bay Morgan. The rain started, and he didn't expect it to let up all day. Heading back to camp, he wondered whether the Mormon avenger could even ride, and if so, for how long. The leg carrying the bullet was in bad shape. He needed a doctor. But Bonham wasn't going to trust his fate to a Missouri physician—Hawkes knew that without asking. But if Bonham didn't receive medical treatment soon the leg might be lost, if not life itself. Hawkes briefly considered trying to remove the ball himself—then decided against it. Not that he was squeamish about such matters. Even if he was successful the operation would surely render Bonham incapable of travel for at least a day or two. And staying put that long was unwise for all concerned.

Bonham was tough as old leather. He had to be in constant, grinding pain but he didn't let on. He declined any of the coffee Gilmartin had brewed, drinking only a little water from the creek, and eating nothing. Hawkes had met some tough characters among the trappers and traders of his world, but Bonham measured up to the toughest. He seemed impervious to pain, thirst, hunger, and exhaustion.

Being of such caliber, Bonham quickly assented to let Hawkes set the broken leg. It was a clean break and Hawkes was finished in no time, using stout sticks and strips torn from the bottom of Bonham's trouser leg to secure the makeshift splints. An hour later Bonham was in the saddle. He stayed there all day and never faltered, though by the time they reached their next campsite, more than thirty miles away, there was fever in his eyes. Hawkes cut away the man's trouser leg and checked the bullet wound by the campfire's light. He saw red streaks in the swollen flesh radiating out from the hole encrusted with black blood.

"Can't wait any longer," he told Bonham. "Either I take the bullet out now or you lose your leg for certain. Maybe even your life."

"Take it out," replied the cold-nerved Mormon. "I want to live long enough for one more shot at Lillburn Boggs."

Hawkes turned to Gilmartin. "This looks like a

good night for you to go out and steal a wagon. At least the rain's stopped."

"Steal a wagon?" Gilmartin was incredulous. "You've lost your mind, hoss."

"He won't be able to ride for a spell. I saw a wagon trace and chimney smoke about five miles back."

"You know," said Gilmartin dryly, "I once entertained thoughts of going back to St. Louis one day. Quitting the high country and living a civilized life again. I see now that it won't happen. I'll never be able to come back."

"Take my horse," suggested Hawkes, ignoring his musings.

Shaking his head, Gilmartin climbed aboard the dun mustang and rode off into the deepening night, leading his mule.

Having no whiskey on hand for sterilizing the wound or his knife, Hawkes held the blade of his Bowie knife in the campfire's flames for a moment. Bonham removed his belt and handed it over. "Use this to tie off my leg," he said. "Cut me off a piece first."

Hawkes cut off a strip—which Bonham placed between his teeth—and heated the blade a few minutes more while Bonham applied the belt as a tourniquet above the knee. The wound being a few inches below the knee, Hawkes removed Bonham's boot and tore the trouser leg open.

"You ready?" he asked.

Bonham nodded, his eyes devoid of fear.

Holding the leg down and straight, Hawkes made a deep lateral cut across the bullet hole and probed for the ball with the point of his knife. Bonham's body went rigid but he made no sound. A moment later Hawkes had the half ounce of lead out. He let the wound bleed while he heated the knife's blade yet again, then laid the hot steel across the incision he had made. Bonham's body jerked again, and a growl escaped from the man's throat. Once more Hawkes put the blade into the fire, once more applied it to the Mormon's suffering flesh. He looked up to find that Bonham had passed out.

Removing the belt tourniquet and the strip of leather from between Bonham's teeth, Hawkes stabbed his knife into the ground a few times, wiped it on his leggings, and settled back to have a drink of water from his canteen and pack his pipe with Ol' Virginny. After a while his nerves settled down. When he was finished with his smoke, Hawkes used part of Bonham's torn trouser leg to bandage the wound. That done, he let the fire die down, stretched out on his blanket, and listened for Gilmartin's return.

Several hours later he heard the wagon. Gilmartin wore an expression of grim amusement as he sat on his heels near the fire that Hawkes had resurrected.

"You'll never guess who that old spring wagon belongs to," said the fur trader. "One of those Missouri boys we ran across a few days ago. Told him if he'd been worth his salt and killed Bonham here he wouldn't be short a wagon now. Oh, and that other mule there is his, too. I admit it made me feel some better about my thievery."

"First light will be in a couple of hours," said Hawkes. "We better get moving pretty soon."

"I don't think he'll be coming after us, hoss, if that's what you're worried about. Didn't seem to hanker for another scrape with our friend here. You know, you could be right—a Missouri posse won't come for us if we're with these Mormons. That is, if we get that far."

"We will."

Gilmartin was gazing at the unconscious Bonham. "Think he'll pull through?"

"I wouldn't bet against him."

They were on their way before dawn, under a gun-metal-gray sky that threatened to unleash a deluge, and the smell of rain was heavy in the air. Bonham traveled in the back of the spring wagon, his Morgan bay tied on behind. Gilmartin handled the rig. About midday the rain came, just as Bonham stirred, sat up, and looked about him.

"You'll come to a creek soon," he said. "Cross it and follow it west to the Missouri. Ten miles up the river you'll find a ferry. It's a place called Council Bluffs. We've got camps on both sides. Winter Quarters is west of the river. That's where you need to take me." Then he lay down and was soon asleep again.

The following morning they reached the ferry that the Saints had constructed some miles north of where the Platte River converged with the Missouri. The ferry was guarded by a squad of well-armed men whose steely eyes were filled with suspicion as Hawkes and Gilmartin approached. But when they saw Bonham rise up in the back of the spring wagon their fingers eased off the triggers of their guns.

"These men are with me," said Bonham. "I'll abide no harm coming to them."

With that they were allowed to board the ferry immediately, even though there were a number of wagons lined up waiting to cross. Reaching the west bank of the river, they traveled several miles up a trace to a large camp. Axes and mallets rang out as work crews harvested a nearby stand of timber and threw up small, one-room cabins. This was Winter Quarters, where Brigham Young and his Saints planned to pause in their mass westward exodus.

Chapter 9

Dozens of log huts had been erected, and dozens more were going up daily. They were all built to the same simple, functional design—twelve feet square with one door and no windows. Many sported an Osnaburg wagon tarpaulin for a roof. The floors were usually dirt; occasionally, rough planking was laid down in those quarters where the dirt was prone to turn into mud when it rained. Wide streets had been marked off, and these were deeply rutted by the passage of numerous wagons. Beyond the encampment, herds of oxen, mules, horses, and cattle grazed, guarded around the clock. This was Indian country, Nebraska Territory, but Hawkes wasn't sure it was Indians that the Mormons were really worried about. He wondered, too, why they were establishing a semipermanent camp now, in the middle of the summer. Bonham had called the place Winter Quarters, but winter was still some months away.

As one of the ferry guards escorted them through the encampment, directing them to John Bonham's hut, Hawkes got a good look at the Saints. Somehow he had expected them to look different from ordinary folks. But they didn't. A deep weariness mixed with grim determination marked their features. The hardship of the four hundred miles of trail from Nauvoo on the Mississippi River was etched into every face.

The guard bade Gilmartin to stop the wagon in

front of a hut, from which emerged two women. One was older than the other, perhaps in their forties, her black hair graying, the bloom of youth gone forever from her hollow cheeks, the joy of life absent from sun-faded eyes. The other was much younger, tall and willowy with chestnut brown hair and big hazel eyes and a dusting of freckles across her nose. Her skin was quite fair—the kind of complexion that burned instead of tanned. Hawkes thought for an instant that she must be Bonham's daughter. Then he remembered that the holy killer had mentioned his *two* wives.

Bonham sat up when the wagon stopped. The older woman's face became animated, and she rushed to his side. "Praise the Lord," she said. "He has delivered you safely."

"This time the Lord had some help, Lizzie," replied Bonham.

She glanced at Hawkes and Gilmartin. "Gentiles? Why would they help you, husband?"

"Not all Gentiles are bad. Doniphan, for one, proved that."

Hawkes dismounted into the muck of the street—it had rained again at daybreak—and moved to help the ferry guard assist Bonham into the hut. "He needs a doctor, ma'am," he told the woman named Lizzie.

"We have no physicians among us."

"Where are they?" asked Gilmartin.

"The Lord our God is the source of all healing. I will summon Brother Jacobs and he will lay hands upon my husband's wounds. If it is God's will he be made whole then it will be so."

Gilmartin was stunned. He'd seen clear evidence that dysentery, malaria, and black canker afflicted these people. Among the hundreds of Saints he had seen as he passed through the camp there were an unusually large number of sick people. But he made no further comment. There could be no profit to be had from remarking on the peculiarities of these people. All he wanted to do was head west. Out yonder lay the plains and the trail back to the mountains. He was ready to put this country and all of its troubles behind him.

Hawkes and the ferry guard had carried Bonham into the hut, with Lizzie on their heels. The young woman remained standing just outside the door, trying to watch Gilmartin without seeming too forward.

"You're welcome to come in," she said shyly.

He'd paid her no attention at first, but now he took a closer look—and for some reason could not bring himself to look away again, even though his intense scrutiny made her more self-conscious than she'd been in extending the invitation.

All thoughts of the plains and the mountains beyond vanished from Gilmartin's mind as he jumped down off the wagon. His landing splattered mud over her shoes and the hem of her faded gingham dress.

"I'm so sorry," he gasped, mortified.

She smiled, looking away. "I don't mind. Truly."

Gilmartin nodded and gestured lamely at the door. "After you, miss."

She turned inside and he followed, noticing how lustrous her chestnut hair was, done up in a careless bun, and he thought how pretty it must look hanging loose around her shoulders.

The small single room was crowded with trunks and barrels and sacks of provisions, harnesses and tools and a few pieces of good furniture—a table with six ladder-back chairs, a rocking chair by the simple stone hearth, a four-poster bed, and a chest of drawers. The floor had been packed down a good ten inches above street level and so it remained fairly dry. With six people in such cramped confines there was barely room to move around, so Gilmartin settled down on a balltop trunk just inside the door and watched.

Hawkes and the guard were placing Bonham on the bed.

"Patience," snapped Lizzie, "fetch a cup of water."

The young woman dipped a tin cup into a bucket of water and carried it to the bed. Bonham drank gratefully, and then glanced at the ferry guard.

"Go find Brigham Young. Tell him I am here. Did the rest of my men come back? What of Lyman Thomas and his family?"

"They all arrived safely," Lizzie told him. "Simon Parker told me what you had done. He wanted to go back for you but Brother Brigham forbade him to do so." Her voice was sharp with resentment. "He said he did not want another war with the Missourians."

"He was right to stop Simon," replied Bonham. "Brother Brigham must concern himself with the welfare of twenty thousand Saints, wife. Against that, what do I matter?"

"You matter to me. What would become of Patience and me if you had not returned?"

"In time you would be sealed to another man."

"I do not wish to be, though I cannot say with any certainty that Patience feels the same as I in that respect."

Bonham looked at Patience, but neither of them said a word. Gilmartin felt a cold knot in the pit of his stomach. Patience was Bonham's second wife! Unlike Hawkes, it hadn't occurred to him that she could be. One so young and innocent and lovely, married to an assassin who had the blood of many men on his hands?

The guard departed on his errand. Hawkes turned to Gilmartin. "We'd better get going. We're burning daylight."

"I am sure Brother Brigham would like to meet you," said Bonham.

"Well, I . . ." Hawkes glanced at Gilmartin. "I think my partner wants to get on down the trail."

"Please stay awhile," said Patience. "We don't have much, but you're welcome to share what we do have. Would you like some milk and cornmeal?"

"I don't see any harm in staying over a day," said Gilmartin.

That was the last thing Hawkes had expected to hear from the fur trader, but he made no comment.

"Milk and cornmeal sounds just fine," Gilmartin told Patience, even though it didn't sound the least bit appetizing. In truth, though, the gruel wasn't half bad after Patience had mixed it with a little honey. Hawkes and Gilmartin were seated at the table, just finishing up, when three men arrived. One was the ferry guard. A second was a slender young man with dark hair and hooded eyes that disguised the fact that he was as alert as a mountain cat. He wore Colt Patersons in cross-draw holsters beneath his frock coat. The first impression Hawkes had of him was that he was just a kid; then he took a closer look and saw a killer's edge to him. He was John Bonham fifteen years ago.

The third man was tall and stocky, with golden hair and a full beard framing a sunburned face set off by bright blue eyes. He was clad in black broadcloth, the trousers tucked into high mule ear boots to protect them from the muddy streets. Hawkes could tell by the way Patience and Lizzie acted that this was someone very important—it had to be Brigham Young. It was more than respect they demonstrated, something akin to awe.

"John Bonham," said the golden-haired man, his voice a deep and gravelly rumble, "Simon here told me what you had done. I can't say that I was surprised that you did it—or that you survived."

"I might not have, without the help of these two men. Gentlemen, this is Brigham Young, President of the Quorum of the Twelve Apostles. The man we rely on to lead us to the New Jerusalem."

"And who are you men, exactly?" asked Brigham Young.

"Could be those Gentile spies Colonel Stout keeps talking about," drawled Simon Parker. He smiled at Hawkes as he said it, but the smile didn't fool Hawkes. Parker was smart and lethal and not one to underestimate.

Bonham chuckled. "Spoken like one of Hosea's whittling deacons."

"Whittling deacons?" asked Gilmartin. "Danite Angels, Twelve Apostles—now whittling deacons." He shook his head in wonder. "Sorry, friends, but I'm getting more and more confused."

"Members of Colonel Hosea Stout's police force," explained Bonham. "Simon used to be one of them, until I recruited him for my outfit. They're called whittling deacons because you always see them loitering about, keeping an eye on everything that goes on while whittling a stick with those Bowie knives."

"It is the opinion of Brother Hosea and others," said Brigham Young, "that the Missourians have sent spies to find out what we are doing."

"That's not us," said Gilmartin. "My partner and I are from the high country. I'm Dane Gilmartin and this is Gordon . . . Henry Gordon. We came to Independence to sell plews. On our way back we met up with Mr. Bonham. He introduced himself by shooting one of my mules."

"I wasn't aiming for the mule," confessed Bonham. "The sun was in my eyes. I thought they were Missouri Pukes. But they aren't. I'll vouch for them, Brother Brigham."

"That is sufficient for me," said the Mormon leader. "From the mountains, you say? They are our destination. I would like to speak to you both at length about the trail that lies ahead—and what we can expect at the end of that trail."

Hawkes looked to Gilmartin, eyebrows raised in a silent query. But the fur trader wasn't paying any attention, fixing his gaze instead on Patience, who was busy cleaning away the table.

"Well," said Hawkes, "I guess we can spare a day." Though eager to get back to Eliza and Cameron, he was curious about the Mormons and wanted to learn more about their plans.

"My thanks to you," said Brigham Young. "Walk with me, then. Brother Bonham, rest yourself. I will look in on you again soon."

He turned and left the hut. Hawkes slapped Gilmartin on the back in passing. "Shake a leg, Gil."

Simon Parker gave Bonham a nod, touched his hat brim with a smile at Lizzie and Patience, and also took his leave. As Hawkes and Gilmartin fell in step with Brigham Young, the "whittling deacon" strolled along a dozen paces behind. Hawkes wondered what Parker was up to. Was he keeping an eye on a pair of Gentile strangers or protecting the Mormon leader from other possible threats?

Plodding through the mud, Brigham Young brooded silently for a moment, his hands knotted into fists as they swung at his side. As the eyes of all the people in the street turned to him, Hawkes got a sense of the immense responsibilities that this man carried. Thousands of people—tired, sick, and hungry people—had been driven from their homes and faced an uncertain future. And every last one of them, it seemed, depended on Brigham Young to lead them as Moses had led the Israelites—out of bondage and to the promised land.

"Do you gentlemen believe in miracles?" he asked abruptly, catching both Hawkes and Gilmartin by surprise.

"I don't think I've ever witnessed one," was Gilmartin's lame reply.

"No?" Brigham Young smiled grimly. "I suspect you know something about our history. Many of us left Nauvoo over four months ago—it took us that long to get this far. The people you saw in the wagons waiting at the ferry are those who left after we did. In fact, we are strung out across the breadth of Iowa. Word has just come to me that the last few families put Nauvoo behind them only a few weeks ago. They were driven out by Illinois mobbers.

"A thousand of our people were there when the 'wolf packs' came. We put up barricades and fought them for three days while the women and children escaped across the Mississippi. In most cases they took with them only what they could carry on their backs. I sent wagons to assist them, but the rains have been unusually heavy all summer, and the roads, such as they are, are in terrible shape. For many days the refugees huddled without food or shelter in a place we will remember forever as Poor Camp. Our people died by the dozens, for you must understand that those who lingered in Nauvoo were the old, the sick, and the lame. When the wagons did finally arrive at Poor Camp there was simply not enough food to go around. But the Prophet told us that signs shall follow those who believe. Suddenly a flock of quail descended on the camp. They ran past the wagons and the people caught them in their hands. They flew away, and came back to run through the camps again—and then again. Just as manna from heaven saved the Children of Israel as they wandered in the wilderness, so the quail saved the people of Poor Camp from death by starvation."

Hawkes didn't know what to say. He thought the story highly suspect. On the other hand, Brigham

Young was not a man prone to exaggeration or flights of fancy.

The Mormon leader stopped and turned. "You are wondering why I have told you all of this. I suppose it is to persuade you that we believe strongly in miracles. We know that the Lord God will provide for us. We know as well that through sacrifice and suffering we earn the Almighty's grace."

Brigham Young paused to look along the street and beyond, to the plains that stretched to a far horizon.

"There will be much more sacrifice in the weeks and months to come. And I think we will need a few more miracles if we are to reach our destination."

Chapter 10

Hounded from state to state, persecuted at every turn, the Mormons had decided a year earlier that their only hope for survival lay in the West. In September of 1845, the Twelve Apostles had promised the state of Illinois that the Saints would depart the following spring. They redoubled their efforts to finish the temple at Nauvoo. Suspicious outsiders wondered why, if the Mormons were leaving, they worked so diligently on that temple. They simply did not understand.

By December the temple was far enough along that the "endowments" could be taken. Saints filed in day and night to be initiated as members of the New Dispensation. This ritual was holy and secret; it lighted the one true way to the Keys of the Kingdom, an anointing similar in importance to the Gentile baptism.

At the same time, the Saints prepared for the long westward exodus. Oak was cut and dried in kilns and then used in the construction of remarkably sturdy wagons. Hickory was soaked in brine and fashioned into iron-hard axles. The women kept busy accumulating stores of dried fruits, pickles, vinegar beans, and cornmeal. They made squash cakes by the barrel. Parley Pratt, one of the Twelve Apostles, posted the requirements needed by every family going west—a wagon, three yoke of oxen, two cows, several sheep, a thousand pounds of flour, and twenty pounds of sugar. He added coffee, tea, and one keg of alcohol, even though the Saints had been advised not to partake of such refreshments in the Words of Wisdom, penned by their martyred prophet, Joseph Smith.

By the end of the year more than three thousand families were inventoried, and were divided into companies of one hundred families each. It was then that Orson Pratt, brother to Parley and another of the Apostles, returned from the East with a crate of Allen pepperbox revolvers and a rumor that the United States government planned to prevent the Saints from going west, for fear that they were bound for disputed Oregon with the intent to volunteer their services to the British at Vancouver. Both the United States and Great Britain coveted Oregon, and quite a few people in both camps expected a war to break out. Another rumor was floating about—that federal marshals carried warrants for the arrest of the Twelve Apostles. It was decided that Brigham Young and the other Mormon leaders would be in the first company to cross the Mississippi.

When word spread that their leaders were going, many of Nauvoo's residents opted for an early departure as well. By early summer there were five hundred wagons on the trail, and a lot of the families were not fully prepared. Rest camps were established along the route that ran from east to west across the middle of Iowa—places like Garden Grove and Mount Pisgah became way stations where weary travelers could rest and recuperate. It was rough going. The summer was a wet one and the trail, all too often, became a river of mud. Flood also became a problem, and the Camp of Israel's leaders went to the extreme of sending wagon loads of goods and herds of livestock into northern Missouri, hoping to trade with the Gentiles for provisions.

Even now, there were wagons rolling into Winter Quarters or one of the smaller camps around Council Bluffs on the other side of the river. Twenty thousand travelers strung out across four hundred miles, tired and sick and undernourished. The scope of this mass migration was almost more than Hawkes could comprehend. The average wagon train heading up the Oregon Trail might contain at most a hundred or so prairie schooners and several hundred souls. But twenty thousand people in five thousand wagons across fifteen hundred miles of plains and mountains? It seemed impossible.

To complicate matters there was the war with Mexico. Hawkes had learned about the outbreak of hostilities from emigrants on the Oregon Trail prior to reaching Independence, but the news was of little import to him. For the Mormons, though, the war was a significant development because the United States government made it so. A Captain James Allen, escorted by three blue-coated dragoons, had come from Fort Leavenworth in search of Brigham Young a few weeks earlier. President James K. Polk was asking for five hundred Mormon volunteers to join General Stephen Watts Kearny's Army of the West, bound for a campaign against Santa Fe and points west.

Polk's decision to seek Mormon aid raised Gentile eyebrows, but Brigham Young knew exactly what the president was doing: securing the loyalty of the Mormon host while extending his help to them, in a very subtle way. The wages the Mormon volunteers would earn—and a good portion would be paid up front—could go to help the rest of the Saints buy the provisions they so desperately needed. After all, the once prosperous Mormons had been forced to sell the property left behind in Illinois for ten cents on the dollar. Polk wanted to help the Camp of Israel, but he couldn't just proffer aid without receiving something in return. Besides, as many a Missouri or Illinois mobber could testify, the Mormons could fight. They even had their own army, Charles Coulson Rich's Nauvoo Legion.

So Brigham Young had agreed to the president's request with alacrity. This problem lay in persuading five hundred men to sign up. There was a lot of resentment toward the United States among his followers. Where had the government been in all the years past when Mormon pleas for protection fell on deaf ears in Washington? Not many men were eager to leave their families to face the difficulties of the westward trail by themselves. Brigham Young admitted to Hawkes that it took him the better part of a month of hard recruiting to fill the five companies of the Mormon Battalion. Soon he would receive more than five thousand dollars in cash—the first installment of wages for the volunteers who, in the Mormon way, were turning every last dollar over to the Church to use as it saw fit for the good of the whole.

"With Battalion money," said Brigham Young, "I will be able to purchase much in the way of supplies at St. Louis."

"That will happen none too soon by the looks of things in this camp," remarked Gilmartin. He still hadn't quite recovered from his shock at the condition of the residents of Winter Quarters.

They had walked through the encampment to the western fringe, and now sat at a fine walnut dining table ringed with chairs which stood incongruously beneath a large tarpaulin tied at one corner to a sapling, and at the other three to stout poles. A few trunks lay about, and a bed made of canvas was pulled taut over a low wooden frame. These were Brigham Young's quarters.

The president of the Quorum of the Twelve Apostles did not even have a hut to call his own. His wives and children lived for the time being in wagons a hundred yards away, beyond a small grove of trees. Simon Parker stood at the edge of the grove, just beyond earshot but not pistol range. He leaned against a tree and, sure enough, whittled on a stick. From the tent, located as it was on high ground, one could see across the bustling Winter Quarters—a muddy, crowded sprawl of huts—to the serpentine road that led to the river marked by a distant line of trees.

"We are suffering, as you can see," said Brigham Young. "We are desperately short of food. But I know not where else to turn."

Hawkes had an idea. "There's food on the hoof west of here."

"We cannot begin to slaughter our oxen or our milk cows."

"I don't mean that herd. I'm talking about buffalo."

"Where can these buffalo be found?"

"Well, that's the trick. You never know for certain. You just roll your wagons west and keep going until you find them."

"How far, in your estimation?"

Hawkes squinted at the western horizon. "Last sign I saw was maybe two weeks by wagon from here. But that doesn't mean you'd find a herd in two weeks. Could take longer. Or less time. You just can't tell."

"But there is a chance. The Lord will provide for His people." Brigham Young leaned forward. "How many men and wagons would it take?"

"To feed all the folks in this camp?" Hawkes shook his head. "I have no idea. Let's say a dozen of your best marksmen, twice as many wagons, and two dozen more men to do the butchering in a timely fashion."

"And would you lead them?"

"I reckon I could."

"Wait a minute," said Gilmartin. "What are you doing, Gordon? I thought you wanted to get back to

Eliza and your boy. They can find a herd of buffalo without our help. A buffalo herd is kind of hard to miss. You either find one or you don't."

"You can move on if you want, Gil."

Gilmartin grimaced. "Excuse us a minute," he said to Brigham Young as he got up from the table and walked away. Hawkes followed. The fur trader halted twenty paces down the hill and turned on Hawkes. "I know what you're doing," he said, "but just because you feel like you turned your back on your mother doesn't mean you have to help these people."

"One has nothing to do with the other."

"The hell you say."

"Gil, you looked into the faces of those folks down there. They're in trouble and I'm going to lend them a hand. A few weeks won't make much difference. I can still get home before the snows come. Why don't you just go on without me?"

"I can't believe this is happening to me."

Hawkes wore a faint smile. "I bet you'll stick around, though."

"You're a gold-plated fool."

"Me? I'm not the one making eyes at the wife of a Mormon avenger. Are you tired of living or what?"

"I wasn't making eyes at anybody. You don't know what you're talking about."

"You better come hunt the buffalo with me, Gil. If I leave you here, you're liable to be worm food by the time I get back."

"I might go with you and then again I might not," said Gilmartin crossly. "I might stay here and I might head west. I don't know exactly what I'm going to do. Know one thing, though. I'm going to have to find a blacksmith around here someplace to make that stolen wagon I've ended up with more trail-worthy than it is. If I don't, I'll be sitting in a pile of kindling somewhere between here and Fort Laramie, waiting for an Indian to come along and lift my hair."

"You lost a mule and a wagon on my account, and got a cracked skull into the bargain. I'm beholden to you. That's why I feel it is my duty to keep you away from Patience Bonham," Hawkes said, trying to keep a straight face with only mediocre success. "First Eliza, and now this woman—you have a bad habit of hankering after married women. But I reckon I'm a lot more tolerant than John Bonham will be."

"You're imagining things," groused Gilmartin. "I'm not the least bit interested in her."

But he was lying and they both knew it.

Brigham Young had the men and the wagons ready to go the next day. There had been no need for hard recruiting in this case. Many more volunteered than were needed. Among the marksmen was Return Redden, a noted shootist with a checkered past that included a notorious career as a Mississippi River outlaw. Notwithstanding this, Redden was a devout Mormon. Simon Parker was also coming along. Hawkes couldn't shake the feeling that the young whittling deacon was charged with the task of keeping a close eye on the two Gentile strangers.

In addition, an Omaha Indian named Loud Talker was attached to the expedition at Brigham Young's request. Loud Talker was a tall, skinny, and eccentric man who wore eyeglasses on the tip of his Roman nose. Hawkes was given to understand that the Mormons had reached an agreement with the Omahas. Winter Quarters was located on Omaha land, and the Indians had agreed to let the Saints stay in return for a little help now and then against their perennial enemies, the Pawnees. Loud Talker wasn't a chief or medicine man, or even a particularly great warrior, but he still had a lot of influence. As best Hawkes could make out, he was a kind of roving diplomat, well known among other tribes in the region, and empowered to speak for the Omaha nation. He would go along in case the expedition ran into trouble with Indians of another tribe. Loud Talker could probably convince them that the Mormons respected the red man, regardless of his tribe, and were sincere in wishing to live in peace—which was more than could be said for many other whites. In fact, many of the Saints believed that the Indians were descendants of the Lost Tribe of Israel and therefore deserving of special consideration.

Hawkes had never met an Indian quite as garrulous as Loud Talker. The Omaha rode with Hawkes on the first day and never shut up for more than two minutes. He waxed eloquent about the sun, the sky, the grass, the water in the rivers and the creeks, and the birds and beasts of the prairie. He told Hawkes more than the latter had ever wished to know about Omaha legends, and their history and way of life. The sun, explained Loud Talker, lived in a splendid white lodge beyond the Big Water. Every night, after his slow crossing of the sky, the sun would go into this lodge decorated with the images of magical beasts unlike any seen by human eyes. He lived in the lodge with his wife, the moon, and his son, the morning star. Lightning was a giant bird that flew with his eyes closed, said Loud Talker. When Lightning opened his eyes a bright flash of light struck the earth. The raven had great wisdom and sometimes spoke to chosen humans, telling them of the future or the meaning of past events. Wolves were highly respected allies of the Omahas, noted for their skill in tracking and fighting; the sign for "scout" in Indian hand talk was the same one used for "wolf." Sometimes the wolf would warn an Indian friend of the presence of his enemies. All of these things Loud Talker spoke of—and much, much more.

Gilmartin also rode with the hunting party. He left the stolen spring wagon behind and borrowed a horse from Lorenzo Young. On the morning of the third day, Hawkes pulled him aside.

"I'm going on ahead," Hawkes told him. "I can't stand one more day of listening to Loud Talker rattle on."

"Want some company?"

"You'd better stay. I don't think that Parker fellow would take kindly to both of us riding out. I don't think he trusts us, for some reason."

"Can't imagine why a Mormon wouldn't trust our kind," said Gilmartin wryly.

"I'll be back before dark."

"Keep your powder dry."

Hawkes was pleased to get off alone. He breathed deep the smell of the earth and the grass warmed by a hot spring sun. The day was plenty warm, but a steady breeze from the south made a difference, cooling the sweat on his skin. An endless sea of grass rolled off to the shimmering horizon in every direction. Out here there were few landmarks—a grove of trees, an occasional ridge line. He headed due west, into country he had never seen before. The Platte River was somewhere to the south, and the Oregon Trail south of that. It occurred to him that if the Mormons stayed on this side of the river as they moved west, they could avoid contact with the Gentiles who seemed to give them so much grief. The Platte would be as easy to follow on its north side as on its south. But on the north side, Brigham Young wasn't likely to run into anybody except Indians.

He hadn't gone too far when an old familiar itch between the shoulder blades began to plague him. He supposed other hunted men developed the same inexplicable survival instinct. Checking his back trail from time to time, he saw nothing. But it sure felt like he was being followed.

About an hour after he first felt the itch, something hit him in the back with such sudden force that it knocked the air out of his lungs and pitched him out of the saddle. He landed facedown on the ground, rolled over slowly, and passed out. Unconscious for only a few minutes, he came to sobbing for air, realizing only then that he had been shot. His whole body felt numb. He couldn't lift his head—it was all he could do to raise an arm enough so that he could get a hand on the pistol on his belt. The sun hammered him from its zenith, but he didn't feel its heat and that scared him more than anything else. It seemed like he could actually feel the life leaking out of him.

Who had shot him? He wondered if he would find out at least that much before he died. When he felt a vibration in the ground beneath him he knew he was going to get his chance, and pushed the .41 caliber percussion pistol under his hip. He had but one shot, and was determined to make it count. There was no fun in dying alone.

The horse drew near but Hawkes didn't turn his head. He kept completely still, eyes narrowed into slits. A shadow passed over him—a dark shape blocked the blazing sun.

Geller grunted in surprise when he saw that Hawkes was still breathing, albeit short and labored breaths.

"You're harder to kill than most," he observed.

Hawkes opened his eyes and recognized the man from the lawyer's office—the big man with the eyes like cold brown marbles. The wind whipped the tattered black greatcoat against Geller's rawboned body. A long gun cradled in his arms, he slowly and carefully scanned the horizon.

"Usually I work up close," he said, "but it's kind

of hard for a man to get close in this country without bein' seen. Rather do business in a dark alley. Still, I wasn't going to let ten thousand dollars go without a fight. More than ten thousand now, I reckon. See, they think you killed that slick-talking lawyer man, too."

Hawkes said nothing. It was getting even harder to breathe, and he fought to stay conscious. Just a minute longer . . .

"Wasn't about to ride into that Mormon hive after you," continued Geller. "So I just bided my time. Real obligin' of you to ride out alone like you done." He reached down and drew the Bowie knife that Hawkes carried sheathed on his belt. The sun flashed off the twelve-inch blade as Geller admiringly turned the knife this way and that. "You look to be sufferin'," he said mildly. "I'll put an end to that."

He dropped down to one knee beside Hawkes and was putting the blade to his victim's throat when Hawkes shoved the pistol against the side of Geller's head and pulled the trigger. The ball entered his left temple and blew a big hole on the right side, taking brains, blood, and skull fragments with it. Geller died instantly, collapsing across Hawkes. Lacking the strength to move the corpse, Hawkes couldn't breathe at all now with the dead man lying on top of him. He had an instant to think about Eliza and Cameron before passing out.

As he slowly regained consciousness, Hawkes heard a voice as if from a great distance. The voice came closer, louder, and he opened his eyes and tried to focus. All he could see through the haze was a flash of light. The brume gradually diminished and Hawkes recognized Loud Talker. The Omaha was sitting on his heels, the setting sun a fiery red orb that seemed to be perched on the Indian's shoulder, its light flashing off the wire rims of Loud Talker's pince-nez.

"I am glad he did not scalp you," said Loud Talker.

"Then you would have come back as a ghost and haunted this place forever. If a Pawnee rode by here and saw a whirlwind of dust he would know it was you. You might have even come back as a skeleton able to walk. I have seen with my own eyes dead men walking."

Hawkes mumbled something and Loud Talker tilted forward. "I cannot hear you," said the Indian. "Speak louder. I do not want to miss your last words."

"I said shut up," rasped Hawkes, "and get him off me."

Loud Talker lifted up Geller's corpse and let it drop on the ground beside Hawkes. "This one will make a big ugly ghost," decided the Omaha.

Gilmartin appeared, leaning over Hawkes with his hands on his knees. "I was getting worried, so Loud Talker here tracked you down," he said, then glanced at Geller. "Knew we should have killed this bastard back in Independence. Has he killed you, Gordon? Damn it, you better stay alive. I'd hate to be the one to tell Eliza you were dead."

"I'll live," said Hawkes.

Chapter 11

Loud Talker rode back to the wagons, bringing one over to the place where Hawkes lay wounded. By then it was dark, but Gilmartin said they couldn't wait—they had to get his friend to a doctor. Then Gilmartin remembered that there were no physicians among the Mormons. And he couldn't haul Hawkes off to the nearest settlement, or even to Fort Leavenworth, because of the price on his head. The only choice was Winter Quarters, about fifty miles east.

It was decided that Loud Talker would lead the rest of the hunting expedition west in search of buffalo. Return Redden would be in charge. Gilmartin and Simon Parker took turns driving the wagon that carried Hawkes. They paused only to rest the mules. Sometimes one or the other would lie down in back beside Hawkes and try to sleep. For Gilmartin, sleep was an elusive thing, for he feared that Hawkes would die, a fear that gnawed at his guts every minute, every mile, so that time and again he checked his friend to make sure Hawkes was still breathing.

At best Gilmartin could tell, the ball from Geller's long gun had struck Hawkes high in the back on the left side above the shoulder blade, and was still lodged within him. It had been too high to damage a vital organ, but that didn't mean it wasn't a potentially fatal wound. For one thing, the lead was still in there somewhere, and Gilmartin though it likely that ligament and bone had been damaged to some extent.

Somehow, Hawkes hung on. He was awfully pale, and it worried Gilmartin. His skin was cold and clammy to the touch, and his pulse was rapid but weak. He remained unconscious much of the time, and when he did come around he seemed dazed and disoriented, asking for water all the time. Gilmartin gave him a little, but was afraid to give him too much. By the time they got to Winter Quarters, Gilmartin was an exhausted wreck—but Hawkes was still alive.

They moved Hawkes into John Bonham's hut at the Mormon avenger's request. Bonham was already up and around after only four days of bed rest—four days on a feather mattress was all he could stand, he said. He was able to put a little weight on the leg with the bullethole, enough to maneuver himself outside to a chair by the door, using a set of hickory crutches. They put Hawkes on the bed and moved him to the table the following day so that Simon Parker could remove the bullet. A few days later, Gilmartin concluded that his friend was going to live.

Lizzie Bonham seemed put out by the inconvenience of her home being turned into a hospital, particularly on a Gentile's account, but she didn't openly complain because it was her husband's wish that Hawkes recuperate under his roof. One favor deserved another, supposed Gilmartin. Hawkes had saved Bonham's life and now the holy killer was squaring accounts.

Unlike Lizzie, Patience Bonham went out of her way to tend to Hawkes. She was tender and untiring in changing bandages and nursing Hawkes through a bout of fever following Parker's surgery. As he spent a lot of time watching over his friend, Gilmartin had ample opportunities to watch over Patience, too. She could not help but be aware of his scrutiny, and she didn't seem to mind. Fortunately, no one else seemed to notice.

Four days after the surgery, Hawkes came to, clear-headed, and Gilmartin was there along with Patience. Bonham was sitting in his chair outside. Lizzie had gone to visit friends.

"You're going to live, hoss," said Gilmartin happily. "You've weathered worse."

"What about the others?"

"They went on with Loud Talker."

Hawkes looked around, taking stock of the situation, and when he saw Patience he laughed.

"You know, my wife had a dream about you. She dreamed I was shot and an angel came to take care of me."

Patience blushed. "I haven't done anything, sir."

"Don't believe that," said Gilmartin. "She hasn't rested since you arrived. She's an angel indeed. I almost wished I'd been the one to get shot."

"I'm glad you weren't, sir," she said.

Gilmartin was pleased, though he warned himself not to read anything into her comment.

A figure blocked the light coming through the open doorway. It was Bonham, balanced on his crutches. Patience returned to the fireplace, where she was heating a kettle of water. Bonham wobbled into the hut and eased down into a chair, scowling.

"The weather's changing," he said. "I can feel it. Brother Brigham has woodcutting crews at work laying in firewood. Brother Pratt's gone to Fort Leavenworth to collect the Battalion's wages. We must waste no time in storing provisions for winter. Thousands of our people are still scattered across Iowa," Bonham said, shaking his head. "And here I sit. I can barely make it to the street and back. I had planned to join the Battalion, you know. As soon as I returned from

Missouri I was going to ride to Fort Leavenworth. My name had already been placed on the rolls."

"Your injuries need time to heal," said Patience.

"I had not intended to sit in this hut all winter long," said Bonham crossly.

"Nor had I," said Hawkes. He glanced at Gilmartin. "You should give thought to going on, Gil. You leave now, you'll get to the mountains before first snow."

"What about you?"

"I'll come along when I'm able. You can take word to Eliza that I am well."

Frowning, Gilmartin thought it over—and shook his head. "Wouldn't feel right to go back without you, hoss, after all we've been through. Reckon I'll stay. Write a letter to Eliza. I'll ride down the trail and give it to the master of the first wagon train I find. Tell him to deliver it to Jim Bridger. Old Gabe will see that Eliza gets it."

"Well, there's no point in arguing with you," said Hawkes. "You're a hard-headed cuss." He wanted to tell Gilmartin that he knew there was another reason the fur trader was set on staying. But that would have been unwise in John Bonham's presence.

The hunting expedition returned two weeks later. All the wagons were loaded to capacity with buffalo meat and hides. They'd found a herd of shaggies near where the Loup Fork branched off from the Platte River. At about the same time, Parley Pratt and Orson Hyde, two members of the Quorum, returned from Fort Leavenworth with six thousand dollars in cash money, the government's first installment for the services of the Mormon Battalion, which was by now on the march with General Kearny's Army of the West. Brigham Young immediately sent trusted associates to St. Louis with orders to buy provisions for the Saints. Meanwhile, more emigrants straggled daily into Winter Quarters. Disease was on the rise, with malaria, dysentery, and the severe scurvy called black canker the most common afflictions of the malnourished Mormons.

Summer was over. The wind came blasting down off the northern plains. In four or five weeks the rain would come and, a few weeks after that, the first snow. Hawkes wrote the letter to Eliza and Gilmartin rode off to find someone on the Oregon Trail who would agree to carry it to Fort Bridger. The prospect of spending the winter away from his family was an unpleasant one for Hawkes. But there was nothing he could do. His wound had been serious and his recovery was slow. When Gilmartin returned, they were given a hut of their own in which to spend the winter. Hawkes was glad—he'd been a burden to the Bonhams for entirely too long. Gilmartin, though, wasn't happy about the new arrangements because the hut was on the other side of the camp from Patience. He needn't have worried. She visited nearly every day. Hawkes was her patient and she would tend to him until he was completely mended.

Hawkes was up and moving about in two weeks, though his left arm remained very stiff, causing him pain when he removed it from the sling Patience made for him. He considered trying for home in spite of the lateness of the season. But he wasn't up to it, and if a blizzard caught him on the High Plains there was a fair-to-middling chance he would never see his wife and son again. He started reading his mother's Bible to while away the hours. This resurrected old unwanted memories of childhood nights spent by the hearth in an Irish cottage listening to Mary Hawkes reading Scripture—but he stuck to it just the same.

The Book of Exodus was of particular interest to him, for it seemed in his view that the tribulations of Israelites in flight from Egypt, beset by enemies on all sides, wandering in the wilderness, seeking the promised land—the whole business was very much like what the Mormons were enduring now. It was a comparison the Saints themselves often drew. They called themselves the Camp of Israel. They sought a New Zion. Was this sacrilege? Hawkes couldn't say. But these people weren't the demons that Lillburn Boggs had portrayed. They had some peculiar customs and beliefs, but then so did the Indians, as Hawkes learned firsthand while living among the Absaroka Crows for nearly a year. He thought perhaps that experience gave him an open mind where the Saints were concerned.

In a few weeks, when he was able to ride, Hawkes volunteered to help bring in the rest of the Mormon stragglers. He was restless and needed to get away from the encampment. Wagons were dispatched eastward to bring as many of the Saints into Winter Quarters as possible. Others herded the livestock into the shelter of the Missouri bottoms before the first winter storm struck. The camp was divided into wards, and a log council house erected. Brigham Young finally consented to the building of a hut for himself and his family, now that most of the others had sufficient shelter. The wagons filled with provisions purchased in St. Louis arrived safe and sound.

The camp was policed by whittling deacons like Simon Parker, who took their orders from Hosea Stout, as stern and hard a man as Hawkes had ever met. The treatment his people had received embittered Stout, and his soul had been darkened even further by recent tragedy. He'd departed Nauvoo with his three wives and three children; soon all were sick. His son Hyrum died in his arms at Garden Grove and another son, William, perished along the trail. His wife Marinda died in childbirth, as did the child. Stout blamed his afflictions on the Gentiles, and it did not sit well with him that there were two men of that description in camp.

He paid Hawkes and Gilmartin a call—a square-built scowling man armed with a Bowie knife, a brace of pistols, and an abrasive attitude. He carried a black-snake whip coiled on a shoulder, and it was said that he did not hesitate to use it on lawbreakers—and even his own men when he thought they shirked their duties. The whip prejudiced Hawkes against Stout from the first, reminding him of Captain Warren and his cat-o-nine tails. Hawkes had felt the sting of the "cat" on his back more often than he cared to remember.

"I come here to tell you I don't like you," said Stout. "don't like you and don't like your United States of America. I didn't like it when Brother Brigham organized the Battalion and sent it off to fight with Kearny. My opinion, our men ought to be fighting on the Mexican side. If Mexico does win, I'll give three cheers. What do you think about that?"

"I don't think Mexico will win," said Hawkes, well aware that Stout was trying to provoke them.

"This is the last time we run from trouble," said Stout. "The last time, I promise you. When we get settled out West, you and your kind had better keep your distance. We won't pack up and leave our homes anymore. We'll fight to the last man."

When Stout was gone, Gilmartin stood fuming in the hut's doorway. "That son of a bitch is sure spoiling for a fight."

"Just leave it alone, Gil."

"He's got no call talking about the United States that way."

"I didn't know you were such a patriot."

"Aren't you?"

Hawkes shrugged. He'd avoided a clash with Hosea Stout and was just as keen to avoid one with Gilmartin. Truth was, he felt no strong allegiance to the

United States. He felt stronger ties to the Absaroka Crows than he did to America, and he'd never really thought of the mountains he loved as being part of any nation.

"I'll tell you one thing, Gil," he said. "Stout will be keeping a sharp eye on us. Better watch your step."

"What does that mean?"

"You know what I'm talking about."

Sparks of anger lit up Gilmartin's eyes. He knew Hawkes was talking about Patience Bonham. "I'm all grown up and I can take care of myself. I'd like to see Stout try to lay that blacksnake on me."

With a sigh Hawkes dropped the subject. There was no reasoning with a man in Gilmartin's lovestruck condition. And there was nothing he could do to change things. All he could do was hope for the best.

Because if Gil got into trouble over Patience, Hosea Stout and his blacksnake whip would be the least of his friend's trouble. John Bonham was an invalid, but he was still more dangerous than a den full of lions.

Chapter 12

On the final day of March, in the year 1847, a dance was held in the Mormon encampment at Council Bluffs, across the river from Winter Quarters. The festivities marked the imminent departure of the first group of Saints to head west in search of the New Jerusalem. This advance party, hand-picked by Brigham Young himself, would blaze a trail that the rest would follow later. Acting as scout for the vanguard would be Gordon Hawkes. The company would consist of seventy-two wagons and one hundred and fifty souls—all but five of them men. Brigham Young would also travel with the group, and the rest of the Quorum of the Twelve Apostles, as well, with the exception of the trio that had been sent east on a mission that would take them to England, where they were to spread the word among the Mormons there of what was transpiring in America. It was the hope of the Apostles that *all* Saints would congregate in the frontier Zion.

The purpose of the vanguard was vital to the survival of the entire Camp of Israel. They would find the New Jerusalem and then immediately begin planting crops. There was no time to waste. Hawkes told Brigham Young how harsh winters in the Rockies could be, and how early they sometimes came. Careful planning was required if all the Saints who would arrive in the promised land this year were to have enough to eat over the long winter. Brigham Young did not intend to take thousands of his people westward just so they could starve in the high country snows.

In addition, the vanguard, called the Pioneer Camp, would try to deal with any and all problems along the trail, smoothing the way with Gentiles and Indians alike for the rest of the Saints. No one could predict what lay in store for them on the way west. Hawkes figured there was no reason to expect trouble. But considering what the Mormons had endured in the past, he couldn't really fault Brigham Young for expecting the worst.

It was in this frame of mind that the Mormon president had selected the members of the advance party—twelve times twelve men, all of them fit and faithful, reliable, and resilient. Men like Brigham's brothers Lorenzo and Phineas, Stephen Markham, and Heber Kimball. Strong, steely-eyed men from the Nauvoo Legion like Norton Jacob, and from Hosea Stout's police force, like Simon Parker, were also chosen. Jacob was an artillery officer and was charged with the care of a six-pounder cannon that would accompany the group. John Bonham was coming along, too.

Over the winter Bonham had fully recovered from his injuries, though he walked with a slight limp and would continue to until the day he died. Lame or not, Brigham Young knew he needed Bonham to go along. The holy killer was his thunderbolt. If diplomacy failed, there was always John Bonham to hurl at the enemies of the Church. Brigham Young thought so highly of the Danite avenger that he gave Bonham permission to bring one of his wives with him. Bonham chose Patience; Lizzie would come with the rest, traveling with her sister's family. Patience had no family, and Bonham did not want to burden strangers with her care. Lorenzo Young was given leave to bring his wife and two children, while Brigham Young chose wife Clarissa, who was the daughter of Lorenzo's wife, Harriet. These were the only noncombatants among the Pioneers.

Hawkes didn't care if it turned out that they had to fight every inch of the way—he was dead set on going. The uneventful sojourn at Winter Quarters had nearly driven him to madness. He missed his family terribly. And he missed his mountain home. It was all he could do to refrain from leaving by himself at the first hint of spring. But Brigham Young had persuaded him to act as guide. There wasn't a single soul among the Saints at Winter Quarters who had ever been to the high country or, for that matter, all the way across the plains along the route they intended to take. Hawkes simply could not turn his back on these people. It wasn't that he thought they were right, and the Gentiles wrong. His decision had nothing to do with religion or politics, neither of which he cared much about.

All through the month of March preparations were made at a feverish pace. Finally Brigham Young announced the departure date—April 7. The Saints were in high spirits, even those left behind to test their mettle on the overland trek in the weeks to come. This was the year that they would find the home God had prepared for them. The horrors of last year's flight from Nauvoo could not dampen their spirits, nor could the discomfort and privations of the long winter months they had just endured. Hundreds of Mormon graves lay between Winter Quarters and Nauvoo. Perhaps there would be hundreds more to dig this year. But none of that mattered. They expected God to chastise them in order to be certain that they were worthy to receive His blessings. Those who had died—and who would die—were to be glorified forever in the annals of Church history as heaven-bound sacrifices necessary for the achievement of Mormon destiny.

As far as Hawkes could tell, he was the only one who didn't relish the idea of a celebration. He was worried on Gilmartin's account. Over the winter his friend had completely forgotten about Red Renshaw and the fur trade and the two or three Indian maidens he was known to gallivant around with. He gave not a care for anything except his next glimpse of Patience Bonham. After Hawkes recovered from his wound, those glimpses became very rare. Gilmartin was looking forward to the dance just for the chance to see Patience again. But what really caused Hawkes to fret was the news that John Bonham would not be present at the festivities. Brigham Young had sent him eastward on some mission the day before. That was the same as giving Gil enough rope to hang himself. Wishing to reserve celebration until he was reunited with Eliza and Cameron, Hawkes nonetheless resigned himself to the task of attending the Mormon jubilee for the purpose of keeping an eye on Gilmartin. He clung to a slender hope that Patience would be absent since her husband was away. Unfortunately, she was there.

Captain Pitt's Brass Band provided the music at the grand open air cotillion, playing Virginia reels and Copenhagen jigs with great flair and accomplishment. A grand feast had been laid on—a number of tables laden with food, including plenty of pies and cobblers, since the wild plums and strawberries were abundant. The festivities commenced in the early afternoon on a warm and sunny day, the kind of spring day tailor-made to lift even the most downcast of spirits. It would continue well into the night, and torches driven into the ground were fired when the sun sank below the skyline.

Hawkes was impressed by the good cheer of the

Saints. They danced and sang and laughed like people who didn't have a care in the world. A good many had lost loved ones since the abandonment of Nauvoo, and many more had lost much in the way of property. But that could not deter them from celebrating life and the future.

After a long winter spent with these people, Hawkes no longer felt like a stranger. The Saints had accepted his presence among them and made him to feel welcome. Well, most of them had. There were a few like Hosea Stout who refused to trust any outsider. Stout was at the dance, of course, with a squad of his whittling deacons, keeping an eye on things. Quite a few of the women present had absent husbands, many of whom were with the Mormon Battalion, and Stout considered it his solemn duty to guarantee their fidelity.

That made Hawkes worry even more about the attention Gilmartin gave Patience Bonham that day. The pair of them seemed to Hawkes to be spending entirely too much time together. Patience rarely danced with anyone else but Gil, and when they weren't dancing they were talking or walking or eating together. It was obvious to anyone with eyes to see that Gilmartin was infatuated with the young woman. Worse, he didn't look to be in the least concerned with appearances. Upon further reflection, Hawkes decided that Patience wasn't either. Still, he didn't interfere. If Gil wanted a taste of Stout's blacksnake medicine it was his own medicine. Might even do him some good. Besides, Hawkes doubted that intervention on his part would change anything. If Gil was cast out of the camp, Hawkes was resolved to go, too. But he kept an eye on things in case Gilmartin was threatened with something worse than a whipping. Then, Hawkes knew, he would have to step in and do something.

Shortly after sundown, Patience informed Gilmartin that she was expected home. Lizzie had frowned on her attending the dance and had ordered her to return when it got dark.

Though he'd spent hours with Patience he wasn't ready to part company with her and petulantly resented the early end to the best day he'd ever had. "She's not your mother, for heaven's sake," said Gilmartin, and instantly regretted the words.

"No," said Patience, suddenly pensive. "My mother and father are dead."

Gilmartin was mortified. "I'm awfully sorry. I didn't mean to . . ."

She touched his arm, smiling. "I know you meant nothing by it." Her hand lingered longer than necessary, and then she withdrew it with furtive glances left and right to see if anyone had noticed.

"I'll take you home," he said.

"You don't have to bother."

"Please let me."

She nodded and they set off for the line of wagons which had been provided to transport inhabitants of Winter Quarters across the river by means of the ferry. A wagon was just pulling away, and they jumped aboard to join a half dozen others who were quitting the revel early. The cotillion was still going strong. Having just concluded a reel, the band accompanied a young woman singing in a clear sweet voice. Gilmartin figured there were still at least a thousand Saints present. As he sat on the wagon tailgate beside Patience, watching the flickering torches recede, he wondered for the first time all day what had become of Hawkes. He'd completely forgotten about his friend. In fact, he'd forgotten about any and all things, so beguiled was he by Patience Bonham's company.

They made the journey back to Winter Quarters in silence. All day they had made small talk, touching on every subject under the sun, save the one that was of any real consequence to Gilmartin. He desperately wanted to know whether Patience had any feelings for him. Clearly she enjoyed his company, and he imagined there might be more to it than that since she had permitted him to monopolize her entire afternoon. She was the prettiest woman at the dance and would not have wanted for partners had she gone her own way. Yet in a matter of such import a man could not trust mere impressions. He needed to hear the words from her lips as confirmation that he wasn't indulging in wishful thoughts. But a wagon filled with people was not the place for that kind of conversation.

The wagon deposited its cargo at the outskirts of Winter Quarters. Gilmartin knew the way through the sprawl of huts and rutted streets; he'd spent all winter wandering around the encampment, disliking his own drab quarters except on the occasions when Patience had come to visit, checking on his friend's recovery or bringing them food. Tonight he walked very slowly. The camp seemed nearly deserted and he was glad of that. One problem remained—he didn't know exactly how to break the silence.

Patience rescued them both from embarrassment. "My parents lost their lives in the troubles down in Missouri. And my husband lost his first wife and children. Then he married Lizzie, but God saw fit to deny them offspring, so later I was sealed to him. I had grown up in the care of my uncle, but he later deserted the Church in Illinois. John Bonham asked the Prophet to provide him with a wife who could bear him children, and it was decided that I would be that woman. The Prophet himself came to speak to me about it. That was shortly before he was murdered in Carthage."

"Did you have any choice in the matter?"

She gave him a strange look. "The Prophet made the request personally."

"What you're telling me is that you did *not* have a choice." Gilmartin recalled that Joseph Smith—the Prophet—had been killed in the summer of '44. That was nearly three years ago. In that time, so far as he knew, Patience had failed to provide Bonham with children. He wondered why. But such a question could not be put directly. Neither could he be so forward as to ask Patience whether she was in love with her husband. "So," he said, hedging, "are you . . . happy with your situation?"

"We're nearly there," she said, avoiding the question. "Come—we can cut through here."

She turned off the street between two huts, and he took her arm to stop her.

"Patience. Are you happy?"

She refused to look him in the eye. "I am content with my lot."

Gilmartin thought she was lying. She tried to free herself from his grasp and he let her go, mumbling an apology. Then she looked up at him, very earnestly, her hazel eyes bright in the darkness.

"What do you want from me?" she whispered.

"A kiss, for starters," he replied, emboldened by sheer desperation.

Without hesitation she stood on tiptoe and kissed him. Then she stepped back, lips parted breathlessly, and even in the shadows he could see her fear. Not fear of him, or of someone seeing this indiscretion—but fear of the feelings stirring within her. Whirling, she ran away. He called out her name but she didn't stop, and he did not give chase.

Part Two

Chapter 13

April 6 marked the seventeenth anniversary of the founding of the Church. Ten days later the Pioneers departed Winter Quarters—one hundred and fifty Saints in seventy-two wagons with more than two hundred mules, oxen, and horses. And Norton Jacob's cannon, too, which Hawkes considered a lot of trouble for nothing. They camped the first night between the Elkhorn and Platte rivers. The weather, warm and dry, was good for travel.

By the time they reached the Platte and turned to follow its northern bank, a certain routine had been established. A bugle sounded at five o'clock in the morning, and by seven they were on the move, having had their breakfast and even cooking their dinner so that the noonday halt would be of short duration. Every man was ordered to keep his weapons close at hand, and no one but the scouts was to stray too far from the camp without permission. At night the wagons were circled, and usually the livestock was corralled within the circle. At eight thirty in the evening the bugle would sound again. By nine the fires were out, and all save the guards had turned in.

The wagons were filled with supplies for the long journey—biscuits, flour, beans, bacon, dried meat and fruit, oats and corn for the livestock. In addition there was seed for planting, hundreds of pounds of it, as well as the implements that would be required to sow that seed in the promised land—plows, hoes, spades, and scythes. Then, too, there were axes and whipsaws and log chains, kegs of gunpowder and plenty of lead, and extra harnesses. The most peculiar cargo was a leather boat, christened the *Revenue Cutter,* and a telescope belonging to Apostle Orson Pratt, a bookish man who was something of an amateur scientist. They were as well equipped as they could be, having learned valuable lessons during last year's flight from Nauvoo.

The men made a good impression on Hawkes. Brigham Young had chosen only the bravest and the fittest. More than half of them were young and unattached, in their late teens or early twenties; these lads were assigned to certain wagons as teamsters, strong and sober boys inured to hard work and peril. The others, though older—men like Brigham Young and his brother Lorenzo, or John Bonham and Return Redden—were just as tough and determined, not to mention more experienced when it came to dealing with trouble. Hawkes didn't doubt that every last one of them would stand his ground and deliver in a scrape.

The valley of the Platte made for good traveling. It was ten to fifteen miles in width, hemmed in by low bluffs and ridges that were often thick with cedar, and presenting few major obstructions to wagons. Hawkes depended on making fifteen miles a day as long as the weather held, and in the beginning it was rare for the party to fall short of that mark. He knew the going would get rougher and slower farther on.

Hawkes and Gilmartin usually scouted well ahead of the wagon train, often accompanied by Loud Talker. The Osage had joined the group at the last minute. He refused to commit to just how far he would go with the Pioneers, but Hawkes was happy to have him along. As for Gilmartin, he'd left the stolen spring wagon behind. Brigham Young had provided him with a sound horse and the promise of a wagon and mule team at the end of the trail in appreciation for his services—an offer Gilmartin readily accepted.

On the seventh day Hawkes and his friend did not return to camp until after sunset, when the first stars were appearing in a cold green sky. Hawkes had killed an antelope and the carcass was draped over the front of his saddle. This he turned over to the women—Patience, Clarissa, and Harriet. Gilmartin offered to help them with the skinning and butchering, even though he knew they were perfectly capable of doing the work without his assistance. Lorenzo's wife, Harriet, being the oldest of the three women, had taken charge of the tiny detachment of female Pioneers. She informed Gilmartin in no uncertain terms that his help was unnecessary, thank you very much. Gilmartin just stood there for a while, at a loss, watching Patience and not wanting to leave her presence. With John Bonham around, Gilmartin's opportunities to be in her general vicinity were few and far between.

Seeing all of this, Hawkes just shook his head and walked away, heading for a nearby campfire where Brigham Young was sitting with a dozen other men. He realized it was time to have a man-to-man talk with Gil. But it would just have to wait. He had important news for Brigham Young—news that *wouldn't* wait.

"Spotted some Indian sign today," he told the Mormon president and the others present, among them two of the Apostles and the young killer, Simon Parker. "I figure we're getting into Pawnee country now."

"I have heard the Pawnees are the worst when it comes to skullduggery," said one of the men.

"They've been known to become nuisances," said Hawkes, nodding, "but you might say they've got good reason. They are enemies of the Sioux, and the

Sioux have been getting the upper hand on them for the past few years. The Pawnees are also on the outs with the Comanches to the south. Problem for them is that the Comanches, like the Sioux, are a stronger tribe than the Pawnee. And, as if that wasn't bad enough, the tribes that the United States relocated west of the Mississippi were for the most part placed on Pawnee hunting grounds. And, of course, the Oregon Trail runs right across Pawnee country, so they've been hit pretty hard by the white man's diseases. You could say that the Pawnees are catching hell from all sides."

Brigham Young scanned the firelit faces of the other Mormons. "I think we can sympathize with their plight."

"I'm not saying we won't have trouble," warned Hawkes. "The Pawnees have been pushed around a lot lately and you usually catch them in a bad mood. But it's worth trying to get on their good side—especially since so many more of your people will be passing through here in the months to come."

Brigham Young nodded. "If you will take me to their village I'll see if we can't reach some sort of agreement with them. We'll take Loud Talker along to interpret."

"No, not Loud Talker. Not this time. The Pawnees would as soon kill an Osage as look at him."

"I don't think you should be the one to go, Brother Brigham," said one of the other men. "It's too risky, and we can't afford to have anything happen to you."

"I'm going." Brigham Young's reply was brusque. Hawkes had noticed that the Mormon leader had a short fuse. He didn't like to be questioned or second-guessed by subordinates. When he wanted someone else's opinion he asked for it. "I'll be safe enough with Hawkes and his friend to look after me."

Hawkes wished he could be as confident about the outcome.

The next morning he rode out earlier than usual to locate the Pawnee village. Loud Talker came along, vowing he would turn back as soon as they crossed sign.

"I do not care for the Pawnees," said the Osage gravely. "They are uncivilized. Did you know they sacrifice their captives to their god, Tirawa?"

"No, I didn't know. Thanks for telling me."

"It is true. They crucify them on poles and shoot them full of arrows. Then they pull all the arrows out slowly and cut their chests open, and paint their faces with their blood. Sometimes the prisoner is still alive. Then they set fire to the brush piled up at the foot of the poles and burn him to death." Loud Talker shook his head. "Such practices give Indians a bad name."

They found fresh tracks within the hour—three unshod ponies heading west along the river. Hawkes surmised that the Pawnees were already aware of the Mormon company's proximity. "I reckon their village is on the river just ahead," Hawkes told Loud Talker. "Go on back and send the others."

"I hate to leave you to go on alone," said the Osage. "The last time you went alone you nearly became a ghost. But I do not want to be sacrificed to the Pawnee god." Loud Talker turned his paint pony around and galloped east.

Hawkes proceeded with due caution. Pausing in a stand of willows and cottonwoods two miles farther on, he saw a cluster of beehive-shaped earth lodges. They were large structures, made of sod, and supported by a framework of posts and willow branches. Several families lived in each lodge, so Hawkes counted the big cones of dirt and multiplied by fifteen. That meant there were probably four or five hundred Pawnees in the village, maybe a hundred of them warriors. The day was nearly an hour old and there was much activity among the lodges. Hawkes slipped away unseen and rode back whence he had come, meeting Brigham Young, Gilmartin, John Bonham, and Simon Parker.

"You might as well go back," Hawkes told the Danite avenger and his young protégé. "If the Pawnees turn on us they'll kill five as easy as three. Won't make a difference to them—or us."

"They won't kill us quite as easy," said Bonham.

"May be that bullets can't kill you, like your Prophet said," remarked Gilmartin, "but I wonder if the same applies to Pawnee arrows."

Bonham smiled coldly. "Let's go find out."

Hawkes was tying a strip of white cloth to the barrel of his Plains rifle.

"How do we go about communicating with them?" asked Brigham Young.

"Like as not some of them speak English," replied Hawkes. "There was a mission operating not far from here a while back. If not, I know the hand talk pretty well."

They rode through the stand of trees, and as they emerged out into the open an alarm was raised in the Pawnee village. It took only a few minutes for a dozen braves to grab their weapons and leap on their ponies and gallop out to confront the white intruders. Hawkes knew that this was the most dangerous moment of all. Would the Pawnees understand the meaning of the flag of truce? And even if they did, would they honor it?

He got his answer quickly enough. The Pawnee horsemen encircled him and his companions, staring belligerently and making loud noises, helping to provoke a hostile move. But Hawkes had steady nerves, and so did the others. The Pawnees, as it turned out, were not without honor; they could not fall upon men who had come to talk peace unless there was adequate provocation. They didn't get it, and moments later an older warrior arrived. A few sharp words from him cooled the fervor of the young braves. Hawkes figured the older fellow was a sub-chief. Like most men of the southern plains tribes, his head was shaved but for a scalp lock. Eagle feathers dangled from a horsehair roach dyed red—these signified war honors. He wore leggings and breechcloth and a long bone breastplate on his chest. The length of the breastplate and the number of bones it contained indicated that he was a very prosperous warrior. And one prospered in Pawnee society by meeting with success at war.

His name was Comanche Killer, and he spoke a little English. Hawkes introduced Brigham Young as the chief of a tribe known as Mormons, who were widely regarded for their friendship with other Indian tribes. The Mormons sought peace with the great Pawnee nation, and their chief desired a meeting with the chief of the Pawnees. Comanche Killer listened gravely. When Hawkes was finished he gave a curt nod, told Hawkes to wait, and returned to the village to deliver the message. The young braves remained behind to guard the white strangers. They were silent and watchful. Bonham asked Hawkes what would happen next.

"One of three things, I reckon," said Hawkes. "Either the head man will talk to us, or they'll send us away—or they'll kill us."

Bonham nodded. He appraised the young braves who surrounded them, and Hawkes got the sense that the Mormon avenger was picking out the ones he would kill first if things took a bad turn.

Comanche Killer returned to them and told Hawkes that Buffalo Horn, the great chief of the Pawnees, had consented to a parlay.

The entire tribe turned out to watch the goings-on.

They crowded onto the sloping roofs of the earth lodges. Wearing a buffalo horn bonnet and an otter skin necklace adorned with bear claws, the chief received them in front of his lodge at the center of the village. Sub-chiefs and principal warriors like Comanche Killer were on hand, as well as an old shaman, scarcely more than skin and bones, but with eyes that were ageless and piercing in their intensity.

Ascertaining that Buffalo Horn knew some English, Brigham Young took his cue from Hawkes and explained that as the chief of the Mormons, he wished safe passage for his people as they moved west through Pawnee land. They were seeking a new home where the mountains stood. Buffalo Horn asked if they had been driven from their old home by the Great Father and his bluecoat warriors. This Buffalo Horn could understand, for he knew that the Cherokee, Creek, Choctaw, Chickasaw, and other eastern tribes had been moved against their will onto Pawnee hunting grounds. Brigham Young explained that the Mormons were no longer welcome in the East, but that they had no intentions of intruding on Pawnee land. He had brought some salt and flour, and some powder and lead, as a token of Mormon friendship. Buffalo Horn considered these gifts insufficient. He wanted guns. The Pawnees had many enemies, on all sides. They owned a few old trade guns but these weren't good enough and there weren't enough of them anyway. Brigham Young confessed that the Mormons did not have any guns to spare. The Pawnee chief insisted, and when the Mormon president refused, Buffalo Horn abruptly terminated the meeting. He retired into his earth lodge without shaking hands with Brigham Young. Comanche Killer gave them safe conduct beyond the trees and then left them without a word.

Brigham Young watched him go and sighed. "I fear that did not go well, my friends."

"You did the only thing you could do," said Hawkes. "You couldn't very well give them guns knowing they might turn them on the wagon trains that will follow."

"You think they'll attack us, hoss?" asked Gilmartin.

"I doubt it, unless we give them an opening. We'll swing north around the village and keep our eyes open. Put extra men on night guard, and keep together at all times. If anyone strays off, they'll likely not be seen or heard from again."

That night passed uneventfully, and the next day they reached the ruins of the Pawnee Mission on Plum Creek, abandoned the previous year and burned by the Pawnees. The Loup Fork crossing gave them some trouble. The river was notorious for its quicksand, and there was a delay until Hawkes could find a ford that angled across a sand bar. The following morning, guards ran off a handful of Pawnees who were trying to steal some horses. Two ponies turned up missing the day after. Nerves were on edge, and a man accidentally discharged his rifle, killing another horse. Brigham Young let the pressure show by losing his temper. The only man who seemed oblivious to the crisis was Apostle Orson Pratt, who spent much of his evenings peering at the stars through his telescope.

Two days west of the Loup Fork several Indians suddenly appeared as the wagon train was preparing to strike camp. From a distance they fired their rifles at the Mormon wagons. Shouting, men grabbed their rifles and dove for cover. Hawkes and Gilmartin were sitting at a cook fire drinking coffee—they no longer ventured out early to range far ahead of the wagon train. Under the circumstances that would just be asking for trouble. As the shots rang out, Gilmartin dropped his cup, picked up his rifle, and took off running for the Bonham wagon. He knew Patience was there—he seemed to have developed an uncanny knack for knowing her exact whereabouts at all times.

The only person who did not react violently to the gunfire was Hawkes. He finished his coffee as some of the Mormons started shooting back at the Indians. The only problem with this was the fact that the Indians had abruptly disappeared.

Brigham Young, John Bonham, and a few of the others converged in the middle of the wagon circle to talk things over. Seeing Hawkes at the campfire, they walked over to him.

"Some of the men want to go after those Indians," said the Mormon president.

"That would be a mistake. It's exactly what they want."

"You mean they've set a trap?" asked Bonham.

Hawkes nodded. "They're not going to attack us head on. We're too strong. Best they can hope for is to draw some of us away from the wagons."

"So what do you suggest we do?" asked Brigham Young.

"Nothing."

"They just took shots at us!" said one of the other men. "Somebody could have been killed."

"They weren't going to do much damage. Not at that range, with trade muskets."

"So we just sit here and take it?" asked the man, perturbed.

"That's my advice," said Hawkes. "Take it or leave it."

"I think we should pursue and punish them, Brother Brigham," said the man.

"No. We'll do as our friend suggests. I'm sure he knows best in these circumstances."

"They want rifles," explained Hawkes. "You wouldn't

give them any so they aim to try to take them—out of your dead hands, if need be."

"What about those of our people who come this way later?" asked Bonham. "We should at least warn them that they might have trouble with these Pawnees."

"We'll send someone back with the word," said Brigham Young.

"He'd better ride a wide loop to the north or south of Buffalo Horn's village," suggested Hawkes. "He should travel only at night to begin with, until he's well out of Pawnee country."

"I heartily wish to be out of Pawnee country, as well," said Brigham Young. "To your wagons, my friends."

Everyone dispersed but Bonham, who was gazing intently across the encampment. Hawkes followed his gaze, and saw Gilmartin standing with Patience beside the Bonham wagon. Returning his attention to the Mormon avenger, Hawkes tried to read the man's expression. But there was nothing to read. Bonham was perfectly inscrutable. Pouring himself a cup of coffee, Hawkes wondered if he should say something, but decided not to. A moment later Gilmartin walked away from Patience. Only then did Bonham start toward his wagon.

Mounting up, Gilmartin brought the dun mustang to Hawkes. Loud Talker came over to join them, astride his pony. Hawkes doused the fire with what was left of his coffee, kicked some dirt over the embers, and turned to his horse. He checked the cinch and then climbed into the saddle.

"That woman is going to be the death of you, Gil," he said.

"I know," said Gilmartin pensively.

Hawkes shook his head and rode on. He wasn't going to waste a lot of breath lecturing his foolish friend. Gilmartin wouldn't stay away from Patience anyway. Somebody was going to get hurt, sooner or later.

Chapter 14

Beyond the Loup Fork the land began to change. It was dustier, more broken and arid. The grass was the short and curly variety known to some as buffalo grass. Timber became far more scarce, and they used buffalo chips in lieu of wood for their campfires. The Mormons saw their first prairie dog town and their first herd of shaggies.

As April moved aside for May the days got warmer—some were real scorchers, and a hot dry wind didn't help matters any. Past Wood River they woke one morning to see a curtain of smoke stretched across the western horizon. It was a prairie fire, said Hawkes, maybe two days ahead of them. The prevailing wind was from the south, so the wagon train was in no immediate danger, unless the wind shifted. There was no way of knowing how the fire had started or how long it would burn.

Though they had put Pawnee country behind them, there was still plenty of Indian sign—the hunting parties of a half dozen tribes were on the trail of the buffalo. Hawkes could not give Brigham Young any guarantees regarding how a particular hunting party or tribe would react to the presence of the Mormon expedition. Things were a whole lot different now with the Indians than they had been ten years ago, when Hawkes had first come west. In the old days, a white man could pretty much depend on a friendly response from most tribes unless he did something wrong—with the notable exception of the Blackfoot Nation, which from the first had been implacably hostile to whites. Occasionally a trapper or trader would get into a scrape with a bunch of Absaroka Crows or Shoshones, but many Indians were willing to tolerate the presence of a few white men—especially those of the mountain man variety, who learned to respect Indian customs and even adopted many of their ways.

These days, though, it was a lot more complicated. You couldn't take any Indian's good nature for granted. For one thing, the aggressive expansion of the Sioux Nation had turned the High Plains into a battlefield. Tribes were constantly clashing, and sometimes whites got drawn into these conflicts. For another, the rapid influx of increasing numbers of emigrants had become a source of grave concern for the Indians. More and more of them were becoming convinced that the pioneer tide had to be resisted if future generations of Indians were to retain their homelands. Fortunately, these firebrands remained a minority around tribal council fires. But Hawkes figured that sooner or later, a full-scale war would break out between the Plains tribes and the whites.

"It occurs to me," Brigham Young told Hawkes, "that the Camp of Israel and the Indian tribes have much in common in one respect—once we have found the New Jerusalem, we will have ample reason to regret the coming of more Americans, just as the Indians do. There will be some Saints, I fear, who will want to encourage the tribes to war upon the Gentiles. And can you blame them? History gives us fair warning of what will happen when the Gentiles come and covet our property."

"You'd help the Indians make war on other white men?" asked Hawkes. There was no condemnation or even surprise in his voice. He just figured it was in his own best interests to know what to expect from the Mormons if they were going to share the high country with him.

"I would never condone that," replied the Mormon leader sternly. "I am firm in my belief that the Church must reach some understanding with the United States. We must somehow learn to coexist with the Gentiles. But bitter hatred runs strongly in the veins of many of my brethren who have seen their homes destroyed and their loved ones slain." Brigham Young sighed. "When this war between whites and Indians that you speak of comes to pass, I must somehow keep my people out of it. And that won't be easy."

"If anyone can do it, I reckon you can," said Hawkes.

Brigham Young was startled. "I am humbled by your high regard for my talents, friend. I wish I deserved it."

"You do. Not one man in a million could hold up under the responsibilities that you've taken on. With all the problems you're dealing with, what's one more?"

Brigham Young's smile was rueful. "Perhaps the straw that breaks the camel's back?"

In the first week of May, when the wagon train had reached the Platte River, Hawkes halted the company at a place where an easy crossing could be made.

"This is a shallow ford with a good bottom all the way across," he told the Mormon president and the other Apostles. "There won't be any more chances like this."

"You mean you think we should take the Oregon Trail from here on out?" asked Orson Pratt.

"It's probably easier going over there, and better graze."

Brigham Young conferred with the rest of the Quorum. When the meeting was over he delivered the decision to Hawkes—a decision that, ultimately, was his to make.

"We believe it is our solemn duty to the thousands of Saints who will follow us to make a road for them to follow. We've decided that between the Indians on the north side of this river and the Gentiles we would meet on the south, the Indians are the lesser threat. We will stay on this side of the Platte."

"Suit yourself."

"I can tell that you don't approve. It isn't necessary that you remain with us, my friend. We are grateful for all the help you have given us thus far, and we realize that we have no hold on you, and no right to detain you further. I know you have family waiting. Go home, with my thanks and my blessing."

Hawkes was sorely tempted. He owed these people nothing—and at the same time owed Eliza and Cameron everything. Brigham Young and the Mormons could get along just fine without him. The same could not be said for his wife and son. They had to come first.

And then there was Gilmartin, and his obsession with another man's wife. That in itself was bad enough, but the other man was John Bonham, of all people. Hawkes was strongly inclined to leave Gil to face the consequences of his folly all by himself.

Yet Gilmartin had risked life and limb in Independence on his account, and that weighed heavily on Hawkes. The fur trader was in more trouble than he knew, and Hawkes simply could not abandon him. The only thing that might profit Gil was the fact that Hawkes had probably saved Bonham's life by removing the bullet from the holy killer's leg. If Bonham felt he had any sort of obligation to Hawkes, it might work in Gilmartin's favor. Maybe, just maybe, Bonham wouldn't kill Gil because the trader was a friend of the man who had kept him alive.

As for the other Mormons, Hawkes decided he couldn't leave them to their own devices. Chances were they'd make it without him, but if he went along, those chances were even better.

"I'll stick with you," he told Brigham Young. "At least until we get to the mountains. We're all heading in the same direction anyway, so we might as well travel together."

"But you could make better time on your own," said the Mormon leader.

"No. I'll stick."

Moving on, the expedition kept close to the river, hoping the wind had driven the raging prairie fire northward. But toward the end of the day they were blocked by a wall of flames leaping as tall as a man and moving more rapidly than a person could walk, so they beat a hasty retreat. The Apostles reconsidered crossing to the south side of the Platte. Was the fire a sign from God that they should follow the advice of their guide and continue west on the Oregon Trail? Brigham Young said he would pray over the matter and make his decision in the morning.

That night it rained, and the prairie fire was quelled.

A few days later they reached the place where the Platte split into northern and southern forks. A Mormon named William Clayton, who served as the Quorum's clerk in charge of keeping an up-to-date inventory of the expedition's supplies, had calculated that the wheel on Heber Kimball's wagon made exactly three hundred and sixty revolutions per mile. Tying a rag to the wheel, he spent an entire day counting revolutions. At that night's camp he made some more calculations and put up a marker—a cedar post with a message carved into it for those who would later pass this way: *From Winter Quarters, 300 miles, May 8, '47. Pioneer Camp all well.* He erected another marker on the following day. There was some debate about the exact distance they had traveled; some of the others were certain they had come farther than three hundred miles. Hawkes wasn't sure himself, being accustomed to do his own figuring based on the number of days it took a horseman to go from one landmark to the next. He surmised that they were six weeks from the mountains—a reckoning that was accurate enough to suit only himself.

Clayton's idea of measuring the trail they were blazing appealed to the others, and in no time at all a carpenter named Appleton Harmon had designed and built a wooden roadometer. This ingenious device was attached to the hub of a wagon wheel. Six revolutions of the wheel turned a screw one revolution, and the screw turned a cog wheel with sixty teeth—hence, one full turn of the cogwheel was equal to three hundred and sixty revolutions of the wagon wheel. One needed only check a mark on the cogwheel once every so often to count the miles. Later, Harmon added a second gear that would indicate the miles traveled in a day.

Following the north fork of the Platte, they found good graze for the livestock, though the valley was narrow. Sometimes the bluff closed in too close, forcing them to negotiate the wagons over steep gravel slopes. Loud Talker spotted Indian sign, but could not identify it. Hawkes could. The Indians were Sioux; he could tell the way the moccasins had been made by their prints.

The land became more arid—sand, rock, and cactus, an occasional sandstone formation sculpted by eons of rain and wind. Two weeks from the forking of the Platte they spotted Chimney Rock. Soon they would arrive at Fort Laramie. Though nearly fifty miles away, it looked much closer; Clayton calculated that the landmark was about four hundred and fifty miles from Winter Quarters. That night the company was allowed to celebrate, dancing to the music of fiddles and a Jew's harp. Since there were only three women with the expedition, men resorted to dancing with one another. John Bonham brought Patience up to where Hawkes and Gilmartin were standing, off to one side observing the festivities.

"Neither of my legs work as well as they used to," said Bonham. "For me, I'm afraid, dancing is a thing of the past. But my dear wife is young and spirited. I do not wish her to be deprived of one of life's little pleasures. Perhaps one of you gentlemen would take my place and dance with her."

"I never learned how to dance," said Hawkes.

Gilmartin stared at Bonham for a moment. Uneasy, Patience spoke up. "John, I'm really not in the mood."

"Sure you are," said Bonham curtly. "You need not be concerned with my feelings. I want only to make you happy."

"Okay," said Gilmartin, extending an arm to Patience. "I'll dance with her."

She took his arm, not knowing what else to do. The impromptu band was playing a lively reel, and Gilmartin led her to the edge of the circle of dancers. Taking her into his arms, he swept her into the stream of whirling couples.

Hawkes watched Bonham out of the corner of an eye. The Mormon killer had a strange smile on his face as he observed Gilmartin dancing with his young wife. What was the man thinking? What did he think he was doing, arranging it so that Gilmartin and Patience were together? That wasn't the sort of thing a jealous husband would ordinarily do. Bonham was like a cat playing with mice. And when cats played with mice, the mice usually lost.

"What the devil is he up to?" muttered Gilmartin. He was paying more attention to Bonham than to his dancing partner, trying to catch glimpses of the holy killer through the couples who swirled around him.

"I'm afraid," whispered Patience.

"No need for that. I won't let him hurt you."

"I'm afraid for you, not for myself. You must leave before he kills you."

"Leave? You mean run away? Not a chance."

"Please. For my sake, go."

Gilmartin was silent for a moment. "I'll go—if you'll go with me."

"I can't do that."

"Do you love him?" He gazed earnestly into her eyes. "Tell me the honest truth, Patience. If you say you love him then I'll go away and never see you again."

"I . . ." She couldn't say it. Even though she knew that if she lied, Gilmartin's life might be spared. But the thought of never seeing him again was more than she could endure. "No. No, I don't love him. God forgive me."

Gilmartin could tell she was on the verge of tears. "Don't cry, Patience. None of this is any fault of yours. I want you to come away with me. I can make you happy. I know I can. I—"

"Don't say it!" she gasped. "Don't say you love me."

"I don't have to, do I? You know perfectly well how I feel about you. Can't you tell by now?"

"Yes."

"Then say you'll run away with me."

"He will track us down. No matter where we go, how far we run, he *will* track us down. And then he will kill you."

"I'm willing to take that chance," said Gilmartin, his voice strident with desperation. It was not love but fear that held Patience to Bonham, and fear was just as powerful of a motivation. "I'll take any chance to be with you. Maybe it's just that you don't feel the same way about me."

"That isn't fair."

"No, it isn't. I'm sorry. None of this is fair. But I can't help it, Patience. I love you. I want to be with you, always. I want to take you away, take care of you, make you happy."

The band finished playing and the dancers applauded. Gilmartin didn't, though—he took Patience by the shoulders and gazed earnestly into her eyes.

"Gordon said you were going to be the death of me," he said. "I guess he's right. Because I just can't walk away."

She looked around, trying to locate Bonham, but she couldn't see him from where they stood in the midst of the other dancers.

"I do love you," she whispered. "You're all I dream about. But I just don't know what to do. I just don't know. All I can think about is what it feels like to be in your arms. John doesn't love me. He just . . . just uses me . . ." Nearly in tears, she broke free of his grasp and ran away. Her sudden departure brought unwanted attention Gilmartin's way. Fuming, he stalked out of the press of dancers. His fists were clenched when he reached Hawkes.

"Where is Bonham?" he rasped. "Where did he go?"

"Calm down, Gil."

"I won't calm down. I'm going to have it out with him. You saw what he did. He already knows, so why not have a reckoning? Right now he's just toying with us. I won't stand for it."

"Get hold of yourself. Bonham will kill you."

"I'm going to get a gun and settle it once and for all," said Gilmartin resolutely, turning away.

"Gil?"

Gilmartin turned—and Hawkes hit him hard, a

sharp uppercut connecting at the point of Gil's chin. The fur trader was out cold on his feet, and sagged forward. Hawkes caught him and put him down on the ground, leaning against a wagon wheel.

"Love sure makes fools of us all, sooner or later," muttered Hawkes as he picked up Gilmartin's hat and put it over his friend's face.

Chapter 15

They reached Fort Laramie two weeks later.

It had started as an outpost for the Rocky Mountain Fur Company. According to legend, William Sublette had picked the site and one of his men, William Anderson, had produced a bottle of champagne which was consumed in a ceremony held to mark the laying of the fort's cornerstone. The magnanimous Sublette had decided to name the post Fort Anderson in honor of a fellow endowed with such remarkable foresight that he could produce a bottle of French wine in a wild and remote place so far removed from civilization. Such a man, said Sublette, was certain to go far in life. But Anderson insisted the outpost be called Fort Sublette. Someone else suggested a clever solution—and the post was christened Fort William in honor of both Sublette and Anderson. Ultimately this was all for naught—the American Fur Company soon took over the place, which came to be known as Fort Laramie.

Fort Laramie stood at an important crossroads, where an ancient north-south Indian trail met the Oregon Trail. Surrounded on all sides by sagebrush desert, the outpost offered abundant grass, plenty of cottonwood groves, and the good water of Laramie Creek. There was plenty of activity when Hawkes and the Mormon Pioneers arrived.

Several hundred Sioux lodges stood below the bluffs

where the creek joined the North Platte. In addition, two emigrant trains had made their camps close by one another just east of the fort. And a caravan of Taos traders had arrived only the day before, to participate in the bustling summer trade.

Hawkes told Brigham Young it might be wise for him to enter the fort without the company of any Mormons, just to test the water. He had Lillburn Boggs in mind, knowing that Boggs had probably passed this way last year with Owl Russell and the Donners. Boggs—and no doubt some others—had probably spread the word that the Mormons were westward bound, and who could say what kind of reception the Saints would receive as a consequence? Brigham Young agreed that discretion was the best course, and camp was made six miles east of the outpost.

Gilmartin and Loud Talker accompanied Hawkes. The former had indulged in sullen silence for most of the way since the confrontation at Chimney Rock. Hawkes was willing to take the brunt of Gilmartin's resentment since the punch he'd delivered had apparently knocked some sense into his friend. At least Gil hadn't challenged John Bonham, as he had planned to do in a reckless moment of love-blind insanity. It seemed the fur trader had realized just how foolish, not to mention fatal, such an action would be. As far as Hawkes knew, Gil was even steering clear of Patience. Maybe, then, the crisis was over. Even so, Hawkes liked to keep Gilmartin within reach as much as possible. As for Loud Talker, curiosity explained his craving to visit Fort Laramie.

They approached from the northeast, so that Laramie Peak soared into the sky as background when they caught their first glimpse of the fifteen-foot-high adobe walls with a blockhouse located at two corners. The walls enclosed a square more than a hundred feet to a side. Inside, an inner courtyard was ringed by adobe buildings—living quarters, storehouses, several blacksmith shops, a trading post, and a council hall. Beyond this was a large corral where livestock could be held in the event of an attack. The entrance to the fort had two gates, one in the perimeter wall and the other barring access to the inner courtyard. Hawkes explained to Loud Talker that this was intended to keep Indians who came to trade from entering the courtyard, the outpost's inner sanctum. Loud Talker nodded solemnly and voiced his opinion that this was probably a wise precaution. From what he could see of the Sioux, they were not to be trusted very far.

The sheer number of Sioux present surprised Hawkes. Ten years ago you would never have seen Sioux in this part of the country. He figured there had to be five or six hundred of them here. The place was crawling with them. A party of seven warriors, their faces blackened, their ponies painted, rode up to Hawkes and his companions, uttering ear-piercing shrieks and brandishing lances adorned with scalps. They sat their pivoting, wild-eyed ponies for a moment, shouting loudly, and then galloped away in a cloud of dust.

"Those look like Pawnee scalps to me," said Loud Talker. "Their faces are painted black because they have gone on the warpath and killed their enemies. The fires of revenge have burned out, leaving only ashes. This, I believe, is what the black face means. They must do this before they enter their lodges, to show the others that they are no longer in the mood to kill their enemies. A warrior should not come home still thirsting for blood."

Loud Talker rattled on about war paint and the significance of tattoos among his own people, the Osage, but by now Hawkes had learned to block out the Indian's interminable ramblings. Yet he'd come to value Loud Talker's company. The Osage had peerless skill as a tracker. The man missed nothing. He was reliable, too—the kind you wanted backing you in a scrape. Hawkes had no idea how long Loud Talker intended to ride with the Mormons. One thing was certain—he would return to his people with a wealth of information about the land and the tribes to the west of his homeland.

The bourgeois of Fort Laramie was a man named Papin, but he was making his annual trek to St. Louis to sell the furs that had been accumulated at the outpost since the previous summer, floating them down the river in a fleet of bullboats. Running the show in Papin's absence was a French-Canadian *engagé* called James Bordeaux, who met Hawkes, Gilmartin, and Loud Talker in Papin's room, located off the courtyard. The room was spartan—a few chairs and a table, and some furs on the walls and floor. Bordeaux was suspicious of the trio, until Hawkes informed him that they were guides for a band of Mormons—the first contingent of thousands who would pass this way during the year. Bordeaux's dark eyes lit up and the furrows of concern disappeared from his brow.

He did not know enough to associate Hawkes and Gilmartin with Jim Bridger and the Rocky Mountain Fur Company, arch-rival of the firm that employed Bordeaux and owned Fort Laramie. All he saw was future profit from the companies of Saints headed his way. He called for whiskey, and a plump Indian woman arrived with glasses and a jug of Taos Lightning. Quite some time had passed since Gilmartin had drunk from an honest-to-God glass, and he gazed at it in wonder as Bordeaux filled it to the brim with New Mexico redeye.

"Of course, I have heard that the Mormons are coming," said Bordeaux. "Let your friends know that they are all welcome here. Have they met with any trouble on the trail?"

"They blazed their own," replied Hawkes. "On the north side of the Platte. I just hope we don't have any problems right here. I noticed a couple of wagon camps yonder."

"I will do all in my power to keep the peace," pledged Bordeaux, "but I can only make guarantees for those who live in the fort itself. You understand, I'm sure. You said you've come up the river on the north side? I regret to inform you that the north bank is impassable for many miles. You will have to cross to the south bank. I will ferry them for a small fee—say, fifty cents a wagon?"

"Let's say twenty five," said Gilmartin. "They won't pay extortion."

Bordeaux looked pained. "It is my job to make money for the company," he said with an apologetic shrug.

"We're talking about a lot of wagons," said Hawkes. "Thousands."

Bordeaux's eyes gleamed with avarice. "You are quite right. Fifty cents a wagon is too steep."

"What about the Sioux?" asked Gilmartin. "Should we expect any trouble from them?"

"The Sioux will not bother you if you give them a little foofaraw. But the Crows are another matter entirely. Two weeks ago the Crows stole our whole caviarde. You cannot trust them, *mon freres*."

Gilmartin glanced at Hawkes. He knew that no Crows would mess with Gordon Hawkes. He was a white brother to the Absarokas. Of course there was no purpose to be served in enlightening Bordeaux on this subject, so Gilmartin kept his mouth shut.

"Have you any news of Kearney's Army of the West?" asked Hawkes. "Five hundred Mormons joined Kearney at Fort Leavenworth. The people I am with desire some word of them."

Bordeaux slapped his forehead with the palm of a

hand. "But of course! *Mon Dieu,* you must forgive me. Sixteen Mormons arrived a fortnight ago. They are from the Mormon Battalion, part of the Sick Detachment, as they call themselves. It was from them that I heard you would be coming this summer. I believe they are camped on the other side of the river, so I will send word to them that you are here."

Hawkes nodded. "We'll be camped a few miles east of the cottonwoods. Thanks for your hospitality."

"If I can be of any service," said Bordeaux with a slight bow.

Gilmartin had finished his whiskey and noticed that Loud Talker hadn't touched his drink. "You going to drink that," asked the fur trader, "or just look at it?"

"The white man's water would make a good horse liniment," said Loud Talker, dipping two fingers in the Taos Lightning and dabbing it on his cheek. "But it is not good for Indians to drink. It makes them stupid."

"Does the same thing to white men," remarked Hawkes.

Loud Talker nodded. "Yes. But a white man who drinks this wakes up with a bad head. An Indian who drinks it wakes up without his horse or his land."

Gilmartin took the glass from Loud Talker, knocked the whiskey back, put the glass on the table, and nodded at Bordeaux. "Mormons don't drink much liquor, either," he said grimly, and with that sallied forth into the courtyard's sunshine.

Soon after Hawkes and his companions returned to the Mormon wagons, two horsemen galloped in. They were greeted with enthusiasm by the Saints. Robert Crow and George Therlkill were members of the Sick Detachment's advance party, and they brought welcome news about the long-absent Mormon Battalion.

The Battalion had arrived in Santa Fe last October. General Kearney and his dragoons had been there for several weeks previous, having departed Fort Leavenworth before the Battalion was fully organized. Kearney had moved on to California, believing New Mexico to be adequately pacified. A few days later, the Battalion had moved west under the command of Lt. Col. Philip St. George Cooke, also bound for the Pacific coast. The Sick Detachment remained behind in a winter camp in southern Colorado.

On December 10, the Battalion was proceeding along the San Pedro River when a herd of wild cattle appeared, mixing with the Battalion's livestock. The wild cattle were cut out and driven away—straight into the guns of a Mormon hunting party returning from a fruitless search for game. The hunters opened fire without thinking, stampeding the *ladrones* back into the ranks of the Battalion. The Mormons had been marching with empty rifles for safety's sake. Now, before they could load, the wild cattle were teeming among them, scattering the men. A saddle horse and a team of mules were killed. Fortunately, no human life was lost. Thus ended the only action engaged in by the Mormon Battalion during the entire campaign.

The Battalion marched on across the arid wastes, arriving in San Diego at the end of January, shoeless and starving. Crow and Therlkill had been spared that ordeal, having spent the winter in the sick camp, but a courier had brought them news of the Battalion having reached the Pacific. All in all, four Mormons had died, all of them from natural causes—though Therlkill was of the opinion that the ministrations of the sick camp doctor, a Gentile, had something to do with the fatalities. Spoken, Gilmartin told Hawkes wryly, like a true Mormon.

Crow and Therlkill rode back to collect the rest of the former Battalion members; they would join the Pioneer company in its trek west. That night, the sound of horses alerted the camp. Hawkes assumed it must be Therlkill and the others returning. But he was very wrong. It was Billy Ring, with two of his buffalo runners.

Brigham Young had admonished everyone to take extra care, keeping eyes open and weapons near at hand, since no one could be sure how the Gentile emigrants in the nearby wagon trains would react to the news that Mormons were nearby. So Billy Ring found himself looking down the business end of a dozen rifles as he entered the camp. He wisely remained in the saddle, scanning the faces of the company with his crooked eyes until he spotted Hawkes—at whom he stabbed an accusing finger.

"You!" he roared. "I've come to kill you, you son of a bitch!"

Brigham Young quickly interposed himself between Ring and the object of the buffalo hunter's wrath. "What is the meaning of this, sir?"

"That man there kilt my brother last summer," said Ring. "I swore vengeance over Charley's grave. I knew one day we'd meet again. I've been checkin' everyone who passes this way, and when I heard that someone fittin' Gordon's description had shown up at the fort today I come out to have myself a look. That's him, no question. Henry Gordon. The man who kilt my brother Charley. I'll have his balls for breakfast."

Simon Parker had slipped up behind the mounted men without being noticed. He'd filled his hands with the brace of Colt Patersons he carried in cross-draw holsters.

"Give the word, Brother Brigham, and I'll see to it he's reunited with his brother," drawled Parker.

Billy Ring gave a start, jerked around in the saddle, and glowered at the slender youth with the deadly smile.

"Hold on," said Hawkes, stepping forward. "This is my fight."

"Not necessarily," said John Bonham, strolling into

the ring of firelight, Northwest gun in one hand and Allen pepperbox in the other. He wasn't aiming the weapons at anybody in particular, but then he didn't have to. The buffalo runners could take one look at him and know Bonham would kill them in a heartbeat.

"Brother Bonham is right," said Brigham Young. "We need you as our guide. And even if that were not the case, you are still our friend. We stand with our friends."

"This quarrel is between him and me," explained Hawkes. "I've got to settle it on my own terms."

Billy Ring's grin was a singularly unpleasant sight. "Had me worried. For a minute there I thought you was a coward, hidin' behind your Mormon killers."

"Name the time and the place, Ring."

"The mouth of Laramie Creek. Dawn tomorrow. Be there, or I'll track you down even if I have to follow you straight down into hell."

With that Ring spun his pony around and rode away, followed by his cronies.

Gilmartin walked up to Hawkes, shaking his head. "You're an idiot, Gordon. You should have let Parker kill that bastard while you had the chance."

"Maybe I should have," conceded Hawkes. "But I couldn't."

"Perhaps you should have given some thought to Eliza and Cameron before you accepted that challenge. What if Ring kills you? What happens to them?"

"I was thinking of them, Gil. Ring won't rest until he's had his revenge. I don't want him following me home. It's better to end it here and now, one way or the other." Hawkes glanced at Brigham Young. "Has to be this way," he told the concerned Mormon leader. "That's just the way of things out here."

Brigham Young nodded and walked away.

Chapter 16

Hawkes was at the dueling site well before daybreak, and as the sun daubed the eastern skyline with strokes of pink and orange he stood at the edge of the river watching the Sioux village awaken on the other side. Women came down to the river's edge to draw water. Some smiled tentatively at him, others watched him warily, wondering what he was doing there. Hawkes wondered the same thing. He'd spent a restless night. When he did finally sleep, he dreamed about Eliza. He hoped she'd gotten the letter sent from Winter Quarters. If she hadn't, she quite possibly believed he was dead. There was a very good chance that he would be before the day was out.

When Charley Ring had died, Gilmartin had voted to kill Billy Ring, too. In retrospect Hawkes thought maybe Gil had been right, for once. Sure, it would have been cold-blooded murder, but that was what the Ring brothers had fully intended to commit themselves that day. Billy Ring had sworn vengeance, and Hawkes could not fault him for it. Neither could he refuse Ring's challenge, or hide behind Mormon guns. Billy Ring wouldn't rest until they had met for a final reckoning, and Hawkes sure wasn't going to let the buffalo runner track him all the way to the mountains, where Eliza and Cameron might get into the line of fire.

Behind him, the dun mustang whickered softly, and

Hawkes turned to see a rider coming through the cottonwoods that grew along Laramie Creek. Taking a deep breath, Hawkes tried to force thoughts of his wife and son from his mind and concentrate on the task at hand—killing Billy Ring. He'd been forced to kill before—men who'd been bigger, stronger, and meaner than he was. But there was something about Billy Ring that worried Hawkes and made him think that his surviving this confrontation was something of a longshot.

But it wasn't Billy Ring who rode out of the woods. At first, Hawkes was surprised to see John Bonham. Then he was angry.

"What are you doing here?" asked Hawkes. "I thought I told you this was my fight."

"Won't be a fight today. Ring isn't going to show up."

"Damn it, what have you done?"

Bonham leaned forward in the saddle, his eyes like steel, his voice sharper than a skinning knife. "I've done what Brother Brigham told me to do. I always do what he tells me. He wants you kept alive. You see, we need you to guide us through Crow country. That tribe won't bother us if you're along."

"Is Billy Ring dead?"

Bonham shook his head.

"Then I've got to settle it here and now. As long as he's alive my family won't be safe. Where is he?"

"Safely tucked away. A couple of Therlkill's men will watch over him for a spell. He's not going to be a bother to anybody."

"You don't seem to understand—"

"No, it's you who doesn't understand. We need your help. And you won't be much help to us six feet under."

"What if I decide not to help you anymore?"

"You're no shirker," said Bonham confidently. "You won't quit a job that's only half done."

Hawkes tried to cool his temper. Brigham Young was only doing what he had to. His first priority was the well-being of the Saints, and he wasn't going to let anything get in the way of that—even if it meant putting the family of his indispensable guide in jeopardy.

"Give the word," said Bonham, as Hawkes turned to the dun mustang, "and I'll go finish Ring. Then you won't have to worry what he might do to your family. It's entirely in your hands."

"No it isn't," said Hawkes bitterly, mounting up. "I can't do that. But then I don't expect it makes any sense to you."

Bonham started his horse eastward, in the direction of the Mormon camp. He looked over his shoulder and asked, "Are you coming?"

Hawkes swung the mustang around and followed the holy killer.

There was no time to waste in getting across the river and proceeding up the Oregon Trail. Riders brought reliable word to Fort Laramie that dozens of wagon trains were coming, with estimates running as high as two thousand wagons that would be passing this way in a matter of weeks. More emigrants than ever before were coming west this year and Hawkes, among others, wondered if there would be enough grass for all the livestock that would accompany them. Brigham Young was eager to press on. So far, the Saints had had no trouble with Gentile pioneers—but he wasn't one to push his luck.

Hawkes had another reason for wanting to leave in advance of the summer tide of emigrants. That man Geller had told him that he was now suspected of killing the Independence lawyer, Ira Taggett. It was bad enough that he was wanted for one murder that he hadn't committed. Now he had a second murder charge hanging over his head. So long as he remained with the Mormons, who kept themselves isolated from others, he felt fairly safe. And he'd heard no mention of Taggett's murder at Fort Laramie. But sooner or later the word would spread even this far from the scene of the crime—quite possibly carried by one of the thousands of pioneers coming up the trail this season. Under the circumstances, then, he did not care to linger.

In spite of sporadic rain, they made the crossing without mishap, making Bordeaux a fair profit as he was paid two bits per wagon in return for the use of his ferry.

They were entering rough country now, broken by numerous tributaries of the Platte, and Brigham Young dispatched work crews to clear the road of rocks and level out the approaches to fords. This was done for the Saints who would come after, even though it was also beneficial to the Gentile emigrants. That couldn't be helped.

In this seared land of sagebrush and bunch grass, good campsites with plenty of water and graze and firewood were sometimes hard to find, and on several occasions the Mormon Pioneers found themselves camping in close proximity to Missouri wagon trains. The Saints were wary, but kept the peace. So did the Missourians.

Coming to a crossing of the North Platte, they found the river running deep and strong, a hundred yards wide. The *Revenue Cutter* was employed to carry over the contents of the wagons, but getting the prairie schooners themselves across proved to be a difficult proposition. A crew was sent south into the foothills of the snow-capped Laramie Mountains and returned with a harvest of poles to be used in the construction of rafts. In the meantime, the Saints tried to get one wagon over with outrigger poles lashed to either side, but the current turned the wagon right over. Two wagons were then lashed together and sent across. But they, too, were overturned. The rain came again with a fury, driven by a hard wind, and the river was ice cold. A ferry was made to transport the wagons to the other side.

A hundred Gentile wagons reached the south bank just as the Mormons finished their crossing. Though some of the Saints had no desire to lend aid to the emigrants, Brigham Young saw an opportunity and seized it. The Mormon ferry was put to work again, and Young left ten men behind to operate it. Their orders were to let everyone cross, and to keep the ferry going until all the Saints had passed through. All wagons would be charged a small fee for use of the ferry. In this way, some badly needed funds would be raised for the Church. In addition, if relations with the outsiders could be improved with this service, what harm could there be in that?

It was time to leave the Platte, the river they had followed for six hundred miles. The next fifty miles, from the crossing to the Sweetwater River, were the worst yet—rugged desert watered by alkali streams. As they crossed an alkali flat east of the Sweetwater range, Hawkes warned them to keep the livestock away from the shallow pools of brackish water found along the way. It was said that this water would cause an animal to bloat until it burst.

After that they came to Independence Rock, one of the most famous landmarks along the Oregon Trail. Shaped like a whale, this elongated dome of gray granite rising up out of the flats was used by the emigrants as a place to mark their passing. Many names had been carved or painted onto the rock. Next came Devil's Gate, where the river cut through a deep gorge.

Following the Sweetwater, they saw the majestic Wind River Range to the north. They were climbing steadily now, and as they reached higher altitudes, the summer nights turned cold. Finally they crossed the divide at South Pass.

On that day Brigham Young called a halt and held a service to commemorate the third anniversary of the murder of Joseph Smith, the Prophet. Gilmartin pointed out that they were no longer in the United States proper—this was the far western boundary of the old Louisiana Purchase. Hawkes had been blissfully unaware of this fact, and upon further contemplation, decided it was a mere technicality of little real consequence. If the country west of South Pass wasn't part of the United States yet, it soon would be once the Mexican War was over. He had no doubt that the United States would prevail in the battles currently raging down south and, in all likelihood, in the rich province of California, as well, since Kearney's conquering Army of the West had reached the Pacific. The only question remaining was how much of Mexico's northern provinces would the United States lay claim to? To the victor went the spoils. The word along the trail, carried by the Missouri wagon trains, was that many Americans wanted to annex all of Mexico. Whatever happened, the United States would soon extend from sea to shining sea, and no one with a brain in his head could doubt that for a minute.

Six miles beyond South Pass they reached a fork in the trail. Sublette's Cutoff continued west to the Big Sandy and thence to the Bear River. The other fork veered southwest to Fort Bridger. A number of wagon trains were taking the latter route, for at Fort Laramie a man named Lansford Hastings was claiming to know of a shortcut to California beyond Fort Bridger, one that circled around a salt lake and rejoined the main trail beyond the Bear River.

Hawkes advised Brigham Young to take the left fork to Fort Bridger. He wasn't sure about Hastings's vaunted cutoff, but he knew Jim Bridger could be relied upon to give the Mormons good guidance. He experienced a gnawing anticipation, for they were but a week to ten days shy of Old Gabe's outpost. For Hawkes, that was almost like being home. It was possible that Eliza and Cameron were there. At the very least, Bridger would have news of his family. Hawkes chafed at the slow progress of the Mormon Pioneers. But the livestock suffered from the stifling heat of the day and the shortage of good grass and potable water. The Saints were weary, too. The country was rough and it was all they could do to make ten miles in a day.

He could sense, too, that the Mormons were becoming more anxious about finding the promised land. They had come nearly a thousand miles from Winter Quarters in a little less than three months, and many wondered how much farther they would have to go before reaching their destination. Surely the promised land could not be anywhere near. This was a barren and inhospitable country, ill suited for cultivation.

Brigham Young could detect the festering discontent of the Pioneers. He asked Hawkes if it would not be better to turn northward, to put the desert behind them and search for the New Jerusalem among the mountains above the Wind River Range. There, at least, they would find plenty of timber and fertile valleys and clean high country streams that never ran dry.

"That's the path to Oregon," replied Hawkes. "Were you to live to the north you'd have to deal with all the people you call Gentiles who will pass through. Eventually they'll stop passing through and start settling down. Then, too, there are the Indians, chiefly the Blackfeet. You don't want to tangle with them—or the Sioux, for that matter—if you can avoid it. I reckon we'll have a full-blown Indian war in the north before too long. And you'd be caught right in the middle of it."

"I'll trust your judgement on all of that," said Brigham Young, plainly disappointed. "We'll continue in this direction."

That the Mormon leader put such faith in him made an impression on Hawkes and reinforced his determination to stay with them until they found a new home.

The next day they saw two riders heading toward them. Keen eyesight permitted Hawkes to identify them as white men from a good distance. He got a feeling that he knew these men. There was something familiar about them. When they got closer he recognized them both: Red Renshaw and Jim Bridger. Hawkes almost shouted with joy and kicked his dun mustang into a gallop, eager to be reunited with his own kind—and to hear news of his family.

Chapter 17

"Eliza and Cameron are well," Bridger told Hawkes. "They stayed for a spell at the post after you left, and then went home. I took 'em, and worked things out with the Absarokas. Hoss, them Crow friends of yourn have been watchin' out for your people better than I ever could. No way any harm was goin' to come to them."

Hawkes was nearly overwhelmed with relief. "I'm obliged for all you've done."

Old Gabe grinned and just waved the gratitude away. "I got your letter early this spring and took it straight off to Eliza personally."

"This spring! Why, I wrote it before last winter."

"It got as far as Fort Laramie and no farther until the snow was gone. The first emigrant train brought it through."

Hawkes sighed. "So Eliza went all winter without knowing whether I was alive or dead."

"She made no complaint that I heard. She's the damnedest woman I've ever known. Did you get that package you was after?"

"I got it."

"Well, I won't ask what was in it. Ain't none of my business. But I hope it was worth the trouble you went to." Bridger glanced beyond Hawkes at the distant wagons. "Who's that you brought along with you?"

"Brigham Young and the Mormons."

"Mormons! Heard they was headed this way. Well, cut off my leg and call me Stumpy. After Eliza read your letter she told me you was holed up with them Mormons, but I never gave thought to the idea that you'd stick with them all this time."

"I didn't plan it that way. Just happened."

"Had much trouble along the way?"

Hawkes shook his head. "Less than I expected. Pawnees stirred up some dust, but nothing since then." He decided to wait until some other time to tell Bridger about Billy Ring and the reasons for Billy's now-postponed vow of vengeance.

"What you didn't mention in your letter was how you came to be shot," said Old Gabe. "Have anything to do with that package you was dead set on gettin'?"

"In a roundabout way," replied Hawkes, and related to Bridger and Renshaw all that had transpired in Independence, the whys and wherefores of Gilmartin walking into a trap at Ira Taggett's office, and what had happened when he'd gone in to make sure Gil was okay, and then about how Geller had stalked him for months, finally catching him alone out on the prairie. "Geller said I was wanted for the killing of that Independence lawyer," he concluded with a grim smile. "Way I see it, Geller must have killed him, because I know he was alive when I left his office. That way, Geller wouldn't have to share the reward."

"So now you're wanted back East for *two* murders?" queried Bridger. He let out a low whistle. "Gordon, you keep this up and you'll come to a bad end. You'd be wise to stay hid up in the high country much as you can from here on in."

"I'm an innocent man and I'm supposed to spend the rest of my life on the run?"

Bridger nodded. "It ain't right, but then what's right and wrong got to do with life?"

"Here comes Gil," reported Renshaw, pointing with

his chin at three riders coming from the Mormon wagons. "That sorry son of a bitch better still have my share of the proceeds from those plews." The epithet belied the fur trader's tone of voice; he was pleased to see that his partner was still above ground.

"One of the reasons we were headed for Fort Laramie was to see if they had any word of you and Gil," explained Bridger. "Who are them other two pilgrims?"

Hawkes turned in his saddle to identify the men who rode with Gilmartin.

"The one with the beard is John Bonham," he said. "The other one is Brigham Young. He's the leader of the Saints."

"They ain't anywhere close to being saints, from what I've heard," said Renshaw suspiciously.

"My advice is to keep those sorts of opinions to yourself while Bonham is around, Red," said Hawkes. "You see, he's a Mormon avenger. An assassin. In fact, he's the one who tried to kill Lillburn Boggs, the governor of Missouri."

"You don't say?"

"I had the dubious pleasure of meeting Boggs," added Hawkes. "He was with the Donner wagon train."

"Donners!" Bridger looked startled. "You met the Donners?"

"A few days shy of Independence. Why?"

"I guess you ain't heard. Just got the news myself. George and Jacob Donner and about thirty men and twice as many women and children in twenty or so wagons split off from the rest of their party at Hastings' Cutoff. You heard of Lansford Hastings? He's written some damn fool piece of nonsense called *The Emigrants' Guide.* Says he's discovered a shortcut to California. Well, the Donners believed him. And they got caught by the snows in the Sierra Nevada."

"My God," said Hawkes. "Sixty women and children?"

"Yep. They made a camp, planning to wait it out, but when most of their livestock wandered off, their food supplies got low, so they sent some of their number across the pass to California for help. A blizzard hit and some of that group died. Turns out the rest ate the flesh of the dead in order to survive. Eventually about half of them got through to California. More than a month later the first rescue party reached the main camp. It tried to take fifteen people out of the mountains to safety, but *another* blizzard hit and only the strongest could make it. I'm not sure yet just who all made it through, but I've heard more than half lost their lives."

"I'm truly sorry to hear that," said Hawkes. "They struck me as decent folks."

"That's the other reason we were going to Fort Laramie," said Bridger as Gilmartin arrived with Brigham Young and John Bonham. "To take word of what happened to the Donners and leave a fair warnin' to any other folks who might be gullible enough to believe Hastings. Now I ain't saying you can't get to California by his route if you try early enough in the season. But it's already too late in the year to try for that now."

Renshaw pulled his horse alongside Gilmartin's, front to back, and grimaced disapproval at his prodigal partner.

"It's about damned time you got back. Thanks to you I was poor as a pauper at rendezvous. Didn't have two cents to rub together. I missed out on a heap of fun on account of you lollygaggin' around back East somewheres. Bet you had yourself a high old time in Independence, didn't you? Had a drink or two for your old partner while you was at it, I hope."

"I'm just tickled pink to see you again, too," replied

Gilmartin dryly. "Gordon here saved our plews from a couple of thievin' scoundrels, the Ring brothers. So when he got hurt I felt obliged to stay with him. Reckon you would have just left him to die." Gilmartin tossed Renshaw the money pouch. "There. That's every cent of what I got for the furs. Haven't spent any of it."

"Well," said Renshaw, somewhat mollified, "it still don't do me no good now that rendezvous is over."

"There'll be plenty of Taos Lightning for you when you get to Fort Laramie, Red," said Hawkes.

"I'm obliged to you for savin' the plews, Gordon."

Hawkes made the introductions all around. Brigham Young's ruddy face lit up when he heard Jim Bridger's name.

"They say you know this country better than any other man living, Mr. Bridger," said the Mormon president, leaning forward in his saddle. "Perhaps you know of a place where twenty thousand peace-loving people can settle. God has prepared a place for us, a New Jerusalem for His chosen ones. But we have got to find that promised land, sir. Can you assist us?"

Old Gabe rubbed his beard-bristled jaw. "Well, I don't rightly know," he said, carefully noncommittal, throwing a querulous glance at Hawkes, who knew exactly what Bridger was thinking. "I'll have to put my mind to that proposition, Mr. Young. It's hard to find much besides desert 'tween here and the Sierra Nevada."

"Mormons are a resourceful people," replied Brigham Young. "We've had to be. If necessary, we will make the desert bloom. But come, Mr. Bridger. We will make camp here, and you are more than welcome at our fires."

"Thanks for the offer. I think I'll take you up on it. The miles are gettin' hard on these old bones."

The Mormon president wheeled his horse about and

returned to the wagons with John Bonham at his side. Hawkes started the dun mustang in that direction, too, and Bridger fell in alongside him. Gilmartin and Red Renshaw brought up the rear.

"Heard a lot of palaver about these Mormons," remarked Bridger. "They seem to have a natural talent for attractin' trouble. Can't say I'm sure whether I want 'em in this neck of the woods or not, to tell you the truth."

"Listen, Old Gabe. They've got some peculiar ways and I don't agree with them on all counts, but by and large they're good people. You have my word on that."

"But I keep thinkin' about that Bonham feller. Hear tell there are a lot of Mormons like him. Cold-blooded killers."

"They've been through hell and back again. They've been chased all the way across the country, and for no good reason that I can see. In my opinion they have a need for men like Bonham. But I won't lie to you, my friend. There are some Mormons who despise the rest of us and wish us ill. They are angry and bitter because they've been driven from their homes and a lot of them have seen members of their families killed. Look, this is a big country. There's bound to be room for the Mormons somewhere out here. All they want is to be left alone. In that respect, they're not much different from you and me, Old Gabe."

"A pretty fine piece of speechifyin'," said Red Renshaw. "But me, I don't want nothing to do with them. Gil, I say we ride out of here right this minute. Let's go to Fort Laramie and kick up our heels."

"I've just been to Laramie," replied Gilmartin. "You go ahead without me."

"Don't tell me you've gone all sweet on these Mormons, like Hawkes has."

Gilmartin smiled ruefully. "Just on one of them."

"Huh?"

"I happen to have fallen in love with a certain young lady."

"In love?" Renshaw gaped in disbelief at his partner. Then he threw his head back and guffawed—a sound that in Gilmartin's opinion bore a striking resemblance to the unpleasant braying of a knobhead mule.

"As a matter of fact, Red," continued Gilmartin, bristling slightly, "we're going to have to go our separate ways, you and me. I'm no longer interested in the fur trade."

Renshaw abruptly stopped laughing. "What? You're pulling my leg! You are—aren't you?"

Gilmartin adamantly shook his head. "I have hankering to see California."

"California? What in hell for? You want to get your head shot off? They're still having a good bit of trouble over there, even though it's been a year since John Fremont grabbed the place away from the Mexicans."

Gilmartin shrugged, supremely indifferent to the perils that might lurk in California.

"We're finished, Red. No hard feelings, I hope. I'll take my share of that money and we'll be all square."

"I'll be damned," muttered Renshaw, incredulous. "You're serious."

"Never been more serious in my life."

Renshaw rode on a ways in brooding silence. Finally he said, "Women! They sure know how to foul every goddamn thing up."

Chapter 18

Brigham Young had not one but three men taking notes as Jim Bridger rambled on and on for more than two hours about the country that lay to the west of the Big Sandy. The Mormon president wanted to gather every last bit of intelligence he could glean from the legendary mountain man. He and more than a dozen other men gathered around the campfire to listen attentively as Old Gabe told them that the Bear River Valley might not suit the Saints, though in his opinion the Utah Valley was a more likely place for them to settle. But farther north, in the basin of the Great Salt Lake, well, Bridger said he would pay a thousand dollars for a barrel of corn if someone managed by some miracle to raise a crop in that godforsaken country. The nights were too cold and the soil too alkaline, in his opinion. Of course, he was no farmer. "I haven't laid hand to plow since I was a boy, thank the Lord," he said fervently.

On seeing Bridger, Hawkes had entertained the fleeting notion that maybe he could turn the Mormons over to Old Gabe and head for home. In ten days, maybe less, he could be back with Eliza and Cameron. But Bridger had made up his mind to go to Fort Laramie and set the record straight about the folly of Hastings' Cutoff. As for Renshaw, he made the sudden decision to forego the pleasures of Fort Laramie and resolved to return to the mountains. The decision by

Gilmartin to break up their long-standing partnership had taken the wind out of Red's sails. Though the two of them were always bickering, it occurred to Renshaw that Gil was just about the only real friend he had. But now Gil was tossing that friendship away. And all on account of some woman. Red tried briefly to talk Gil out of such folly, but as soon as he voiced the opinion that no woman was worth messing up prime fixings like they had, Gilmartin lost his temper and told Red to shut the hell up.

Hawkes could sympathize with Renshaw. Red knew instinctively that the only reason Gil was thinking about California was on account of the woman. And Red was right in pointing out that he and Gil had invested a good deal of time and effort in establishing their trade with the Indians. Maybe they didn't make a whole lot in the way of profit, but they earned enough for the lives they led. Hawkes wondered what Renshaw would have thought had he been made aware of the fact that the woman Gil was so wrapped up in was married. Red didn't ask for particulars, however. Frankly, he didn't *want* to know who the woman was. Bitterly disappointed, he divvied up the money in the pouch with his ex-partner and rode out that same day, promising Hawkes that he would swing by and tell Eliza that her husband was alive and well and would be home before too much longer—certainly before the first snows fell. Hawkes had to be satisfied with that. Brigham Young was depending on him to guide the Pioneer Camp to the valleys which Jim Bridger had suggested. And Hawkes had not come with the Saints to leave them now.

Bridger took his leave the following morning, wishing Hawkes and the Mormons luck. Hawkes thanked him, realizing that the only reason Old Gabe had been so helpful to the Saints was because he relied on Gordon's assessment of their character. As far as Bridger was concerned, if Hawkes said they were good people then that was all he needed to know. Hawkes promised they would meet next summer, when he made his annual visit to Fort Bridger.

The Pioneers continued westward, with the snow-capped peaks of the Uinta Range to the south and the majestic Tetons visible far to the north. But the country they crossed was nothing but sand and sage-brushes and dry gulches, as inhospitable as any they had yet seen, and in spite of Bridger's optimistic descriptions of valleys that lay somewhere up ahead, doubts reappeared on the gaunt, sunburned faces of the Saints. On the second day they had to push more than twenty exhausting miles to reach the Big Sandy because there wasn't enough water and grass anywhere along the way to make for even a tolerable campsite.

To make matters worse, some of the Pioneers fell prey to spotted fever, an affliction marked by a high temperature and a terrible aching in the joints. When they reached the Green River and found it running high, the expedition was forced to stop and build rafts. That gave the ailing ones a chance to lie in tree shade and recuperate—something exceedingly difficult to do when you were laid out in a moving wagon and every bump and jolt sent spasms of excruciating pain through your tormented body. While crews worked constructing the rafts, other men spent their leisure moments fishing, and met with unexpected success, landing numerous fat trout. The trout were a pleasant change from a monotonous diet of beans, biscuits, and salt pork.

As they crossed the Green, thirteen men appeared on the eastern bank. They turned out to be members of the Mormon Battalion, on the trail of mule thieves, with news that the Battalion had been mustered out, having served its allotted time in the service of the

United States, and were in the process of coming west in search of the Pioneer Camp. Their leader was a Sergeant Tom Williams. Williams and his men threw in with the Pioneers, since the trail of the thieves seemed to be taking them in the same direction that Brigham Young and his company were traveling.

When they arrived at Fort Bridger, William Clayton figured they had traveled nine hundred miles from Winter Quarters; he'd been faithfully reading Harman's roadometer and putting up markers for two-thirds of the way. Seeing Old Gabe's post made Hawkes both sad and happy—happy because it signified that he was on the last leg of his long journey home, but sad because it served to remind him of that scene, down by Black's Fork, where he had told Eliza about Taggett's letter and his decision to go east for the package containing his mother's Bible. It stunned him to realize that fourteen months had passed since he'd ridden out of Fort Bridger on that mission. More than a year since last he'd held sweet Eliza in his arms. He wondered in what ways Cameron had changed in that time. A boy could do a lot of growing up in fourteen months.

It was discovered that Tom Goodale, the leader of the mule thieves that Sergeant Tom Williams had been tracking, was holed up among the Shoshones who, as was their custom, had set up their lodges under the big cottonwoods along Black's Fork. Unfortunately, the rest of the gang had pushed on in the direction of Oregon with the purloined livestock. Williams was dead-set on arresting Goodale, but Brigham Young prevented him from doing so. Goodale was a criminal, surely, but he was also an American citizen. Since there was no duly constituted court out here which could try Goodale, what did Williams propose to do with his prisoner? If he were tried, convicted, and punished according to Mormon justice, that would just incense other Gentiles. Williams had to settle for confiscating Goodale's horse. Even then, Brigham Young forced him to provide the thief with a receipt for the appropriated pony. That galled Williams, and many of the other Saints scratched their heads in bewilderment. It wasn't like their president to go easy on those who preyed upon his people. Hawkes, though, believed he knew what Brigham Young was doing. The Mormon leader didn't want to raise a ruckus with the local inhabitants since he hoped they would be his neighbors.

At Fort Bridger they learned that the Utes were active in the Utah Valley, which Old Gabe had recommended as their best bet for a place to settle, so Brigham Young decided their only recourse would be to take a good hard look at the area north of Ute country, around the salt lake. But a hundred miles separated them from that place—a hundred hard miles over rough terrain crossed by few wagons. Circling Bridger Butte, they crossed the Bear River Divide, passed a sulfur spring and an oil spring, and camped in Echo Canyon. At the other end of the canyon they found the Weber River. The going was very hard now, as every mile produced a formidable array of obstacles—steep hills, boulders, or thick stands of willow trees blocking passage between narrow canyon walls, rocky creeks to negotiate, and more spotted fever. This time Brigham Young was among those afflicted, and it was decided that an advance party of twenty wagons would proceed while the remainder of the Pioneer Camp stayed behind with their leader. Hawkes and Loud Talker went with the advance party, forty-two men led by Orson Pratt. Gilmartin remained with the others, since Patience Bonham was Brigham Young's nurse during his illness. John Bonham, however, went with Pratt's company at the Mormon president's request. Bonham didn't complain, though

Hawkes wondered what his feelings were as he left Gilmartin and wife behind.

Pratt's men labored mightily to blaze a trail through the virgin wilderness, so that on Sunday, July 18, the Apostle declared a day of much needed rest. Early on the following day, Hawkes and Loud Talker, scouting ahead as was their custom, reached the crest of a high hogback ridge in the Wasatch Mountains and gazed down through a notch at a broad plain, golden in the hazy distance. The valley stretched many miles west, to the base of a faraway mountain range.

"I've never been in this part of the country," admitted Hawkes, "but my guess is that this is the valley of the salt lake."

Loud Talker gazed for a pensive moment at the panorama that lay before them. Then he drew a deep breath and nodded in satisfaction. "So it ends here."

"How so?"

"This is where the Saints will make their new home."

"What makes you so sure of that?"

The Osage shrugged. "I feel it in my bones." He smiled at Hawkes. "Our long journey together has come to an end, my friend. It is time for both of us to go home." He extended a hand. "I hope that someday we will meet again. I have many more things I want to tell you."

"You must be kidding," said Hawkes. He shook Loud Talker's hand.

That day Hawkes took Orson Pratt to the lookout, and Pratt shouted with unrestrained joy when he beheld the broad valley. "Hurry back and tell Brother Brigham that we have reached the promised land. To think that after all this time, all of this suffering, we have finally found the home which the Almighty God has prepared for his people! Hurry, Hawkes. Tell Brother Brigham to make haste as soon as he is able.

We will try to find the best route down from these heights."

Hawkes rode back to Echo Canyon; a stretch that had taken Pratt's party days to cover, he covered in one long day. When he informed Brigham Young of the discovery, the Mormon's eyes lit up. New strength seemed to flood his fever-wracked body. In spite of this, he was still too weak to ride. A wagon was emptied of everything but a pallet and a few supplies. Simon Parker would drive it, and one of the young teamsters would accompany him, with Brigham Young riding in the back. The rest would follow, under the leadership of Lorenzo Young and Return Redden—and Gilmartin told Hawkes he would stay with the main party. Since Patience Bonham was with the main party, Gil's decision came as no surprise to Hawkes.

Two days later, Hawkes led the wagon bearing Brigham Young to the place where he had parted company with Orson Pratt. One man had been left behind to inform those who came later that a route down to the valley had been discovered—a steep and difficult gulch that Pratt had christened Lost Creek Canyon. It was so steep, in fact, that in places the wagons had to be lowered on ropes, one at a time, with all the men straining on the lines. Norton Jacob's cannon, which had been hauled a thousand miles from Winter Quarters, stood abandoned at the camp, as did some of the wagons. Pratt was taking only what he had to in his hasty descent to the valley.

Brigham Young insisted on seeing the valley, and with Simon Parker's assistance, Hawkes took the ailing Mormon president to the top of the hogback ridge. Though he could barely stand upright when he got to the top, Brigham Young was beaming when he gazed down at the golden valley. For a few minutes he was speechless with joy and a vast relief. Finally, softly, he said, "It is enough. This is the right place."

That day they followed Pratt's precarious trail down Lost Creek Canyon. Four men could not lower a wagon down the steepest places, so Hawkes asked for time to find a more suitable route. Brigham Young was too impatient to wait. He insisted on taking to the saddle. Against his better judgment, Hawkes dismounted and helped the Mormon leader aboard his dun mustang. Then he led the horse in the treacherous descent down the canyon.

They reached the valley with everyone still in one piece. Hawkes wasn't sure how Brigham Young found the strength to complete the arduous journey through the rugged Wasatch, but he did, through sheer determination alone, because he was pale and terribly weak. In fact, Hawkes thought he looked like death warmed over. It would be a tragic thing if the Moses of the Mormons perished at the moment of triumph, just as he arrived at the promised land to which he had led his people. But Brigham held on. He actually perked up when he saw that Pratt's party was already hard at work. Several acres of ground had been plowed, and the soil looked rich enough for the seed corn they sowed within it. A creek had been dammed, and irrigation ditches dug. Pratt excitedly told the Mormon president that there were plenty of streams and lots of timber in the foothills. They had even discovered a hot mineral springs. Best of all, there was absolutely no sign of prior habitation, either by red man or white. There was plenty of room in this broad valley for twenty thousand Saints to put down roots. Or even twice that many. And surely, added Pratt fervently, surely this place was sufficiently remote that those who settled it would be left alone for many years to come.

Brigham Young nodded in complete agreement. "The day will come when the Gentiles encircle us. And, if history teaches us anything, then we know we can expect them to covet what we will build here. But we will not be driven from our homes again. If we are given ten years we will be strong enough to withstand any attempt to do so. Never again will we build our temple and then abandon it. I pledge every drop of blood in my veins to this solemn vow. This *is* the New Jerusalem. This is the place the Lord has set aside for His chosen people. All that we have suffered in the past was meant to bring us here. And this will always belong to us. We will make the desert bloom and our children—and their children, and on down through the generations, Mormons from this moment until the end of time—shall prosper from the fruits of their labor in here."

Chapter 19

Brigham Young summoned John Bonham and ordered him to ride back and find the Mormon Battalion, and then lead them back to the valley. Hawkes half-expected the holy killer to protest. Surely Bonham was reluctant to get too far away from Patience, what with Gilmartin lurking about. But if Bonham had any reservations about embarking on the mission Brigham gave him, he didn't show it, and rode out immediately.

The Mormon leader then turned to Hawkes and clasped the mountain man's hand in both his own.

"God directed us here, but you were the instrument of His will. We will forever be indebted to you."

"Reckon it should be the other way around. You took me in with no questions asked. I never told you the whole truth about my past. Maybe you should know that the man who shot me was after a bounty. I'm wanted for murder—well, two murders now. I didn't commit either one of them, but you'll just have to take my oath on that."

"I take it without reservation. There is room here among us for you and your family. You would be safe here."

Hawkes shook his head. "I appreciate the offer, but I don't think I'd fit in."

"A man may live here with us and worship as he please so long as he respects our beliefs. Consider it.

No longer would you have to look over your shoulder. No longer would you be hunted. We do not intend to have any commerce with the Gentiles. We will be free and independent."

"That's how I live, too. And you see, that's why I'm not suited for your way of living. You folks all work for a common goal and the common good. Don't think there's anything wrong with that, if you're the kind of person who's cut out for working with others. But I do for myself, and my family. I'm accustomed to being alone, and answering to no one. That's what the high country breeds in a man, for good or ill. Speaking of which, I think it's time I got home."

"If you ever change your mind," said Brigham Young, "our doors will always be open to you."

"Maybe I'll come see how you've made out in a year or two."

A steely determination hardened the Mormon leader's features. "We'll make out," he replied. "In fact, we will do better than that. We will prosper here as we have never prospered before. Because here, we are no longer hunted."

"I hope that's right, sir."

As Hawkes prepared to take his leave, Simon Parker walked up, that deceptive half-smile lifting the corner of his mouth, as always. After all these months, Hawkes still wasn't sure about Parker. He never could read the young Mormon gunman. Hawkes figured Parker would still wear that easy smile while he was in the process of killing a man. And killing was probably something Parker could do without blinking an eye. Hawkes was just glad there hadn't been an opportunity for Parker to prove whether this was so. John Bonham, at least, took killing to be a serious business; Hawkes didn't think the same could be said for Parker.

"You ought to know that Brother Stout ordered me

to keep an eye on you right before we left Winter Quarters," drawled Parker.

"If I ever see him again I'll tell him you did a good job of that. But I thought you took orders from Bonham these days, not Stout."

Parker shrugged. "Both, sometimes."

"Why doesn't Hosea Stout trust me?"

"Because you're not a Mormon. You know that. He thought you must be up to no good. It didn't make any sense to him that a Gentile would help us. He even thought you might be a spy sent into our midst. Or an assassin with orders to kill our president."

Hawkes smiled wryly. "Well, you now know that he was wrong, don't you?"

"I guess maybe I do. It's been a pleasure knowing you. But I'm still glad you're leaving."

"So am I. There'll be more Gentiles coming along. You folks had better find some way to get along with them."

"That isn't possible." Parker gazed across the sun-hammered valley. "This belongs to us now, and we'll kill anybody who tries to take it away from us."

"So long, then."

Parker nodded. He didn't offer his hand, and neither did Hawkes. Riding away, Hawkes mulled over the whittling deacon's words. The Gentiles *would* come, and if the Saints made this desert bloom, then they would covet what the Mormons had. And Hawkes had no doubt that the Saints would thrive, even here. They were a people accustomed to overcoming tremendous odds, and if they set out to accomplish something, it was good as done.

So there would be a war, somewhere down the line. Hawkes was certain of it. Maybe it was inevitable that men would be willing to fight and die to possess this land. This country had that kind of power over the hearts and imaginations of people. It surely was worth fighting for. But Hawkes had to wonder how the conflicts to come would affect him and, more important, his family. His mountain home would not remain a sanctuary forever. A year ago he might have been able to convince himself that the westward tide of pioneers was so gradual that it would have little or no effect on the high country in his lifetime. Now, having seen firsthand the hundreds of wagons and thousands of emigrants on the trail this summer, he knew better. It was indeed a human flood, and that flood would wash away the life he had known and loved, probably in a matter of a few short years.

All the more reason to get home, then, so that he could enjoy what he had while it remained for him to enjoy. And he promised himself that he would never leave again, as he had done nearly a year and a half ago. A year and a half! Precious days lost forever. He would make the same oath to Eliza if she wanted him to. He would swear it on his mother's Bible.

When he got back to the main party he looked for Gilmartin, knowing that somehow he had to persuade Gil that it was time that he departed, as well. It was time to put aside all those dangerous fancies about Patience Bonham. But Gilmartin was nowhere to be found. Hawkes hunted up Lorenzo Young.

"Your friend left this morning," Brigham's brother told him. "He asked for a wagon and a team of mules, and that I gave him gladly, as my brother had promised, along with some provisions. He headed back up the canyon. If there is anything that I can do for you . . ."

"Did John Bonham pass through here earlier?"

"Yes, early this morning. He did not tarry, but rode east in search of the Mormon Battalion."

Hawkes was on the verge of asking Lorenzo Young if he had seen Patience lately, but caught himself. It was too risky for Gilmartin's sake to pose such questions. Instead, he roamed the camp, searching for the young woman, trying not to arouse suspicion. He didn't find her. A sudden urgency possessed Hawkes and he left the camp, found the tracks of Gilmartin's wagon easily enough. They took him back up Echo Canyon. Gil had a good half-day's head start on him but Hawkes relied on making much better time aboard the sure-footed dun mustang than his friend could do with a team of mules pulling a prairie schooner. Before long he saw by the tracks in the dry, sandy soil that someone else was following the wagon. Hawkes worried about them. John Bonham was gone to find the Mormon Battalion, and Simon Parker was back in the valley with Brigham Young. But there were others in the Pioneer Camp who were nearly as dangerous as those two, and maybe one of them was trailing Gilmartin with some dark design.

Toward day's end, as purple shadows began to fill the canyon, Hawkes caught up with Gil. The wagon was partially concealed in a stand of scrubby trees. Gilmartin was checking the team's harness, evidently intending to put some more miles behind him before calling it a day. When he heard Hawkes coming through the brush he grabbed his rifle out of the wagon, relaxing only as Hawkes broke cover. It was then that Hawkes saw Patience on the wagon seat—and realized that it was her tracks that he had seen. She had followed Gil's wagon, no doubt according to some prearranged plan, and they had rendezvoused here. Her horse was tied to the wagon's gate. Hawkes felt a cold knot form in the pit of his stomach.

Gilmartin handed the rifle up to Patience and resumed his inspection of the team as Hawkes drew near.

"What are you doing here?" he asked, though it was obvious that he knew the answer perfectly well.

"You don't sound too happy to see me," remarked

Hawkes. He smiled and nodded at Patience. "Evening, *Mrs.* Bonham."

Patience looked away, ashamed. Gilmartin fired an angry look at Hawkes.

"Listen here," he said sharply. "I don't need any lectures, so if that's what you have in mind for me you can just forget it and ride on."

Hawkes dismounted. "Look, Gil—"

"No, you look. Patience and I love each other and we're going to spend the rest of our lives together. It may look wrong to you and everybody else, but it's right for us, and frankly I don't care what other people think. You just don't understand. Her marriage to Bonham was a matter of convenience—his, not hers. It was arranged by the Church and she didn't have any say in the matter. She doesn't love Bonham and never has. But she loves me and I can't leave without her. I *won't* leave without her and that's all there is to it."

"So you'll live the rest of your life on the run. Always looking over your shoulder. Don't do it, Gil. Believe me, that's no way to live."

"Go home and mind your own business for a change."

Hawkes drew a long breath, comprehending the utter futility of trying to talk his friend out of making this colossal mistake.

"Okay. So where are you going?" he asked. "I thought you were headed for California. Well, if you are, you're going the wrong way."

"Why do you want to know? So you can tell your Mormon friends?" Gilmartin instantly regretted his rash words. "I'm sorry, Hawkes. That was uncalled for. I know you wouldn't do a low-down thing like that."

"Forget it. I really don't want to know."

"We *are* going to California. Soon as we're out of

these mountains I'll turn south, maybe to Taos. Lie low there through the winter and head west next spring."

Hawkes thought it over, nodded, and extended a hand. "So long, Gil."

Surprised, Gilmartin hesitated, then took the proffered hand. "I know you don't approve, Gordon. I wish . . . well, I don't guess it's fair to expect you to understand."

Hawkes turned to Patience. "I hope you both find happiness."

"Thank you," she said in a small, uncertain voice.

Mounting up, Hawkes took one last look at Gil and then rode on. He tried to put everything out of his mind. Patience and Gilmartin and John Bonham and the Mormons. So much had yet to be resolved, but he told himself that none of it was his concern any longer. He had done what he'd set out to do. His job was finished. Gil and the Saints were on their own from here on out. It was time for him to go home.

Part Three

Chapter 20

"I've got a bone to pick with your old friend, Brigham Young."

Standing in the Fort Bridger trading post and staring at Old Gabe, Gordon Hawkes felt that flood of old memories wash over him. Bridger's raspy words brought it all back to him—vivid images of those days ten years ago when he had led Brigham Young and his Saints in their epic westward undertaking. For a moment he just stood there in silence, his thoughts focused on that long ago adventure. Thinking of the letter that had found him here, at this very place, in the summer of 1846, of the news of his mother's death, of the trek to Independence with Dale Gilmartin and his wagon load of plews, of the scrape with the buffalo-running Ring brothers, of the trap laid for him in Independence, of meeting up with the notorious Mormon avenger, John Bonham, of a long winter spent at Winter Quarters while he recovered from a gunshot wound inflicted by the bounty-hunting Geller. Then there was the journey westward, the situation with Gilmartin and Bonham's wife, Patience, the trouble with the Pawnees, the confrontation with a vengeful Billy Ring at Fort Laramie, the discovery of the valley of the salt lake, and the look on Brigham Young's face as he gazed at long last upon the promised land. That was a lot to come at a man all at once, and Hawkes was a little stunned.

"The feller keeps on about how I'm stirrin' up the Utes to make trouble for the Saints. Hell, Gordon, you know that ain't so. I get along with the Utes about as well as the next man, even traded with 'em a time or two, but I ain't friends with 'em, not the way I am with the Snakes. Still, Brigham suspects me. Reckon it's on account of how I've made sure the Snakes have plenty of good rifles. Now, Chief Washakie and his Snake warriors ain't never given them Saints a lick of trouble, so far as I know. But the Utes have. And the Utes are well-armed. The Santa Fe traders have seen to that, not me. I've told Brigham as much. But he just don't seem to get through that thick skull of his." Bridger drew a deep breath and lifted the jug. "How about another shot of Taos Lightning?"

"Don't mind if I do."

"I ain't talkin' too much, am I?"

Bridger rubbed his grizzled jaw. Old Gabe was older than dirt now. His deeply seamed cheeks were hollowing out, and he had lost a good many of his teeth. His beard stubble was snow-white. Much had happened to Bridger in the decade past. His Ute wife had died. He'd gotten hitched to a Shoshone woman. His daughter had been kidnapped by the Cayuse Indians who murdered Marcus and Narcissa Whitman, and Bridger had never seen Mary Ann again. And then there was all this trouble with the Mormons. In fact, Brigham Young and his Saints had made Old Gabe's life a living hell. He'd said it a hundred times if he'd said it once—he was as sorry as a man could be that he had given the Mormons any help at all back in '47. That was a day he rued, sure as hell was hot. It was what a person had coming when he let greed get in the way of good old common sense.

"I should've known better than to help them Mormons settle so close," moaned Bridger, taking a swig from the jug. "I mean, they've been in the middle of trouble everywhere they go. Now I ain't sayin' they're the ones who always started it, but you can't deny they attract it like flies to horse shit. So why did I think it would be any different this time around? Well, you see, that was the problem. I *didn't* think. Or I should say I didn't think about anything except all the money I was likely to make when all them Saints came rollin' past here on their way to the salt lake."

Hawkes had heard most of this before. Ever since coming home from his sojourn with the Mormons, he and Eliza and Cameron had faithfully made their annual trek southward to Fort Bridger during the summer, so that he could trade his small pack of plews for shot, powder, and percussion caps, and luxuries like coffee, sugar, tobacco for his pipe, and some things for his wife and son. It was the one time in the year that he got much news from the outside world. Even now, with the frontier fast filling up with newcomers, few people ventured deeply enough into the mountains to stumble on the secluded Hawkes cabin. Sometimes he called on the Absaroka Crows, and every now and then he would run across another mountain man, but it was Jim Bridger who was his only real source of news. But it just seemed like Old Gabe was becoming more and more obsessed with Brigham Young and the Mormons. It was about all he talked about anymore.

"But you must admit they've done what you thought couldn't be done," Hawkes reminded Bridger. "They made the desert bloom just like Brigham Young said they would. Did you ever pay that thousand dollars you promised for the first bushel of corn grown out of that valley?"

Bridger scowled. "No, I ain't never paid up, on account of no one has called me on it. They call it Deseret now. What kind of name is that? What does it mean?"

Hawkes shrugged. "I have no idea."

"You ain't never wanted to pay them a visit, hoss? I mean, you're their friend, ain't you?"

"I suppose I am. But no, I've never paid them a visit."

"Well, then, you'll be interested to know that an army of federal troops is on the march and headed for Deseret. I believe we are gonna have us a genuine knock down, drag out war."

Hawkes had been packing his pipe with recently acquired Ol' Virginny tobacco. Now he forgot all about a smoke. Putting the pipe aside, he leaned forward over the counter that separated him from Bridger.

"Are you drunk, Old Gabe?" he asked, suspiciously. "Or am I? I could have sworn you mentioned war."

Bridger nodded. "You thought I was just going to tell you the same old story, didn't you? Well, Gordon, there's a new chapter fixin' to get writ even as we speak. Your Mormon friends are about to catch hell."

Hawkes took a look around. For the time being, at least, they were alone in the trading post. Vasquez had gone off to run a similar post at Deseret, so Eliza, no longer able to enjoy the company of her friend Mrs. Vasquez, was out among the members of an emigrant train that had arrived at Fort Bridger the day before yesterday. Cameron was out there, too, though he no longer sought other children to play with. Cameron was no longer a child. He had grown into a big, strapping young man, now seventeen years old, and a little on the quiet side, strong but silent. Eliza's determination to give her son some book learning had paid off; Cameron was pretty well-educated for someone who had spent his whole life in the mountains. He could read and write and reason well. On top of that he was a darn good marksman and tracker.

"You better tell me everything," said Hawkes, thinking of his family. If there was going to be a war he needed to know enough of the details to keep Eliza and Cameron—not to mention himself—out of the way.

He knew some of the background to the story already. The rest of the Saints had begun to follow the trail blazed by the intrepid Pioneer Camp and settled in the valley of the salt lake in 1848. At the time, the valley had legally belonged to Mexico, but as part of the treaty negotiations of the Mexican War, Utah was ceded to the United States. In 1849 the United States had sent territorial officers that were not to the Mormons' liking. Also that year, the westward flood of emigrants was increased substantially by gold seekers bound for California, drawn by sensational tales of a big strike on the American River. These gold seekers passed through Salt Lake Valley by the hundreds after a difficult trek, pushing their livestock past the limits of endurance, and suffering from hunger, measles, and cholera along the way. In their headlong rush to reach the fabled gold fields, many had embarked on the westward journey ill-prepared for what lay ahead.

That being the case, the Mormons realized considerable profit from catering to the needs of the gold seekers. The latter traded their worn-out livestock for fresh teams, or traded in their wagons and belongings for a good horse and some provisions, and many of them gave little or no thought to how badly they were getting skinned by the Saints. All they were concerned about was getting to California and striking it rich.

The Mormon exodus continued through the year 1852, since many families were reluctant to leave the familiar confines of Iowa for the unknown dangers of the trail. This worked out for the best, allowing those at Deseret to establish the New Zion, gradually increasing the acreage under cultivation, and make arrangements for the feeding and shelter of the newcomers. For the most part, the westering Saints stuck to the north side of the Platte and so managed to avoid the cholera that filled a thousand graves along the Oregon Trail.

Finally, the Gathering was complete. God's "chosen" had emigrated to the New Jerusalem. They had suffered so much to get there, and were so protective of their new home, that any hint of Gentile interference was enough to set them off. As a kind of preemptive strike, Mormons marched to seize the ferries over Green River, but were driven off.

"They came after me next," Bridger sourly told Hawkes. "But you know all about that. One hundred and fifty of 'em, carryin' a warrant signed by some Mormon judge. 'Course I knew they were on their way long before they got here. So they drank up all my whiskey and stole most of my livestock and several wagon loads of my goods. They were Danites. Call themselves avenging angels. Just thievin' cutthroats if you ask me. They had it in mind to burn this post, on account of there had been some talk that I was going to let the United States Army use it, and of course because they had that damn fool notion of me sellin' guns to the Utes. Lucky for me, they were poor arsonists."

Hawkes was feeling worse by the minute. Bridger had never said a thing about it, but Hawkes remembered that Old Gabe had been reluctant to help the Mormons ten years ago, back when Brigham Young and his Pioneer Camp were desperately in search of a new home for the Church. Bridger had heard all kinds of rumors about the Saints, most of them unflattering, but he had cooperated because Hawkes had vouched for the Mormons. Now the old mountain man was sorry he'd ever even heard of Brigham Young, and rued the day he'd suggested that the Pioneers take a look at the valleys west of the Big Sandy. Now they were his neighbors—and they were making life miserable for him.

"You remember back in '54," said Bridger, "when I went up to Fort Laramie? That's when I met up with that Irish lord—Sir George something or other . . ."

"Gore. Sir George Gore."

"You're a heap younger than me, which probably accounts for your better memory."

"I'm also better looking than you are, Gabe," Hawkes quipped.

"That's a matter of opinion. Anyway, Sir George and I got along famously, so I agreed to act as his guide the next spring. We headed on up into the Yellowstone country so that Sir George could do some hunting. He kilt forty grizzlies and more elk, deer, and antelope than I can count. Kilt over two thousand buffalo, too. I can tell you, the Injuns warn't too happy with us over that."

Hawkes tried to conceal the fact that he wasn't happy about it, either. Bridger had told him about his adventures with the Irish sportsman a year ago, and Hawkes had wondered if it even occurred to Old Gabe that by working for men like Sir George Gore he was hastening the day when this country would bear absolutely no resemblance to the land he and other mountain men cherished almost beyond reason. But Sir George was very rich and he paid well, and as much as Hawkes hated to admit it, Jim Bridger had become very enamored of money in his old age.

"Anyhow," continued Bridger, "I stuck with Sir George through the summer of 1856, up around the Rosebud and the Tongue, so I didn't have no run-ins with them Saints. Later I went to Kansas City and got asked to go to Washington, where I was introduced to President James Buchanan himself. The president wanted to talk about the Mormons. He was mad as a hornet about the way Brigham Young had treated the territorial officials, refusing to acknowledge the authority of the United States of America. Sedition—that's what the president called it, and he swore he was going to teach them Mormons a lesson. Well, they're fixin' to get that lesson at long last, and I'd be a goldurned liar if I said I warn't glad of it. There's an army comin', and I aim to meet up with it in a month or so at Fort Laramie. They're gonna pay me five dollars a day to serve as a scout. I'd do it for nothin'—just the satisfaction of seein' Brigham Young's face when we run the ol' Stars and Stripes up over Deseret."

Bridger took another healthy slug of Taos Lightning and passed the jug to Hawkes, who helped himself since he couldn't recall an occasion when he'd needed a drink worse. As he drank, Bridger gave him a speculative glance.

"What about you, Gordon?" he asked.

"What about me?" gasped Hawkes as the whiskey burned his throat.

"Reckon you know the Mormons as well as anybody. Hell, you lived with 'em and rode with 'em for more than a year. The army would be pleased to have you for a scout. I'm sure I could get you five dollars a day in wages."

"I've never worked for wages and don't intend to start. No thanks, Old Gabe."

A man entered the trading post. "Mr. Bridger, I'm needin' that wheel out of your forge. I'm in sort of a hurry to get to California. The mother lode's waitin' for me to get there."

Bridger raised a hand. "I'll be right along."

The gold seeker walked out and Bridger turned his attention back to Hawkes, leaning forward with a squinty gaze.

"You don't aim to side with them Saints, do you?" he asked.

"No," said Hawkes. "If there is going to be a war, I aim to stay completely out of it."

"Oh, I can guarantee there'll be a war," replied Bridger, supremely confident. "But whether you can steer clear of it or not—well, that there's something else again."

Bridger left the trading post to attend to the gold seeker's wagon wheel. Taking one more swallow from the jug, Hawkes made up his mind and went out to find Eliza. He explained the situation to her. She didn't mind at all when he suggested they leave first thing in the morning. If he wanted to go to their home deep in the mountains and wait until the smoke cleared, that was fine with her. The last thing Eliza Hawkes wanted was for her husband to get involved in a war.

Chapter 21

Sitting in a straight-backed chair beneath a cottonwood tree, Brigham Young watched his people mill about the meeting place at Silver Creek, located at the mouth of Big Cottonwood Canyon some miles east of the city they had built beside the salt lake. It was the twenty-fourth day of July, the tenth anniversary of the day the first Mormon had entered this valley. Hundreds of Saints had gathered to celebrate the occasion. There were six bands playing, three open-air pavilions erected, and plenty of food prepared. The people had come in wagons and carriages, on mules and horseback—men, women, and children from the city as well as the little towns that had sprung up all over the valley.

This was an occasion for good cheer and thanksgiving. In just ten years, they had made the desert bloom. At last count, nearly thirty-six thousand Mormons had settled in the valley, thousands coming over from Britain, Ireland, and Scotland. A tabernacle had been constructed in the middle of the city, and a temple was under construction. They had grown crops, planted trees, dug wells, and built houses and halls. Truly this was the promised land, the safe haven God had promised His chosen people. The Saints felt secure here. Once again they could look to the future with confidence. Ten years had passed since last they had been in fear of Illinois "wolf hunts" and marauding Missouri Pukes. The Utes to the south were a threatening presence, but the Indians had come to respect the well-armed and well-trained Mormon militia, and hadn't tried anything beyond an occasional raid on outlying areas.

But Brigham Young himself did not feel secure, or confident in the future. Soon he would have to announce to the Saints who had gathered here that a federal army was on its way. John Bonham had just brought him confirmation of this, and Bonham wasn't one to make mistakes. If he said an army was marching on Deseret, then it was so, as much as Brigham wished not to believe it. Not that he was all that surprised. For some time now he had suspected that it would come to this. He had done everything in his power to delay the inevitable confrontation between the Church and the United States of America, now presided over by President James Buchanan.

Buchanan! Brigham Young grimaced. That gutless wonder lacked the nerve to put down the rebellious southern states, so he hoped to use the subjugation of the Mormons as an example to intimidate the southern firebrands. The South had been threatening secession for some time now, quarreling with the federal government over the issues of states' rights and slavery. Was Buchanan sending an army into Dixie to put a stop to such seditious talk? No. He dared not. He thought the Mormons would be a much easier foe to crush.

Brigham Young had faith—faith in God and in his people, faith in the ability of the Church to stand up to Buchanan and his bluecoat soldiers. If war came—and it seemed certain that war *would* come—the Saints would fight to the last man to keep what belonged to them. But the Mormon president didn't want bloodshed. There had to be a way to keep the peace while maintaining the security of Deseret and the Mormon right to live their lives according to their beliefs.

Several men clad in somber black broadcloth and broad-brimmed hats were now coming toward him, grim purpose in their long strides. Heber Kimball and Daniel Wells, a pair of Mormon fire-eaters who, God help them, actually *wanted* blood. Hosea Stout approached, too—the police chief hated the United States in particular and all Gentiles in general with the unrelenting fervor of a zealot. There were many more vengeful Saints who shared the sentiments of these three men when it came to outsiders.

"Brother Brigham," said Kimball as the three elders reached the shade of the cottonwood. "Do you remember what you told us ten years ago?"

"You said that if our enemies left us alone for just ten years," said Wells, "we would be strong enough to withstand any attempt to drive us from our land, as we have been driven so many times before, in Missouri, in Illinois."

"Well, we've had our ten years of grace," continued Kimball. "Now our enemies are on their way here—twenty-five hundred soldiers with orders to lay waste to our fields and homes, to kill our livestock, to rape our women—"

"Please, Brother Heber," said Brigham Young dryly. "We do not know what their orders are."

"We have transformed the desert into a paradise on earth," said Wells. "Now that we have done so, the Gentiles want to steal everything away from us. The Nauvoo Legion stands ready to defend Deseret to the last man. Give us the word, Brother Brigham, and we will go out to meet this army and, God willing, destroy it."

"I have wives enough to whip such an army," said Kimball contemptuously. "We will fight until there is not a drop of blood left in my veins, if need be."

"We are not entirely blameless in this affair," Brigham Young reminded them. "Against my wishes, an attack was made on Fort Bridger and on the Green River ferries by a group of hotheads who care more about wreaking vengeance than they do about the welfare of the people."

"The Gentiles have insulted us and lied about us from the beginning," protested Hosea Stout, fingering the handle of the blacksnake whip curled over one burly shoulder. "That Judge Brocchus called our women whores, and Judge Stiles lied when he told Buchanan that we burned his records and shut down his court."

Brigham Young nodded. Brocchus and Stiles were two of the territorial officers dispatched by Washington to preside over the Territory of Utah. Neither man had any respect whatsoever for Mormon ways. In fact, they seemed to go to great lengths to antagonize the Church. But, despite the fabrications they had sent to Washington, Brigham Young had tried very earnestly to get along with them, and the rest of the federal officials. Had all his efforts been for naught? That certainly appeared to be the case.

He glanced in the direction of the largest pavilion. There, a Stars and Stripes flew atop a tall pole. It was meant to symbolize the Mormon desire to live in peace as citizens of the United States. And yet now the government in Washington was trumpeting the fiction that the Saints were in open rebellion, stirring all the old resentments to a fever pitch. Their Indian agents even claimed the Mormons were inciting the tribes to attack American wagon trains, and as far as Brigham knew that was a complete falsehood. Just one of many.

Turning his attention back to the three men, Brigham Young sighed. "So what is it that you would have me do, gentlemen? I have already approved the reorganization of the Nauvoo Legion."

"That was a wise decision," said Wells. "The good never wish for war, but are always prepared for it."

"Shall I issue an appeal to President Buchanan? Tell him—and not for the first time, I remind you—that we wish only to live in peace?"

"What good would that do?" rasped Hosea Stout.

"No, there is but one appeal left to make," said Kimball sternly. "An appeal to the God of our fathers to give us strength in the battle to come."

"There must be no battle," said Brigham.

"But we have no choice!" erupted Kimball. "We can defeat this army. I am certain of that. And our scouts tell us they have thousands of head of cattle on the hoof, and hundreds of wagons loaded with provisions and munitions. We could make use of that."

"We must place all of Deseret on a war footing," said Wells, who, unlike the fiery Kimball, did not usually let emotion get the better of judgment. "Once you have made the announcement that federal troops are coming, we should stockpile all food supplies so that we can be certain that everyone will have enough to eat while the war is waged. Last year our southern settlements produced a surplus while those in the north scarcely had enough to go around."

"A prudent suggestion, Brother Daniel," said Brigham Young. "It will be done. Brother Kimball, will you summon the people to gather at the large pavilion?"

Kimball walked away to do his president's bidding, and a few minutes later the music of the competing bands dwindled away, and the Saints began to congregate at the nearby pavilion. Brigham Young waited until nearly all the people present at the festival had gathered together. Then, wearily, he went to a dais wrapped in gaily colored bunting and addressed the hushed crowd in a deep, solemn voice that carried like summer thunder.

"The time must come," he said, "when there will be a separation between this Kingdom of God and the kingdoms of the world, a time when this kingdom must be free and independent of all other kingdoms.

"Dear brethren, we have learned that an army of about twenty-five hundred men are now en route to this Territory. We do not know for certain their intentions. Until such time as we do know, we will cease all transactions with Gentiles. We will not hinder those who pass through Deseret on their way to California, but neither shall we give them any aid. We will not be the first to strike, but we must be prepared to strike back if we are attacked. You must not panic. Go about your daily affairs in a calm and orderly fashion.

"There exists a thread that connects us to the United States of America. The Prophet himself spoke of that nation as one of great promise, where all could one day live free and prosper. I want to believe that is so, even though our experiences thus far do not support that belief. But we must be prepared to cut that thread. I shall take it as a witness that God desires to sever the ties between us and the world when an army undertakes to make an appearance in this Territory for the purpose of chastising or destroying us. We will wait a little while longer to see, but I shall take a hostile move by our enemies as evidence that it is time for that thread to be cut.

"That is all I have to tell you. Go home now. Lift your prayers to heaven and make your preparations with a stout heart and a firm faith in God."

Hosea Stout's whittling deacons moved in to keep the curious away from Brigham Young as the Mormon president left the dais. The crowd was quiet—eerily so for two thousand souls—as it dispersed. Brigham resumed his chair beneath the cottonwood. Kimball sought him out there.

"Wait?" asked Kimball, fuming. "Why must we wait until the invaders pollute our soil with their tread? I say strike them now. Destroy them. We can do it."

"Of course we could do it," said Brigham Young calmly. "That isn't the issue. But if we destroy this army, they will simply send another, ten times as strong, comprised of volunteers, perhaps, whom the federal officers will not be able to control, and they will wreak havoc upon our people." Brigham shook his head. "No. We must wait." He wagged a finger at Kimball. "And you will spread this warning, Brother Heber. I should have hunted down and punished the men who attacked the Green River ferries. Let it be known that if any man or group of men attacks the Gentiles before we have declared war against the United States, I will hang them with my own hands."

Hosea Stout approached with a dark-haired young man that Brigham recognized as the baritone from Scotland, Brother Dunbar.

"I have been inspired to write a song, sir," said Dunbar. "I have not yet finished it, but I thought . . ."

"Sing it for me, please."

Dunbar nodded, cleared his throat, and began to sing:

> *"In the mountain retreat God will strengthen my feet,*
> *On the necks of thy foes they shall tread.*
> *And their silver and gold, as the prophets foretold,*
> *Shall be brought to adorn thy fair head.*
> *Zion, dear Zion, land of the free!*
> *Our hearts shall be ever with thee."*

Brigham Young glanced at Kimball and Hosea Stout. It was obvious that they were as deeply moved as he.

"Thank you, Brother Dunbar," he said. "You have a gift, truly."

"I will complete it quickly, sir," vowed the young Scotsman.

"Do so," encouraged Kimball, nodding emphatically. "It will be our battle cry as we march against the Gentiles."

Brigham shot an exasperated look at Kimball. "As yet we have no need for a battle cry. You may go, Brother Dunbar, with my thanks."

Dunbar left, and Hosea Stout went with him. Realizing that he had gone too far with his bellicose statements, provoking Brigham Young, Heber Kimball also turned to go. But Brigham stopped him.

"Brother Heber, are you returning straight home?"

"That is my intent."

"Be so kind as to send John Bonham to the city. I will expect him there sometime tomorrow."

Kimball ached to know why Brigham Young wanted the Danite avenger, but he knew better than to ask.

Chapter 22

When John Bonham rode up to the Indian mission he was a little surprised to see several saddle horses tied up in front of the small adobe structure. This was a pretty isolated place at the southern end of the valley, a good many miles from the nearest Mormon settlement. From what he knew of the mission, it was rare to find anyone here except Joshua Haldman, the man hand-picked by Brigham Young to establish friendly relations with the Ute and Kanosh Indians. That was no small order, and Bonham had been impressed by the progress the courageous Haldman had made. It helped that Haldman was a widower—his wife and two children had all perished in the summer of 1846, on the difficult trail between Nauvoo and Winter Quarters. That tragedy explained Haldman's bravery; he frankly did not care whether he lived or died. Such sentiments benefited him in his relations with the Utes. Like all Plains Indians, the Utes admired bravery above all else and often refrained from taking a stranger's life on that account alone.

Despite Haldman's magnificent efforts to forge a peace between the Mormons and the Indians, it was a touch-and-go business still, after ten years. Armed by traders out of New Mexico, the Utes had occasionally attacked wagon trains that passed through their country, bound for California. They had made a few forays against the southernmost Mormon settlements, as well. Haldman's chief problem was that the Utes lived in small bands without one principal chief with whom the Saints could hash out a peace treaty. So Haldman's only recourse was to negotiate with each band separately. He had met with better success with some than with others. But as far as Bonham knew, Brigham Young and the Quorum of the Twelve Apostles had no quarrel with Haldman. They were fairly well satisfied with the results he had obtained.

As Bonham reached the adobe, the Mormon Indian agent emerged. He was a tall, rail-thin man with a shock of red hair and a gaunt face. His gaze was direct and piercing. Bonham noticed the pistol stuck in Haldman's belt. He gave some thought to that and decided there was nothing particularly sinister about Haldman greeting him armed. In such a lonely place on a troubled frontier, carrying a weapon at all times was simply a wise habit to develop.

"John Bonham," said Haldman, without enthusiasm. "What brings you to these parts?"

"Just looking things over," was Bonham's ambiguous reply. "How are things with the Indians?"

"They're not happy. A bunch came through here just yesterday, asking for food. Hunting has been poor for them. Children are going hungry. I had to turn them away." Hands on hips, Haldman scanned the heat-shimmering horizon of the arid plain, a sour look on his face. "We must all abide by the proclamation, you know—all food stores must be saved in the event of war. No exceptions."

"You think we'll have trouble with the Utes?"

Haldman gave Bonham a long look. "You never know, do you?"

Bonham nodded. He glanced at the saddle horses, then dismounted, since it was apparent that Haldman wasn't going to proffer an invitation. "See you've got some company. Maybe you could spare me a little water."

"Well, I . . ."

Bonham went right by him and into the adobe.

There were three men inside, one standing at a window where he could watch the goings-on in front of the station through the gun slots in the shutters. The other two were seated at a trestle table in the middle of the room. Bonham recognized only one of them: Griffin Ward was a shopkeeper from Cedar City, the nearest settlement. He also sat at the head of the town's High Council.

"Brother Ward."

"Brother Bonham." Ward was plainly ill at ease.

Bonham realized he'd stumbled into the middle of something, and he wasn't being made to feel welcome.

"Well," he said, with a cold smile. "I've never been one to beat around the bush, so I'll just come straight out and ask. What's going on here? What are you men up to?"

Haldman was standing in the doorway now. "Go ahead," said the Indian agent. "Tell him. Might as well. He'll find out anyway."

Ward and his companions exchanged worried glances. Then the shopkeeper nodded. "Okay. Fine. You might as well know. A wagon train of Missourians passed through Cedar Creek day before yesterday. They demanded supplies. We refused to sell them any. We can't—the proclamation forbids it, and any sort of commerce with Gentiles."

"Not that we would have sold anything to them anyway," said one of the other men.

"I don't know who you are," said Bonham, turning to the man.

"Joseph Mitchell. I'm a farmer." He nodded at the man standing at the window. "That's my younger brother, Franklin." He made the introductions with a degree of belligerence that Bonham found intriguing. He decided that these men were plotting some mischief that they didn't want Brigham Young to know about, so they were leery of the Mormon president's troubleshooter, the man Brigham called his "lightning bolt." Bonham had a well-deserved reputation as a man who would be judge, jury, and executioner if Brigham gave him a free hand—which often happened.

"And why wouldn't you have sold them anything?" asked the holy killer.

"Because they are sons of bitches, that's why. They made hateful remarks about us. Some of the men called themselves Missouri Wild Cats. One of them bragged that he was in the black-face mob at Carthage and that he owned the pistol that had been used to kill the Prophet. I heard him say he was thinking about taking a shot at 'Old Brig' before he left the valley."

"I heard another one boast of being present at Haun's Mill," said Griffin Ward.

Bonham felt a chill run down his spine.

"Story goes you lost a wife and child at Haun's Mill," said Haldman softly.

Bonham drew a long, slow breath. "Tell me the rest."

"The Missourians cursed us," continued Ward. "They sneered at our womenfolk. One of them, a man named Fancher—I believe was the leader of the wagon train—said that when he got to California he would tell the people there what was going on back here and that he'd come back with an army and show us what happens to traitors."

"They camped west of town, at Big Spring," said Mitchell, picking up the narrative without missing a beat. "They stole some chickens and some cows and they poisoned the spring. This morning we found eight cows dead from drinking that water."

"Are you *sure* those Missourians poisoned that spring?" asked Bonham, with some skepticism. "In this country, water can go bad on its own."

"No, they poisoned it," said Mitchell definitively. His mind was made up and, as was so often the case with people, there would be no changing it. "Proctor Robinson was skinning the dead cattle and he came down with a sickness. His eyes swole shut and then his face swole up, too, and he started to puke. I took him home to his father and if he's still alive tomorrow, I'll be surprised. His sickness was on account of the poisons the cows drank."

Bonham was silent for a moment, turning his flinty gaze on the other men, each in turn.

"So why are you here? Tell the truth."

They exchanged blatantly guilty looks. Then Haldman spoke up.

"They came to ask me my opinion about what they ought to do."

"Why should they need your opinion, Brother Haldman?" asked Bonham sternly. "Brigham Young's orders are clear. It isn't possible that you have misunderstood them. You're to leave all Gentiles alone. We will not be the first to strike."

"Fancher's people already struck at Cedar City," replied Haldman. "What does Brother Brigham think we are? Sheep that will scurry away at the first sign of trouble?"

Bonham was getting annoyed and he let it show, hoping to intimidate these men. It appeared to work. He watched the belligerence leak right out of Joseph Mitchell.

"He's right," he said, despondent. "There's really nothing we can do."

"Where are they now?" asked Bonham.

"Moved on towards Mountain Meadows," replied

Ward. "Figure they'll lay up there for a day or two before pushing on across the desert."

"How many are there?"

"Over a hundred, all told. Thirty or forty men, the rest women and children. Between twenty and twenty-five wagons."

Bonham nodded and turned to leave the mission.

"What do you intend to do?" Haldman asked him.

"I don't believe I have to answer to you." Bonham brushed by the Indian agent and walked out into the blistering sun.

He rode west, pushing his horse as hard as he dared, giving it a little water when he needed to, walking it with loosened cinch on occasion. But riding or walking, he was always on the move. Leaving the flats, he entered foothills where groves of trees were interspersed with rocky gulches. By this time he had picked up the trail of the wagon train. They weren't too far ahead of him, and by the time the sun dropped behind the western mountains Bonham knew he was getting close. He continued more cautiously through the broken country.

Mountain Meadows was a small green valley with plenty of grass and numerous seeping springs leaking out of the rocky flanks that were covered with sagebrush, cedar, and scrub oak. Thirty-five miles east lay Cedar City, but there were no habitations in the immediate vicinity. Beyond to the west lay a long dry haul across sagebrush desert. So it made perfect sense that the Fancher company would want to camp at Mountain Meadows, to provide their stock with plenty of water and good graze in preparation for the arduous trek that lay in front of them. This route had been used for a number of years by California-bound emigrants—a clear wagon trace wound through the lush grass.

Bonham spotted their camp from a mile away. He

paused on the rim of the valley's eastern flank, seeing several campfires in the quickly deepening gloom. By the locations of the blaze he could tell they had made a loose camp; the wagons weren't circled but rather spread out to afford the individual families some privacy. Bonham shook his head. These people were fools. They had just provoked the Saints to the east and had to know that the sometimes-hostile Utes were somewhere to the south, and yet they were taking no precautions.

Though the day had been a scorcher, the nights at this elevation—about six thousand feet—were crisply cool, even in summer. Bonham dismounted, loosened his saddle cinch so the horse could blow, and untied his old gray duster from behind the cantle. Donning this, he checked the loads in his pistol and rifle, then sat down on a rock, reins in hand, wincing at the stiffness in his legs. Those old injuries still plagued him when the cold crept in.

There were some old wounds of a different kind that also persisted—the wounds of his soul caused by the loss of a wife and child at Haun's Mill. Could it be that some of the Missourians in that camp down there had really participated in the butchery that had taken place at Haun's? Bonham felt the old hatred well up inside him, burning like bile in his throat. Sometimes he thought Brigham Young expected too much of his people, asking them to restrain from wreaking a terrible vengeance on the Gentiles for all the pain and suffering outsiders had inflicted on the Church. Bonham's palms itched to feel the familiar shape of the Colt Navy Model 1851 percussion revolver he carried these days, and the urge to ride down there and spill blood was overwhelming. But his loyalty to Brigham Young was stronger, wasn't it? He was about to test one against the other.

He had another reason to hate outsiders, for as the

Missouri Pukes had taken his first family away from him at Haun's Mill, so another Gentile had stolen his wife Patience, the girl who had embodied Bonham's last chance for another family. Lizzie was dead now, never able to bear him children. Patience had been his hope for the future. But Dane Gilmartin had stolen her from him. In so doing he had stolen John Bonham's whole future. That was one Gentile that Bonham knew he would kill on the spot, if they ever chanced to meet again, whether Brigham Young liked it or not.

Bonham waited an hour, then another. The camp down below quieted, the campfires burned out, and wagon lanterns were extinguished one by one. Finally, the holy killer rose stiffly to his feet. He took some rawhide pouches from his saddlebags, and placed them over the iron-shod hooves of his horse, securing them in place with thongs. This would serve to muffle any sound his mount might make crossing this stony ground. Tightening the saddle cinch, he led the horse down the slope. At the bottom he mounted up and rode straight into the emigrant camp, his Colt Model 1855 Revolving Rifle across the pommel of his saddle.

As he neared the camp he saw two men huddled around a fire near several wagons. Bonham steered his horse in that direction, holding it to a walk. The two men were sharing a jug and some conversation, and didn't realize they had company until the Mormon avenger passed between two of the wagons and checked his horse a scant thirty feet away. Startled, one of the men dropped the jug and made a move for a shotgun that lay on the ground nearby. The other one just froze, gaping at Bonham, who swung his Colt rifle around to bear on them.

"Pick up that gun and I'll kill you," he said. Both men froze.

"Who the hell are you?" one asked.

"I'm looking for a man named Fancher."

"That would be me." His voice was steady. He had quickly mastered his fear. "Who are you?"

Leading his horse, Bonham stepped closer. "Who I am doesn't matter. I'm here to give you some friendly advice."

"You're a Mormon, aren't you?"

"Maybe he's one of them Danites I've heard tell about," said the other Missourian.

"I am," said Bonham. "But I'm not going to kill you unless you force me to."

"I thought so," said Fancher's companion. "You see, it's the hair. I hear Danites don't cut their hair. They wear it long, like an Injun, and they got beards like Moses."

"What's this advice you want to give us?" said Fancher with a sneer.

"Move out. Now. Don't wait until morning."

Fancher glanced at his companion. "Why would we want to do that?"

"To save your lives."

Fancher scowled. "That sounds like a threat to me. What do you think, Johnny?"

"Not a threat," rasped Bonham. "You've made a lot of people mad at you the last few days."

Fancher grunted. "I'm not scared of no Mormons."

"Then you're a bigger fool than I thought."

Fancher bristled, and he looked down at the shotgun again, thinking about another try.

"Maybe he's right," said the one called Johnny. "Maybe we *should* get a move on. I've got a funny feeling about this place—"

"Hell no!" snapped Fancher. "No goddamn Mormons are going to run me off. We planned to stay here for a couple of days to rest up and let the stock fill up on good grass. It's a hard pull up ahead." He turned his attention back to Bonham. "Besides, I don't trust this feller. Since when did a Mormon—especially a Danite—give a shit about our kind? Answer me that, Johnny. Killing is what they live for. They don't try to save lives. They take 'em."

"Well, I don't know . . ." said Johnny, confused.

Bonham threw a quick look around. The rest of the camp was still sleeping, blissfully unaware of the danger they were in. He had hoped to make Fancher see reason or, failing that, put some fear into him, but it didn't look as though he was going to be able to do either. The thought of the women and children in those wagons, their lives in jeopardy thanks to Fancher and the other men in this company whose actions had provoked the Cedar City Saints, angered him.

"I am a Danite," he said coldly, "and I've killed plenty of men in my time, it's true. But I have never harmed a woman or a child that I know of. Think of your families first. Put foolish pride away and get the hell out of here while you've still got a choice. That's my final word on it."

Keeping the rifle trained on Fancher and Johnny, he mounted up. Wheeling the horse around, he turned in the saddle to keep an eye on them until he had passed through the wagons and beyond the reach of the campfire's light.

Fancher reached for the shotgun, muttering a curse as Bonham vanished into the night, but Johnny was on the move, too, and grabbed the scattergun's barrel, pushing it down and planting himself in front of Fancher.

"I know what you're thinking, Bob," he said. "Don't do it. He'll kill you for certain if you go after him."

"Goddamn Mormons," growled Fancher, venom in his tone. But he let Johnny have the shotgun, and turned to stride angrily toward his wagon.

Chapter 23

John Bonham camped about five miles south of the Fancher company's camp, near the mouth of the valley. He built a small fire to warm his old bones against the night chill. He hobbled his horse and let it graze. For his supper he dined on squash cakes washed down with water from a nearby spring-fed stream. Then he sat with a blanket around his shoulders and watched the fire die down.

His thoughts wandered to his first wife and their beautiful son—the way they had looked alive and happy, and the way they had looked when he carried their lifeless bodies out of the bloody carnage at Haun's Mill. Something inside of him had died that day, something he had never been able to resuscitate. Lizzie hadn't been able to breathe new life into him, either, though she had tried, bless her soul. But when Patience had become his bride, Bonham entertained some hope that he would once again enjoy life, and looked forward to the prospect of more children.

But now Patience was gone. He thought of her often. He missed her, even more than he missed Lizzie, though Lizzie had been with him for many more years. And, obviously, Lizzie had been more devoted to his happiness. But Bonham couldn't blame Patience for running away. He realized now that he had treated her poorly. That was partly because of Lizzie, who had resented Patience, her youth and beauty. And

Bonham regretted the fact that he had seldom been home while Patience had been his. That no doubt accounted for the fact that she had not borne him offspring.

He wondered how Patience was doing these days. Rumor had it that Dane Gilmartin had taken her to California. Bonham hoped she was happy. He bore no hard feelings toward her. As for Gilmartin, well, that was a different matter altogether. Ten years ago he'd carefully considered going to California for the sole purpose of tracking that man down and killing him. But Brigham Young had told him not to. And, of course, as he had done all his life, John Bonham put aside his personal feelings for the good of the Church.

When the fire was reduced to embers, he lay down on the hard ground and covered himself with a single thin blanket. It occurred to him—as happened occasionally when he got to thinking too much—that he'd spent entirely too many nights on hard ground in lonesome camps. Sometimes he tried to imagine what his life would have been like had he been a simple farmer or storekeeper. Instead, God had chosen him for a thankless task. God, and Brigham Young. His job was to protect the Church against its many enemies. Not once had he shirked his duty. The ironic part about it was that many of the Saints—the very people he committed murder to protect—feared him. Like the men he'd found at Haldman's Indian mission. They were afraid of him. And fear bred hate. Not many would pray for his soul when he passed on, that was certain. Maybe Brigham Young would, but not too many others.

John Bonham sighed, rolled over on his left side, and reached out to rest a hand on the Colt revolving rifle that lay beside him. Then he closed his eyes and went to sleep.

When he awoke the first threads of dawn light laced

the eastern sky. He checked to make sure his horse was still nearby, then got up and limped a short distance from camp and back again, trying to limber up his sore legs. Relieving himself, he scanned the brush-covered flanks of the valley and saw nothing out of the ordinary. He decided to get underway immediately, wanting to pay a visit to Cedar City just to make sure Ward and the Mitchell brothers were behaving themselves.

The bullet grazed his side—it felt like a hot branding iron slapped against his flesh—and he spun halfway around and fell. The gunshot rolled across the stillness of the morning. Bonham hit the ground facedown and stayed that way, not moving an inch, ignoring the pain. That wasn't too difficult for a man as accustomed to pain as he. Instead, he concentrated on listening for the bushwhackers. Would they come in close to make sure he was done for? He was counting on it.

It seemed like an eternity for a man whose blood was seeping into the ground, but finally Bonham heard their horses. He wasn't sure how many—at least two, probably three, but not many more than that. The riders checked their mounts a cautious distance away. Bonham strained to hear the telltale sound of a gun's hammer being pulled back. That would be his signal to go into action. Instead, he heard voices. Familiar voices.

"Is he dead?"

"I don't know. Check him, Joe."

The creak of saddle leather. A man stepping closer . . .

Bonham rolled over. He had the Colt Navy revolver in his hand and he drew a bead on Joe Mitchell—the man he had met at the Indian agency. Stunned, Mitchell was a little too slow in bringing his own pistol up. Bonham squeezed the trigger without hesitation. The bullet hit Mitchell in the chest, picking him up off his feet and knocking him backwards. Still mounted, Mitchell's brother Frank shouted incoherently as he watched Joe die, and he fired at Bonham but his horse wasn't trained to stand in the midst of roaring gunfire. He missed his mark as the cayuse jumped sideways. Bonham didn't miss. He fired again and Frank Mitchell performed a somersault over the haunches of his spooked horse. He was dead long before he hit the ground.

The third man wheeled his horse around and took off at a gallop. Grimacing at the pain from the bullet wound in his side, Bonham struggled to one knee and fired a third time. But the rider was bent low in the saddle and Bonham's bullet went high. Cursing, Bonham got up and stumbled back to his camp. The third man was out of pistol range now, so the Mormon avenger grabbed the Colt revolving rifle. He drew a bead on the rider's horse, the larger target. It was a two hundred-yard shot but Bonham took it, just as the horseman reached the skyline. The mount went down and Bonham paused to watch the man get to his feet and begin to run—briefly he was silhouetted against the brightening eastern sky, and then he disappeared down the far side of the rise.

Drawing a knife from his belt, Bonham cut the hobbles on his horse and swung aboard to gallop bareback after the fleeing man.

When he heard the thunder of hooves, the would-be-assassin looked back to see Bonham come tearing over the rise in a cloud of dust, looking like one of the four horsemen of the Apocalypse with his long hair and gray duster flying. Realizing that there was no escape, the man stopped and turned his pistol on the holy killer. He frantically fired all five rounds. But Bonham kept coming. Throwing the empty gun aside, the man stood his ground. Praying, he closed his eyes—and kept them closed as Bonham drew near. He braced for the impact of the bullet. But it didn't come. He opened his eyes to see that Bonham had stopped his horse twenty paces away. He was looking right down the barrel of the Danite's Colt rifle.

"You finished?" asked Bonham.

The man nodded. He thought about begging for his life. But he knew it wouldn't do any good. Besides, if a man had to die he needed to do so with a little dignity.

"What's your name?" asked Bonham.

"Stokes. Leland Stokes. From Cedar City."

Bonham nodded. "You got family?"

Hope filled the man's eyes. "Yes. Yes I do. A wife and children."

"I'll take your body back so they can give you a decent burying."

"Oh, God," breathed Stokes, feeling his knees beginning to go out. "If you're going to kill me, hurry . . ."

Bonham pulled the trigger.

He draped the body over his horse and led the animal back to camp. Saddling up, he went after the mounts of the men who had come to kill him. Finding two, he returned to where the corpses lay. He put two of the bodies across one horse and one over the other pony. Only then did he attend to his wound, going down to a nearby creek and washing away the blood. The graze wasn't too deep. He used his shirt to bind the wound, then put the old gray duster back on.

Only once before had he killed a fellow Mormon. A few years back a man named Creer had plotted the murder of Brigham Young. In a quarrel over the rights to a piece of land, Brigham had testified in court against Creer, and the man had nursed a grudge until it consumed him. Folks said Creer was half mad anyway, and Bonham figured he must have been, for he'd publicized his designs on Brigham Young's life. They had kept Creer in jail for a while, but that didn't cool his fervor, and finally Bonham had taken it upon himself to track the man down and kill him. He had done it without orders from Brigham, but the Quorum of the Twelve Apostles had unanimously approved his actions after the fact.

Now he had slain three more Saints. There had been no other choice. The question remained, had Stokes and the Mitchell boys come after him on their accord? Or were there others involved in the plan? Bonham could think of a pair of likely suspects—Joshua Haldman and Griffin Ward. The second question was, why? Bonham didn't have a clue. But he had every intention of getting to the bottom of it.

He started back for Cedar City, leading the horses that carried the dead men. A few hours later he came upon the tracks of many horses, heading west. The riders had passed this way late yesterday, by Bonham's calculations. Most of the ponies were unshod. That meant Indians. Some, though, were iron shod. Were white men riding with Indians? For what purpose?

Then he thought about the Fancher party—and the more he thought about the Missourians and these riders and the possibility of a connection between the two, the less he liked it. He kept coming back to Haldman, and how Ward and the Mitchell brothers had gone to the Indian agent—for what? Advice? Bonham doubted that. No, there was more to it than that. But what, exactly? What could Haldman offer the three Cedar City men? Only one thing.

The Utes.

Those Indians had been known to prey on emigrant trains.

Bonham indulged in a little more speculation. Haldman had turned down a Ute request for supplies. What if he had also suggested to his Indian clients that they attack the Missouri wagon train? If they wanted food, they could have the livestock of the Fancher party. Not to mention a lot of other loot. And the Cedar City crowd would have their revenge on the Missourians who had so antagonized them—with the added bonus of being able to blame the attack on the Indians.

All nice and tidy. But then it could be all wrong, too. Could be that a band of Indians was planning to attack the Missouri wagons all on their own. The shod horses could be stolen mounts.

One thing was immediately clear to Bonham. He had to do everything in his power to keep Fancher's party safe. Not that he gave a damn about Fancher and the other men in the group. But he did not want to see harm come to the women and children. And he knew that an attack on the wagon train could well trigger full-scale war between Deseret and the United States.

Making sure the bodies of Stokes and the Mitchell boys were firmly lashed down over the saddles, he sent the horses on their way with a couple of pistol shots fired into the air. His hope was that the ponies would go back to Cedar City, and the bodies would be discovered. He resolved to ride to the settlement later and make sure. If the horses strayed, he would track them down. He knew from personal experience how important it was for families to be able to bury their dead loved ones. And Bonham wanted Cedar City to know why the three men had died. That, too, was important in his book. He still didn't know why his wife and child had needed to lose their lives at Haun's Mill. It had been a senseless slaughter, and all the more unforgivable for that.

Freed of the burden of the dead men, the Danite rode hard to westward, following the trail of the war party.

When he was yet a mile from the Fancher company's camp, he heard gunfire ahead, and spurred his horse to greater effort. The shooting ebbed and flowed—at times a flurry, sporadic at others. As he neared the brush-covered rise that marked the eastern flank of Mountain Meadows, he saw a number of men crouched in the scrub, or running from one point to another. They were shooting down into the valley at the Missourians. Bonham didn't see any Indians, and that worried him.

He rode right up to the nearest man, pistol drawn. The man whirled, saw the Colt Navy revolver, and froze. Bonham was aware of a pair of riders galloping toward him along the back side of the ridge, but he kept his attention glued to the man in front of him.

"Who the hell are you?" he rasped.

"Name's John Woodley. Iron County militia. I know you. You're . . ."

Bonham nodded. "I am." The Iron County militia was based in Cedar City. He knew its commander, Colonel Isaac Hale. "What's going on here? Answer me, damn you, or I'll just kill you where you stand and go ask somebody else."

"I—" Before Woodley could respond, the two riders arrived. Both of them carried pistols, which they were aiming at the holy killer. One of them was Griffin Ward. The other was John Rigby, a major in the militia and Colonel Hale's right-hand man.

"Bonham!" exclaimed Rigby. "Put that gun away."

"Not until I get some answers."

"Don't interfere. I have my orders."

"Orders? Hale's orders? Where did he get the authority to start a war, to massacre innocent people?"

"Innocent people?" scoffed Ward. "Are you taking the side of that Missouri scum?"

"Call your men off, Rigby."

"I don't take orders from you."

"Call them off, or die."

Rigby laughed harshly. "You're the one about to die, Bonham. I've got fifty men here. Not to mention twice as many Indians, Moqueta's band. Now drop that pistol."

Never in his life had John Bonham surrendered his weapons, and he wasn't about to start now. He was confident he could take Rigby, and probably Ward, too. But he couldn't fight the whole Iron County militia—and what good would he be to Brigham Young or the Missouri women and children in the valley yonder if he gave his life here and now. So he swallowed his anger and holstered the Colt Navy.

"Let me shoot him, Major," said Ward. "He's too dangerous to let live."

"By the way," sneered Bonham, "the three men you sent to kill me are all dead. Just like you will be when this is over. You'll both hang—unless Brigham Young gives me leave to kill you myself."

Ward raised the pistol, but Major Rigby reached out and grabbed his arm and pushed it down.

"No," he said. "We'll let Colonel Hale decide his fate. Get down, Bonham. Woodley, take his guns."

Bonham dismounted, but when Woodley reached for the Colt at his side, the holy killer gave the man a hard shove.

"Back off, boy!" he snarled.

He unbuckled his gun belt and tossed it at Woodley's feet. Then he drew the Colt revolving rifle from its saddle scabbard and tossed it to the militiaman.

"Now," he said, turning to Rigby, "take me to Colonel Hale. I want to meet the man who has destroyed everything it took us ten years to build."

Chapter 24

Fancher's Missourians had gathered most of their wagons together and thrown up barricades made of anything and everything they could find in their prairie schooners, from furniture and barrels to sacks of flour, trunks and valises, and even an infant rocker. From a high point on the ridge east of Mountain Meadows, Bonham gazed bleakly down at the scene from the cover of several cedars growing around a rock outcrop. Standing with him was Major Rigby and Griffin Ward. Haldman, the Indian agent, was there too. So was Woodley, keeping a rifle trained on Bonham's spine.

The Missourians were firing sporadically—Bonham could see the muzzle flashes through a pall of gunsmoke that hung heavily in the hot summer air. There wasn't a breath of wind today, or a shred of cloud cover, and the sun burned like a demon in a sky the color of brass. Bonham wondered how much water Fancher and his men had in their wagon barrels. The nearest spring was more than a hundred yards away across open ground, and no one was going to get across that space alive. While Rigby's Iron County militia occupied the high ground to the east, the Indians were spread out on the north side of the Fancher camp, hidden in a gully, on the western flank of the narrow valley.

"Moqueta's Indians attacked as soon as we got here

this morning, right about dawn," explained Rigby, scanning the besieged camp with a field glass. "There was no holding them back. The Missourians drove them off and had time to pull their wagons closer together and prepare their defenses before we could prepare a better organized assault."

Bonham glanced at the short, stocky major. He had a hunch Rigby thought of himself as some kind of Mormon Napoleon.

"As you can see, we have left the southern approach open," continued Rigby, smugness in his tone of voice. "I hope to lure the Missourians into making an escape in that direction."

"Fancher isn't that big of a fool," said Bonham.

"You know him that well?" asked Griffin Ward.

"We've met. After I saw you at the mission I came here to warn those people to move on quick as they could. I had a feeling you were up to something."

"No one sent the Mitchell boys after you," said Ward. "That was their own idea, and Stokes went along for the ride."

"You sound like you're apologizing to him," snapped Haldman crossly. "My God, Rigby, you can't let this man live."

"That's what I told him," offered Ward.

"I am in command here," said Rigby tersely. "What do you suppose? That by killing Bonham you can keep what we are doing here a secret? And why would we want to do that? You are acting like criminals, afraid of being caught and punished."

"Oh, you'll be punished, all right," said Bonham. "But so will all our people. Every Mormon in Deseret will suffer for your sins."

Another man joined them—and Bonham knew him instantly, and was shocked to see him here. John Lee was a tall, pale-haired man—and Brigham Young's adopted son. Lee was as loyal to Brigham as Bonham. Or so the Danite avenger had assumed.

"Brother Bonham," said Lee. "I just got word that you were here."

"I'm here—but I can't believe you are."

"Isaac Hale sent word to my home that I should come at once to Cedar City. It was there that I learned what he had in mind."

"And you didn't try to stop him?"

Lee glanced at Rigby and the others, his expression carefully inscrutable. "We talked late into the night. Colonel Hale believes the Quorum will approve of the destruction of those people down there."

"Do you believe that?"

Lee looked down at his dusty boots. "I believe the majority *will* approve it, yes."

Bonham shook his head. "What will he think when he finds out you were a party to this?"

Lee knew to whom the holy killer was referring—Brigham Young.

"I love him as though I were from his own seed," said Lee solemnly. "But he has gone too far in trying to appease the Gentiles."

Bonham seethed. Had he been armed he would have commenced to slaying all those present in a cold rage at what they had done to the Church.

"At least let the women and children go," he said, his voice a harsh whisper. "Give them safe passage beyond the reach of your Indian allies. That may, to some degree, mitigate your crimes."

The other men exchanged looks. "I for one would support such an act of mercy," said Lee.

"We are not committing a crime," insisted Rigby. "There is no need for mitigation. We are at war with the outsiders. They want to take this land away from us. We will not let them drive us from our homes again."

"Waging war on women and children makes you no better than the bastards who massacred our people at Haun's Mill."

"It is because of Haun's Mill, and a dozen other places whose names are seared into our memory, that we are here."

"Blood cannot wash away blood."

"That's an odd sentiment," said Ward dryly, "coming from a Danite avenger."

Bonham took another look at the besieged camp of Missourians. There was nothing he could do here to save them. And he *wanted* to save them, even though they were Missourians. If somehow he could prevent a massacre, it might go easier for Mormon women and children when the wrath of the United States descended, as he knew it must, on Deseret.

There was nothing he could do—not here and now. But if Fancher and his Missouri Wild Cats could just hold on for three or four days . . .

"I've seen enough of this," said Bonham curtly. "Give me my horse, Major, and I will ride away from here."

"Don't do it," warned Haldman. "If you won't kill him, at least keep him prisoner."

"He will ride straight to Brigham Young," said Ward.

"That's exactly what I intend to do," admitted Bonham. "But what do you care if I do? You think you're doing the right thing, isn't that true? If so, then you have nothing to fear. Holding me captive will be proof that you know this is a criminal act, and that you fear a just retribution."

Major Rigby stared at him. Bonham could tell that his argument had made an impression on the major. Or course, Haldman and Ward were right. The smart thing to do would be to kill him. But he was counting on Rigby's misplaced sense of honor, not to mention his self-righteousness.

"Brother Bonham is right," said Lee. "Let him go. It's at least three days' ride to Salt Lake City. Even if Brigham Young wanted to stop this, it will be too late by the time he gets the word."

Rigby made up his mind, and nodded. "You are free to go," he told Bonham. "Woodley, pick one other man and escort Brother Bonham away from here. Do not return his weapons to him until you have gone several miles at least. And when you do, make sure those weapons are empty."

"Yes, sir."

Woodley went off to collect another guard and Bonham's horse.

While they waited, John Lee stepped up to Bonham. "When you see Brigham, will you give him a message from me?"

"No," replied Bonham brusquely. "I do not intend to tell him that I even saw you here."

"Why not?"

"Because it will break his heart."

"You've always been unquestioningly loyal to him, haven't you? You love him, same as I."

"No one else could have brought us this far."

And now we need Brigham Young more than ever, mused Bonham, because only he has a chance of saving New Zion from destruction.

Woodley returned and they were off, Bonham sparing Rigby and the others neither word nor glance. He rode hard, with Woodley and the other militiaman trailing along behind. A few miles away from Mountain Meadows, Bonham abruptly checked his mount.

"I'll take my guns now." It was more a command than a request.

Woodley handed over the Colt pistol and revolving

rifle. "They're unloaded," he said, "so don't get any ideas."

"One bullet," said Bonham. "In case something happens."

Woodley glanced at his cohort, who shrugged. "One bullet can't hurt. There are two of us. He won't try anything."

Woodley nodded. "I don't like leaving him defenseless in this country. Okay." He took one of the loads he had previously removed from the Danite's weapons out of his saddlebags and threw it on the ground. "Don't press your luck," he warned. "Just keep riding east." With that he and his companion turned their horses and headed back for Mountain Meadows.

Smiling bleakly, Bonham dismounted to retrieve the bullet. He loaded it into the Colt revolving rifle and peered after the two Iron County militiamen. Out of rifle range, they had slowed their ponies to a walk. Bonham climbed back into the saddle and went after them.

He was closing in on a hundred yards from them before they heard him coming and looked around.

Bonham was waiting for that. He brought the rifle to his shoulder and fired. Woodley's companion fell sideways out of the saddle. His horse shied away, colliding with Woodley's mount, which pivoted, delaying Woodley for a few precious seconds as he tried to drag his pistol from its holster. He got off one shot, then another, but both went wild. He didn't have much to shoot at anyway because Bonham was clinging to the off-side of his galloping horse like an Indian. Unnerved, Woodley made a run for it. Alone, he knew he didn't have a prayer against a killer like John Bonham—never mind that the Danite avenger didn't have any ammunition. Woodley whipped his horse around and took off like the devil himself was in hot pursuit.

Gripping the saddlehorn, Bonham let his right leg slide off the cantle and made a running dismount. The dead man's horse veered away from him but Bonham caught up the reins and pulled the rifle from its scabbard. Another shot, and Woodley fell. Bonham remounted and rode out to where the militiaman lay. Woodley's horse had stopped running and stood with trembling legs a little ways off.

Woodley was still alive, trying to crawl away, but a glance told Bonham that the Iron County man wasn't going to last long. The bullet had entered through his back near the spine and had torn through Woodley's guts. The Iron County man was already puking black blood. The holy killer felt a twinge of regret for having had to kill these two men. But then he thought about the women and children back at Mountain Meadows. It occurred to him that he had slain five Saints today. Didn't make much sense that he was taking the lives of his own people to save the lives of outsiders. But sometimes life just didn't make a whole lot of sense. He knew that as well as anyone.

"I'm sorry," he said, dispassionately watching Woodley fight to hold on to life. "But I needed your horses."

With one final heaving breath, Woodley was gone.

Gathering up the two Iron County ponies, Bonham visualized the long trail to Salt Lake City. He knew it well. Three long days of normal travel, but he counted on getting there late tomorrow. He would ride his horse into the ground and then switch to Woodley's, and when Woodley's mount bottomed out he would switch to the third pony. In that way he could cover a lot of ground in a hurry, traveling both by night and by day. Even with a fresh wound in his side, John Bonham had no doubt he would make it. The question was, would he make it in time?

* * *

When Woodley and the other militiaman failed to return, Major Rigby started to worry. When they were six hours overdue he summoned Lee, Ward, and Haldman to his command post. It was dark, and the shooting had died down, though now and then the Missourians would shoot at shadows, fearing a sneak attack by the Indians, and occasionally one of the Iron County men up on the ridge would shoot down into the wagons just to harass the enemy.

"There is no time to waste," Rigby told them. "We must resolve this matter quickly."

"Having second thoughts about letting Bonham go, Major?" asked Haldman.

"How do you propose to resolve things?" asked Lee dryly. Since seeing Bonham he'd been having his own second thoughts about this whole business. He fervently wished there was some way to call it all off, to pretend it never happened.

"With your help, Brother Lee," said Rigby. "I want you to go down there and talk to those Missourians."

"Talk to them about what?" asked Lee, startled. "Why they ought to shoot me on the spot? Frankly, I don't think I could give them a good reason not to."

"You will go under a flag of truce. You will tell them that we will guarantee them safe passage away from here."

"You mean lie to them. Try to decoy them out from behind those wagons. No, Major, I don't think so. They wouldn't believe me, in any case."

"Moqueta's braves are getting restless," said Haldman. "If something isn't done soon, there is no telling what the Indians might do. We promised them they could have the Missourians' cattle. They've lost a dozen men already, and they won't go home empty-handed, I assure you."

"What are you saying?" asked Ward. He didn't like the sound of this.

"I'm saying Moqueta may well attack us if we don't give him what we promised."

"What *you* promised," amended Lee.

"It was agreed by all concerned that we would employ the Indians in this endeavor," said Major Rigby. "They were hungry and needed food. We needed someone we could blame this on."

"Think of your family, if nothing else," Haldman told Lee. "The last thing we need right now is a war with the Utes. They could put all the southern counties to the torch."

Lee sighed and turned to Rigby. "I'll do what you ask—if you'll agree to let the women and children go free."

"Damn it," muttered Haldman. "Why can't you get it through your thick skull? None of the Missourians can be allowed to survive—or talk."

"Moqueta attacked the Missourians first," said Lee deliberately. "You can say that you and the Iron County militia arrived without knowing what was going on. That when you did learn the truth, you forced the Indians to back away, and promised the Missourians safe conduct. Now I realize that those men down there have to die. I understand the concept of retribution, of an eye for an eye. But you let the women and children leave the camp first, separately from the men. When the men are dead you can say that the Indians attacked and killed them and you were unable to prevent it."

"I don't know," said Rigby, wavering.

"Major, it's the only way I can see that you can have your vengeance, and still conceivably prevent all-out war with the United States. If it works, President Buchanan will have to reconsider invading Deseret. After all, it will appear that Mormon militia at least managed to rescue those women and children down there."

•

"We've been shooting at those people down there," said Haldman caustically. "You can't explain that away."

"They were shooting at us when we arrived. In the confusion of battle, it took some time to sort things out."

Griffin Ward paused, rubbing his jaw. "You know, it just might work."

"I disagree," said Haldman bluntly.

"Somehow I knew you would," drawled Lee.

"Any number of things could go wrong," insisted the Indian agent. "Why take chances? The safest course is to make certain that no one survives. No one."

"If you slaughter the women and children then you're no better than Missouri Pukes," said Lee.

"Thank you," sneered Haldman. "Your friend Bonham already made that point."

"It warrants repeating."

"You have your orders from Colonel Hale, Major," Haldman told Rigby. "They are clear. No one is to be left alive to dispute our claim that the Indians did this."

"Brother Lee," said Rigby solemnly, "we will do as you suggest. But first you must somehow convince those men down there to surrender."

"I will," said Lee, relieved. "Believe me, I will."

To the surprise of some of the Mormons present, the Fancher party agreed to the terms of surrender that John Lee carried to them under the flag of truce. Much of the credit belonged to Lee; the Missourians could tell he was sincere in his desire to save lives. Then, too, the Iron County boys had no way of knowing how low on ammunition Fancher and his men were. They had failed to conserve it during the long day of skirmishing, and feared what would happen on the morrow, when their guns fell silent. Then the Indians would attack again, and the slaughter would commence. They had no choice but to hope that Major Rigby's promise of safe passage was sincere. Their situation was so desperate that they even agreed to leave their livestock and most of their wagons behind to appease the Indians. The Utes, explained Lee, had to be given something or they would demand more blood.

At dawn on the following day, the young children were placed in one wagon and the wounded in another. John Lee took charge of these, and as the wagons rolled away from the camp, the older children and the women walked along behind. A short time later the Missouri men marched out, guarded by the Iron County militia, led by Major Rigby. As soon as the women were out of sight, Rigby gave the order and his Iron County boys turned on their prisoners. Some of the Missourians lived long enough to make a dash for freedom—a few members of the militia intentionally missed their targets—but a band of Indians appeared and chased them down. None survived.

At the same time, the caravan of women and children entered a hollow ringed with scrub oak, where other Indians lay in wait. As they leaped from cover, descending on the defenseless innocents and the wagonload of wounded with knife and tomahawk, Lee managed to guide the wagon carrying the eighteen youngest children to safety. Several braves pursued, but Lee talked them out of murdering the youngsters. The Utes saw the tears on John Lee's face, and from that point on would know him as *Yogurts*— "crying man."

As he fled the scene with the Missouri children, Lee wondered what had gone wrong. Had the Indians acted on their own in staging the ambush? Or had he been betrayed by his own people—by Haldman and Ward and Rigby? Had they used him to lure the Missourians into a trap? Trying to block out the horrible sounds of the massacre, and the terrible sobbing of the children in the wagon, Lee swore to God on high that he would uncover the truth. Even if it killed him.

Chapter 25

Sitting on a bench in the middle of Portsmouth Square with a copy of the *Chronicle* on his knees, Dane Gilmartin watched the city around him awaken to a new day, and reflected on how much San Francisco had changed in the years since he had set up residence here.

In 1846, when American sailors and marines landed to seize the coveted bay, San Francisco had consisted primarily of a sleepy little settlement on Yerba Buena Cove. The Presidio had already been abandoned. The mission was but a shadow of its former self. Only two hundred people had been living here in those days, in about fifty buildings, with an adobe customhouse the center of commerce and community affairs. It did not extend past the *puertosuelo,* or "little pass," between Telegraph Hill and Russian Hill to the north, or the deep ravine near California Street to the south. A few warehouses and taverns lined the waterfront—now Montgomery Street—with more taverns at the *embarcadero* at Broadway and Battery, an area which had since earned a pretty sordid reputation, and was known to sailors everywhere as the Barbary Coast.

The following year Colonel Jonathan Stevenson's New York volunteers arrived. They had agreed to settle in California when the term of enlistment was up, and two companies were assigned to garrison duty at the Presidio. By mid-1847 San Francisco could claim a population of five hundred, about half of them *californios.* Even then it was obvious to most observers that the town would soon surpass Monterey, the old provincial capital, in importance. The gold rush proved the point. By 1851 the town had become a bustling port city of nearly fifty thousand residents.

In January 1848 a man named James Marshall, employed to build a sawmill for John Sutter on the south fork of the American River, had found traces of gold in the stream. The local rush occurred first—nearly everyone in San Francisco made tracks for the American, including the *alcalde* and the town council. Both newspapers shut down and the public school at the corner of Portsmouth Square closed its doors. By midsummer there was only one store in town still open for business. In May there were eight hundred miners already scouring the Sierra streams. By October there were eight thousand. Gilmartin had been one of them.

Though he had never found much gold, Gilmartin looked back on those days with fondness. He and Patience had lived in a miserable little shanty that leaked badly when it rained, turning the dirt floor into a muddy morass. It made the huts of Winter Quarters look like mansions by comparison. Despite the hideous living conditions, they had been happy. Gilmartin looked back on those days now with fond regard. They'd lived like dogs but made love like rabbits. Though they had nothing but each other they, that turned out to be enough.

Eventually, Gilmartin had realized that he wasn't going to strike it rich panning for gold, so he used the modest amount of gold dust he'd acquired to buy up town lots on the outskirts of San Francisco. He could see that the town was growing by leaps and bounds as an entrepôt for all the gold seekers coming in by ship from points as far away as Russia, the Orient, and South America, not to mention the east coast of the United States, and he was counting on the value of his property soaring. This time he was right on the money. He used his profits to buy more lots, as well as part interest in hotels, shops, and saloons. Everything he touched seemed to turn to gold. Now he was a wealthy man. He wore tailored suits of the finest broadcloth, hats and cravats of the best silk, shirts of French linen, boots of imported leather. He and Patience lived in a suite of rooms at the City Hotel, of which he owned twenty-five percent.

Everything sold at a premium in San Francisco. A town so remote and yet so populated with miners going to or coming from the gold fields operated an economy of scarcity. A blanket or a pair of mule ear boots might cost a hundred dollars. A barrel of flour could sell for hundreds of dollars. Gilmartin made it his business to know what commodities were in short supply, and tried to offer the highest bid on any cargo entering the harbor that fit the bill, secure in the knowledge that he could triple or quadruple his investment.

Strangely, though, as Gilmartin's financial situation improved, his relationship with Patience deteriorated. Something had happened to spoil their love affair, and try as he might Gilmartin couldn't quite figure out why or how. Six years ago Patience had come down with a life-threatening fever. Physicians were another commodity in short supply in San Francisco—they still were—and those who were practicing at the time could not diagnose her ailment. For lack of anything better, they peddled the idea that it was some sort of exotic influenza brought into town by the crew of a foreign ship. A number of people died during the minor epidemic. Patience, however, survived. But eleven months later she suffered a miscarriage. Sixteen months after that she had another, and nearly died from loss of blood.

After that she turned to religion—or *returned* to it—having put aside her Mormon faith on the day she and Gilmartin had decided to pretend they were man and wife. She would not marry him because she was still legally wed to John Bonham. Gilmartin had been willing to go along with this. At the time it hadn't mattered much to him whether they had a certificate of marriage or not. He hadn't needed a piece of paper to legitimize his love for her.

So what had happened to her? Was it the sickness, the miscarriages, or the religion that had driven a wedge between them? Or something else entirely? Gilmartin couldn't say for certain. She was a different person now, though. Silent and melancholy, she seldom left their rooms except to attend a service. There was a small group of Mormons residing in San Francisco. Gilmartin thought they were British, having sailed to California with the intention of joining Brigham Young in Utah, but for some reason they had put down roots here instead. He didn't like it that she was associating with those people, even though she assured him that she wasn't foolhardy enough to tell them about her past. As far as they were concerned she was a new convert.

Worst of all, she had as little to do with him in bed as out of it. They fought often, Gilmartin accusing her of failing in her wifely duties, and she reminding him that they were not legally married. It had gotten so bad of late that he had taken to visiting the prostitutes who plied their trade in the tent city called Chiletown on Telegraph Hill. He favored one woman in particular, a redheaded Easterner named Molly. Her hard-luck story had touched Gilmartin, for she had come to California with her new husband, an argonaut, only to be abandoned. The man, disillusioned by his failure in the gold fields, and frequenting the Barbary Coast to drown his sorrows in rotgut whiskey, had been shanghaied aboard a Portuguese whaler. Gilmartin had taken Molly out of Chiletown and set her up in grand style at a hostelry just blocks away from the City Hotel. He'd never told Patience, and as far as he knew she hadn't been informed of the arrangement by anyone else, but by now he was pretty sure she'd guessed the truth. Some things you simply could not conceal forever from a woman. Not that she cared. She seemed to have forsaken all worldly considerations.

Gilmartin glanced again at the headlines emblazoned on the front page of the newspaper on his lap. A fortnight ago, a wagon train of emigrants bound for California had been massacred at a place called Mountain Meadows. The Mormons were saying that the Indians had done the deed. But others pointed the finger of guilt at the Saints themselves. The whole nation would soon be up in arms. An army had already been on the march against Deseret. Encamped now out of the Mormon kingdom, it awaited orders from President Buchanan. The writer of the long piece—a column and a half—was certain that the president would send the troops in to do battle with the treasonous, murderous Mormons.

Lifting his eyes to gaze in distraction across the sunlit square, with a cool breeze carrying the salty taste of the sea to him, Dane Gilmartin made up his mind then and there.

The news of the Mountain Meadows massacre had only now reached San Francisco, and for the moment the teeming port city seemed to be going about its business in normal fashion. But Gilmartin was confident that before the day was out, there would be speeches and meetings galore as the outraged community worked itself into a frenzy over the heinous crime. The drums and bugles of war would sound, and off the brave men would march to avenge the murders of all those innocent pioneers. Gilmartin decided he would be one of those volunteers.

He had an old score to settle back there in the New Jerusalem, anyway, and now was as good a time as any to settle it. Of course he had a lot to lose, but neither his business concerns nor even his life mattered all that much to him any longer.

That was the funniest part of this whole tragic affair, mused Gilmartin. Now that he had all the money he'd always dreamed of having, it didn't amount to anything. It had no value for him, brought him no happiness. Nothing did, and nothing could, except for Patience reciprocating his love for her. Yes, he couldn't deny it, though many were the times he tried to. He loved her as much today as he had ten years ago. It was like an addiction to opium, he supposed, an attraction he couldn't resist even though he knew it would destroy him. He wished he could hate her, but that wasn't possible. What he hated was everything about the Mormon Church, and everyone associated with it. Particularly John Bonham. He didn't know who or what to blame for what had happened between him and Patience, but the Church was a part of it, and a handy target.

The decision made, Gilmartin stood up, his mind racing with plans. There were preparations to be made. He would need to visit his bank, and make sure dear Molly would be well taken care of in the event that he did not return. But first he wanted to confront Patience with the news. He couldn't wait for her to learn of his plans to strike a blow against her beloved Church—that damned Church that caused him so much grief.

He found her in a chair by the window in their well-appointed suite, gazing morosely through the lace curtains at a forest of ships' masts visible over the rooftops. She scarcely acknowledged his appearance until he tossed the newspaper in her lap.

"Your people have gone too far this time, I'm afraid," he said, unable to keep the triumph out of his voice.

She didn't even look at him. Reading the article, her body tensed. Gilmartin almost felt guilty in relishing the consternation on her face, but he just couldn't help himself. It was odd how sometimes you could hardly distinguish love from hate.

After reading the article twice, Patience let the newspaper slip from her fingers onto the fine Belgian carpet. Gilmartin could tell she was on the verge of tears.

"I know what you're thinking," he said. "That it can't be true. That it must be a Gentile lie, part of a grand design to force the Saints off their land. Well, your Mormons aren't the poor, persecuted saints they make themselves out to be. They've brought it all on themselves. Frankly, I never thought otherwise. I—"

"Do be quiet, Gil."

Gilmartin was stunned. She spoke to him as though he were a misbehaving child.

"I for one am glad this has happened," he said bitterly—even while a part of him, the sane and rational part, was shocked by the spiteful words coming out of his mouth—"because now we can resolve this Mormon problem once and for all. I think we shall have a little war, my dear, and I—"

"Yes," she said flatly. "There will be a war. And I must be with my people when it comes."

Gilmartin was even more stunned than before. This was the last thing he'd expected from her.

"What? You're going back? Back to John Bonham, you mean."

"He would not have me back, even were I so inclined."

"So you don't deny it's what you want."

"Oh, you're such a fool!" she said savagely, leaping to her feet, anger blazing in her hazel eyes. "But there was no point in trying to reason with you. I'm going back to Deseret. I should have done so long ago. I don't belong here."

"No, you don't," he snapped. "Go on, then. I'll take you back there."

"No. I don't want you to."

"I'm going to, nonetheless. Because I'm going anyway. I intend to take part in this war, you see. And with any luck I'll have an opportunity to square accounts with John Bonham. It's probably good that you will be there to see it. I'll kill him or he'll kill me. I guess it's clear enough who you'll be pulling for."

She crossed the room and entered the adjoining bedroom, closing the door softly. A moment later he heard the sounds of her weeping. It tore at his heart, yet gave him satisfaction at the same time.

Chapter 26

Gordon Hawkes was back in a grove of trees not far from his cabin cutting firewood when his son came to tell him that they were about to have company.

What Hawkes did next was purely second nature—he put down the double-headed ax and picked up his Plains rifle, which was leaning against a tree trunk within easy reach. Occasionally they had a visitor in this remote valley, an Absaroka warrior or a mountain man, but it didn't happen very often. Relatively few people knew where to find Gordon Hawkes, and he liked it that way, for obvious reasons. But even though he'd had no unwelcome guests for the better part of twenty years, Hawkes couldn't afford to let his guard down, because he couldn't forget that day long ago when bounty hunters had invaded his sanctuary. He'd killed two of them but the third would have killed him if Eliza hadn't intervened, taking the bounty hunter's life. The events of that terrible day were as clear in his memory as if it had been last week and not almost two decades past. A hunted man could never get careless.

"How many?" he asked Cameron.

"Only one that I can tell. Saw him for just a second through the trees on the other side of the lake."

"White man or Indian?"

"Indian, I think." Such a determination was hard to

make sometimes, as the white "fringe people" who lived in the high country often adopted elements of Indian dress.

Hawkes nodded and started for the cabin, stepping high through the fresh snow that blanketed the ground. It was late October by his best guess, and the first snowfall had come earlier than expected this year, bringing with it the promise of a long and severe winter.

"You stay with your mother," Hawkes told his son. "I'll go meet our guest."

He didn't need to tell Cameron any more than that. He knew he could rely on his son, who had proven himself capable of handling dangerous situations. Two years ago Hawkes had been abducted by the Ogallala Sioux while transporting goods by keelboat from the Upper Missouri Indian Agency to his friends, the Absaroka Crows. The Sioux had decided to adopt him into the tribe rather than put him to death. The Crows had prepared to do battle with the Ogallalas to rescue their white brother, but federal troops, charged with keeping the peace among all the Plains tribes, had prevented them from doing so.

It was then that Cameron had stepped in, promising his mother that he would bring her husband back alive. Recruiting a brigade of rough-and-tumble mountain men, Cameron had ventured boldly into the country of the fierce Sioux, and had fought at his father's side as the mountain men battled a vastly superior force of Indians, holding a strong position on an island in the Powder River for five days, beating back one attack after another.

So Hawkes had no doubt that Cameron could take care of himself and his mother if circumstances required it.

Leaving his son at the cabin, Hawkes gave Eliza a reassuring wave and started down the path that circled the pond. His wife stood in the doorway, watching him go with the Bible that had once belonged to Gordon's mother clasped in her hands. For the thousandth time Hawkes regretted that she had to live a fugitive's life of fear and uncertainty. But she had never once complained. It was a price she was willing to pay to be with the man she loved—and the regret Hawkes experienced at that moment was tempered by a determination to guarantee Eliza's safety, no matter the cost.

He didn't bother with the horses in the corral alongside the cabin, but ran with the fleetness of a deer down the trail that cut through a stand of larch along the banks of the old beaver pond which the cabin overlooked. Where two trees had fallen one atop the other, he took cover, just up a gradual slope from the trail about sixty paces. From here he would have a good close look at the interloper—and a clear shot if such was needed.

In moments the rider appeared, and Hawkes took a deep, calming breath, forcing everything but the matter at hand from his mind. Laying the barrel of the Plains rifle across the top log, he eased back the hammer and put the stranger in his sights.

But it was no stranger—just the last person Hawkes had expected to see up here.

Easing off the hammer, he stood up, vaulted over the logs, and started down the slope, shouldering the rifle. The rider's horse threw its head and whickered, alerting the man on its back.

"Loud Talker!" exclaimed Hawkes. "What are you doing so far from home?"

The Osage nodded gravely. "It is true. I do not like to travel when the Cold Maker has left his lodge of ice. The Cold Maker is white as the snow he brings with him. His horse is white, too. It is now, when the sun is weak, that he rides across the land, and sometimes you do not see him coming because he always moves within a snowstorm."

Hawkes laughed. "By God, it's good to know that some things never change. I'll wager you haven't stopped talking since I saw you last. How long has it been? Ten years, nearly eleven?"

Loud Talker shrugged. "I suppose I will stop talking when I don't have anything more to say." He looked around him at the valley, hemmed in by towering peaks dressed in new snow, that was Gordon's home. "This is a good place to live," he said approvingly. "I always knew that you would live in a good place. I have never seen this part of the world up close before. I will have to tell my people all about it when I get home."

"I'm sure you will. But what brings you here?"

Loud Talker's expression was grave. He hadn't aged a day, it seemed. Some people were lucky in that regard, mused Hawkes, ruefully rubbing his bearded jaw and thinking about all the gray in his own hair, and the deep furrows that had been etched in his brow in recent years.

"I came when I heard what was happening with the Mormons," said the Osage. "I wanted to see for myself what all the shouting was about. I am riding with your old friend, the one called Bridger."

"I thought Old Gabe was scouting for the army."

"He is. So am I. But that doesn't mean I will fight against the Mormons. I am not a fighter, anyway, and when I agreed to scout for the bluecoats, and made my mark on their paper, nobody said anything about fighting Mormons. It is safer to ride with the bluecoats for now. My people and the Teton Sioux aren't getting along."

"The Sioux don't get along with anybody," remarked Hawkes fervently.

"If the Sioux caught me alone they would probably kill me, and I am not ready to be a ghost yet."

"Did Bridger send you?"

Loud Talker shrugged again. "Since I was in this part of the world I wanted to come and see how you were doing. I told your friend this, and he gave me a message to bring to you."

Hawkes grimaced. "I have a feeling I know what it's about. Well, come on up to the cabin. I want you to meet my wife and son."

As they approached the cabin, Eliza and Cameron came outside. Hawkes introduced everybody and Eliza, smiling warmly, put out her hand.

"I remember Gordon speaking of you," she said. "Please come in."

Once they were settled at the table in the common room, and Eliza had put some coffee on to boil in the hearth where a warming fire crackled, Hawkes asked about Old Gabe's message.

"One moon ago," said the Osage, "the Mormons and some Indian friends of theirs attacked a wagon train at a place called Mountain Meadows." Loud Talker shook his head. "I do not know where this place is. But I will know it when I see it. There will be many ghosts. It is a sacred place now. It belongs to the dead."

"Are you sure the Mormons were involved?"

Loud Talker gave one of his expressive shrugs. "Who can be sure? Some people say one thing, some people say another. But the bluecoat soldiers believe the Mormons did it, and if they believe it, what does it matter if it's true or not?"

"You've got a point," allowed Hawkes. "But I can't believe Brigham Young would be involved in something like that."

"Doesn't surprise me," said Cameron.

"You've never even met Brigham Young," said Hawkes. "Why are you so quick to judge?"

"On account of what he did to the men at the Green River ferries, and how he went after Jim Bridger."

"I know Old Gabe thinks Young was behind that, but he could be wrong." Hawkes looked at Loud Talker. "What do you think?"

"I know people can change."

Hawkes took a deep breath and got up from the table. He fetched his pipe from the mantel and packed it with tobacco, deep in thought. Belatedly he became aware of Eliza, standing off to one side watching him. She was trying to hide her feelings behind a mask of impassivity, but Hawkes thought he knew what she was thinking.

"So I guess now there really will be a war," he said as he fired the tobacco in the pipe bowl with a sliver of wood flaming at one end. "Old Gabe will finally get his wish."

"Funny thing about that," said Loud Talker, sniffing at the aroma of the coffee. "Jim Bridger talked a lot about war for many days—until he heard about the massacre. Now he doesn't act like he wants a war anymore. A man should be careful what he asks for."

Eliza couldn't stand the suspense any longer. "So why did he want you to tell my husband about this, Loud Talker? What does he want from Gordon?"

Loud Talker pursed his lips, giving the query careful consideration before answering. "I think he wants your husband to stop the war from happening."

"Oh." Eliza pushed a tendril of pale yellow hair behind one ear. Suddenly, she refused to even look at Hawkes. "Oh, I see." She turned to take the pot of coffee off the fire, holding the handle with her apron bunched up in her hand to keep from burning herself.

She poured the strong fragrant brew into three tin cups already in place on the table.

"Would you like some coffee?" she asked the Osage. "I think we have a little sugar someplace."

Loud Talker very much wanted some sugar in his coffee. He had a terrible sweet tooth. But he shook his head. He knew he was going to be taking this woman's husband away from her, and he didn't want to take the last of her sugar, too. It was going to be a long winter. Holding the cup with both hands so that the heat would thaw his stiff, frozen fingers, he sipped the coffee. It tasted very bitter without sugar.

"Gabe just isn't thinking straight," decided Hawkes. "I have no way of stopping a war. To be frank, I thought it was sure to come eventually. Besides, I can't go scout for the army. I'm a wanted man. Wanted for two crimes back East."

"Bridger said something about that. He said the bluecoats would not know who you were, that he would call you Henry Gordon. And he does not want you to scout for the soldiers. That's his job. He wants you to go see Brigham Young."

"What's going on here, Loud Talker? Does the army know about this?"

"I do not know. But I can tell you what I think. I think the bluecoat chief, a man named Johnston, does not want war either. Not the kind of war that will happen now that there has been a massacre."

"What kind of war are you talking about, sir?" asked Cameron.

"Many men with many guns are coming. I have seen some of them already. They do not wear the bluecoat, so the soldier chief Johnston cannot tell them what to do."

"Volunteers, you mean," said Cameron.

"They will not just make war on the Mormon men," continued Loud Talker. "But on the women and children, too. I think that is why Bridger and the soldier chief want to make a peace. But it may already be too late. This is very good coffee, ma'am."

"Thank you. Would you care for some more?"

"Please. It is a long trail back to the bluecoat camp."

"You're not leaving right away, are you?"

"I should be getting back. I don't want to miss anything that I should tell my people about."

"It's getting late. You may as well stay the night. Then the two of you can get an early start in the morning." She finished filling Loud Talker's cup and turned to look at her husband. "You know you have to go," she said, acting very matter-of-fact to hide her sorrow. "You can't just stand by and let innocent people be killed. Cameron and I will be fine. Now you just sit down and I'll start supper. Cam, fetch me some fresh water, please."

Hawkes sat down. He didn't say anything, because Eliza was right. As much as he hated to admit it, she was right.

Chapter 27

When Hawkes and Loud Talker rode into the camp of the federal army, the cold was so severe that the expedition's herd of cattle was being decimated, dying by the dozens. The first thing Hawkes noticed was that the soldiers were busy building log huts. It reminded him of that winter more than twenty years ago when he had first come west with the Rocky Mountain Fur Company. He and his companions had rushed to build a small post before the winter blizzards struck. The same sense of urgency was evident in the labors of these soldiers. That they were constructing winter quarters was a good sign, in Gordon's opinion. That meant it was likely the campaign against the Mormons had been postponed.

Bridger was surprised to see him. The old mountain man was sitting on his heels next to a crackling fire with several other buckskinners and a couple of Indians, no doubt the expedition's contingent of scouts. When he spotted Hawkes he jumped to his feet and rushed out to meet him.

"Well, hoss, I halfway didn't expect you to show up," admitted Old Gabe. "I figured if anybody could talk you into it, that would be Loud Talker. He has a talent for words."

"Bridger, you are wrong," said the Osage. "His woman told him to come with me."

Bridger was stunned. "Eliza? You're pullin' my leg."

"It's the gospel truth," said Hawkes, dismounting stiffly. It was so cold his bones hurt. He looked around, and allowed himself a small smile. "Snows came kind of early this year, didn't they? Guess that's too bad."

Bridger smirked. "I know that breaks your heart. Fact is, you're glad this here army is snowed in."

"Might be another one of those miracles the Saints talk so much about."

"Yeah, sure. I heard all about how they were losin' all their crops to millions of crickets back when they first started up out here. They claim thousands of seagulls showed up out of nowhere and ate the crickets, and how if that hadn't happened a lot of folks might have starved."

"You don't believe that, Old Gabe?"

"Reckon it's just that I have a hard time believin' anything them Mormons say. But come on over here and warm your butt by our fire." As they headed for the campfire, Bridger leaned closer to Hawkes and pitched his voice low. "Listen here, son. Far as anybody around here knows, exceptin' me and Loud Talker, of course, your name is Henry Gordon."

Hawkes nodded. When they reached the fire, Bridger introduced him to the other scouts.

"You're the man what brought them Mormons out West in '47?" asked a mountain man named Portugee.

"I gave them a hand, but they were bound and determined to come out anyway," said Hawkes, not sure what to expect.

"Then I reckon you know 'em better than anyone else here. So tell me, what kind of fighters are they?"

Hawkes gave that question a moment's thought. He'd never had occasion to see the Saints in action, except for a brief skirmish with Pawnee raiders, and that hadn't amounted to a hill of beans. But he thought about John Bonham and Simon Parker and Return Redden and Hosea Stout. Tough, determined, and dangerous men all.

"They'll fight hard," he replied. "They're God-fearing people, but don't let that fool you. They've been in plenty of scrapes with mobbers in Missouri and Illinois, and they're not likely to turn tail and run at the first sign of trouble."

"They've been on the move," said Bridger. "What Colonel Johnston calls a 'scorched earth' campaign. They set fire to the grass all up in front of us. They had a place called Camp Supply set up east of the Wasatch, and they burned it to the ground just so's we couldn't make use of the buildings for shelter. I'm kind of surprised they didn't put a torch to Fort Bridger whilst they was at it. Ain't had a chance to tell you—just found out about it myself a few months back—but Louis Vasquez sold his half interest in the trading post to the Saints for eight thousand dollars. Can you believe that, hoss? Never would have thought Louis could do a thing like that." Bridger looked positively morose. "But leastways it must mean he's gettin' along right well with the Mormons, and that could be a lucky break for you."

"You know, that really burns my bacon," remarked Portugee, frowning. "We come all this way to have us a ruckus and now Colonel Johnston wants to make peace with the damned Mormons. I don't savvy why you'd march an army all this way to make peace."

One of the Indian scouts, a Shawnee, said something in his own tongue, and Portugee laughed heartily.

"What did he say?" asked Hawkes.

"He said the White Father—that's Buchanan—fights his wars like a woman."

Hawkes glanced at Bridger. "Sounds like you better take me to this man, Johnston."

Bridger accepted a jug the others had been passing around, took a swig, and nodded. "I will. But have a pull on this firewater first. It'll put the feelin' back in your fingers and toes."

Colonel Albert Sidney Johnston's headquarters were located in one of the handful of completed log huts. He was sitting at a desk consisting of a wagon gate laid across a couple of barrels. Looking up from some papers as an orderly brought in Hawkes and Bridger, he put down his quill pen and stood. He was a tall and slender man with a commanding presence. His yellow hair was long around his ears and brushed back from a widow's peak. His thick mustache was of somewhat darker hue, and concealed a severe mouth. His pale blue eyes were steady, his gaze intense.

"Colonel," said Bridger, "this here's the feller I told you about, Henry Gordon. The man who acted as Brigham Young's guide ten years back."

Johnston nodded curtly. He did not offer a hand. "I'm sorry, gentlemen, that I can offer you neither a chair or a drink. I have neither." Turning away, he threw another piece of wood on the fire in a mudstick fireplace. "What are your feelings about the Mormons, Mr. Gordon?"

Hawkes had expected just such a question, and answered readily. "I think that generally, they are good people."

Johnston swung around and fastened his steely gaze on Hawkes. "Do you indeed? Does that include the Mormons involved in the massacre at Mountain Meadows, by any chance?"

"There are some among them who hate outsiders, it's true. One could argue that they have good reason—"

"I know of no reason sufficient to justify the murder of innocent women and children."

"You might let me finish, Colonel. I didn't say they had good reason to kill innocent people, only to hate outsiders—not to mention the United States of America."

"Why would they hate this great country, sir?" asked Johnston. He seemed offended by the very notion.

"Because the government did precious little to protect them when Missouri and Illinois mobbers were burning their homes, trampling their fields, and murdering *their* families. Perhaps you've heard of a place called Haun's Mill."

"I have. But two wrongs do not make a right."

"No, they don't. But bloodshed begets more bloodshed."

Johnston glanced at Bridger. "You didn't tell me he was a Mormon-lover."

"And he didn't tell me you were such a jackass, Colonel," said Hawkes.

Bridger winced. "Lord have mercy, hoss. You been up in the high country entirely too long. You done forgot how to deal with folks."

"That's why I'm up there, Old Gabe—so that I don't *have* to deal with them. Reckon I've wasted enough of my time and yours, Colonel, so I'll just be going."

He turned to leave.

"Just a minute there," rasped Johnston. "It is not necessary that you and I become friends just so we can do business, or even agree on the issues. But we do need to reach an understanding if you're to serve as my go-between with Brigham Young."

"I'm listening," said Hawkes.

"It has come to my attention that armed bands of men are on the march from California and Santa Fe and even from as far away as Missouri. The word of what happened at Mountain Meadows spread like a damned prairie fire. I suppose such is always the case with bad news. These men intend to make the Mormons pay in blood for their transgressions. If they have their way, the entire frontier will be engulfed in the flames of war."

"I thought a war was what you were after, Colonel."

"Not *that* kind. My quarrel is not with Mormon women or Mormon children. These armed bands of which I speak will make no such distinctions, I fear."

"Then you'd better stop them."

"I have three regiments, sir. At best, a little more than two thousand men who are fit to bear arms. Before this damned winter is done with us I may have a lot fewer than that. Still, I may be able to prevent violence and effectively police this frontier—if I don't have to worry about the Nauvoo Legion. In other words, Gordon, I want a peace, or at the very least, an armistice with the Mormons. That's where you come in."

"I'm not sure there's much I can do," said Hawkes dubiously. He knew he was getting in way over his head.

"Bridger here tells me you know Brigham Young as well as anyone who is not a Mormon."

"I guess maybe that's true."

"Will he listen to what you have to say?"

"I don't honestly know. I haven't seen him in ten years. But if he's the same man that he was then, I would say yes, he will."

Johnston nodded. "Good. You will deliver to him my terms for a peaceful resolution of this crisis. First, he must surrender control of the Territory of Utah to a governor appointed by the president. Second, he must permit federal troops to be garrisoned within the territory."

"For how long?"

"Indefinitely, sir. Indefinitely. You are aware, I presume, that the so-called State of Deseret is in the United States. That seems to be a difficult pill for your Mormon friends to swallow. But they are going to have to."

"Is that all?"

"No. The third condition is that all parties responsible for the Mountain Meadows massacre must be brought to justice."

"I don't know if they'll accept those terms, Colonel. You see, they'll figure that once they let your soldiers in, then Gentile settlers will come next. And whenever that happens the Mormons end up losing everything they've worked so hard for."

"The army will not allow that sort of thing to occur."

"Can I give Brigham Young your personal guarantee as an officer and a gentleman?"

Johnston stroked his mustache. Those pale blue eyes were cold as ice. "As far as it is within my power to prevent such occurrences, yes."

"Okay," said Hawkes, reluctantly. "I'll go see him."

"May not be as easy as you think, hoss," warned Bridger.

"Bridger is quite right," said Johnston. "The countryside to the west is swarming with Mormon irregulars. Beyond my picket line I cannot vouch for your safety. Salt Lake City is eighty very dangerous miles from here, sir."

"Well," said Hawkes, "all I can do is try."

For the first time Johnston seemed to relax. He even allowed himself the faintest ghost of a smile.

"I had expected a bit more bravado from you, frankly. Mountain men seem to hold their own abilities in very high regard."

"I could promise you that I'll get through come hell

or high water, Colonel, if that will make you feel better."

"No, don't bother. Just do the best you can. Many lives depend on it."

"That's the only reason I'm here."

Once again Hawkes turned to go—and once again Johnston stopped him.

"Tell me, Gordon. Where are you from?"

The old familiar fear coursing through his veins, Hawkes remained cool and collected on the outside.

"I come from the mountains. That's where my life really began. What happened before isn't important to me and it ought not to be to anybody else."

Johnston gave him a long, searching look, and for an instant Hawkes thought his answer had been too evasive, too defensive, and that the colonel wasn't satisfied with it. There was no reason to think that the colonel had any suspicions about him, or any way of knowing that he was a man wanted for a pair of murders.

But Johnston just sat down at his makeshift desk, picked up the pen, and dipped it in an inkwell. "I'll have a letter for you to deliver to Brigham Young within the hour."

"I don't need a letter. Either he'll believe me or he won't. Your signature won't make any difference. And if the wrong people find such a letter on me it could turn into a death warrant. Mine."

"Very well. Good luck to you, then." Johnston returned to his work.

As they trudged back to the campfire through the fresh snow, Bridger said, "I'd like to go with you, hoss. But since the Saints have such a low opinion of me I don't think I'd be much good to you."

"Don't worry about it."

"Reckon Loud Talker will ride along, though."

"No need for the both of us getting killed."

Bridger pondered that remark for a spell. "You don't think you're comin' back, do you?"

"Guess we'll find out soon enough."

"Well, if you do wind up gone beaver, I'll take care of your family. You know you can count on me for that."

"I know. But there's no need for that, either. Cameron's a man now. He can take care of himself and his mother."

"Sure." Bridger closed his throat. "Wonder, if you do get through, would you take a message to Vasquez for me? Tell him . . . tell him there ain't no hard feelings about what he done. I was madder than a nest of hornets when I first heard he'd sold out his share of the business. But what the hell. Reckon he did what he thought was best. No reason to ruin a friendship over business."

Hawkes smiled and clapped Bridger on the back. "There's hope for you yet, Old Gabe."

"I know what you've been thinkin'. That I done sold my soul for the almighty dollar. Well, maybe I did. I wanted to give my little girl everything I could, and a man needs money to do that. Or so I thought. But fact is, I was so busy makin' money I didn't pay her much attention. Shouldn't have never sent her off to that mission like I did. Now she's gone. I feel bad for not spendin' more time with her." They were nearly to the campfire, where Loud Talker and the army scouts were huddled, so Bridger stopped in his tracks, making Hawkes stop too. "I'm feelin' bad about this, Gordon. About gettin' you involved. It's too dangerous, aint it? I hate to be the one takin' you away from *your* family."

"Gabe, you're not the one who got me into this."

"If I didn't, who did?"

"It just happened, that's all. It happened ten years ago, when I went back to Missouri and ended up with the Mormons. And when I left them at the valley of the salt lake I tried to tell myself that I was finished with them. But down deep I had my doubts. Because I knew they'd never have any peace, and sooner or later this would happen. Their situation is a lot like mine, I guess. I'll never find true peace, either. That's just the way life is. A friend of mine once told me that life never played fair with a person, but it was still worth living. I learned that's true. Now come on. I could use a snort of that redeye before I get going."

Chapter 28

Hawkes was already several miles away from the encampment when Loud Talker caught up with him.

"I thought I told you I wanted to do this alone," said Hawkes.

The Osage gave him a stony, unreadable look. "I am not coming to protect you. But something might happen that I need to—"

"Yeah, I know. That you need to tell your people." Hawkes noticed that Loud Talker had daubed his horse with war paint and wore a couple of feathers in his scalp lock. They were feathers from a turkey vulture, but maybe that was the only kind he could find. "Looks to me like you're all set for the warpath."

Loud Talker shook his head. "I keep telling you, I'm not a warrior. No, I just want to make sure the Mormons can see that I am an Indian. Mormons like Indians, so maybe they won't shoot me."

Hawkes grinned. "I hope it works."

"Me, too."

They rode twenty miles that day, and as the sun began to set they arrived at a place where their trail took them past a line of willows and cottonwoods marking the rocky course of a stream. Suddenly a flock of sparrows exploded out of the top of one of the trees. Then Hawkes heard the hooting sound of a blue grouse's call. Only he wasn't all that convinced that a blue grouse made it.

"I think we've got company," he said, reaching down to draw the Plains rifle from its fringed sheath, which was tied to the saddle beneath his leg.

A heartbeat later a shot rang out—and Hawkes tumbled sideways off his horse.

Loud Talker leaped to the ground, keeping a tight grip on the reins and using his horse for cover as he knelt beside Hawkes.

"You are not a ghost yet," he said, "unless some part of you is made of wood."

Lying on his stomach, Hawkes opened one eye. "Check my long gun."

Loud Talker did so—and saw that a bullet had lodged in the stock of the Hawken rifle. He was certain he'd heard the bullet strike wood. "I think this rifle will still shoot," he said.

"Glad to hear it. Now, if they think they hit me they might come in for a closer look to see if I'm dead. At least it worked for me once before. Now get out of here, Loud Talker, before it's too late."

"They would just come after me and kill me if I tried to run," reasoned the Osage. He stood up and looked toward the trees, then walked a short distance away from the place where Hawkes lay imitating a dead man. He then sat cross-legged on the ground and began to sing a monotonous chant.

A few minutes later Hawkes heard horses and his blood ran cold because of the vivid memories of that day eleven years ago, when the man named Geller had shot him from a distance and then rode in to make sure he was finished. Hawkes knew he'd been lucky that time, and he wondered if he was still lucky.

Loud Talker looked up as the four horsemen checked their mounts, looming over him on all sides.

"What's that noise you're making?" asked one of the men. "A death song?"

"No. It is a rain song, I think. Indians have many songs. There are songs that ask the Great Spirit to bring the buffalo, and songs that ask him to make a war party successful, and to protect a village from sickness, and to ask for rain when it is too dry. Usually there are dances that go with each song. But I am not a good dancer. Since there are so many songs for so many different things, I am a little confused about this one and what it is for, but I'm pretty sure it is a rain song." Loud Talker scooped up handfuls of dirt. "I hope it is, because this land of yours is very dry. I think it could use some rain. You know, the spider will tell you when the weather is going to change. When it is dry the spider's web is thin and very large. But when the rains are coming, the spider's web is—"

"For God's sake, shut up," muttered the man. "Layton, go check that other one." He pointed at Hawkes.

One of the Mormons dismounted and approached Hawkes, a pistol in one hand and a rifle cradled under his arm.

"Way I see it," said the leader of the foursome, frowning at Loud Talker in a very menacing way, "you men must be scouts for the Federals. Which means you're in a heap of trouble."

Loud Talker didn't appear to be paying him any attention. He was studying the dirt in his cupped hands with great interest.

Hawkes waited until the man named Layton was close—then he lashed out with a leg, catching the Mormon behind the knees. Layton sprawled backwards. His pistol, pointed skyward, went off accidentally, and he dropped the rifle altogether. Hawkes was on him in an instant, his knife at Layton's throat and his pistol aimed at the three startled riders.

"No more shooting," he warned. "Or next time somebody really gets dead."

But one of the Mormons wasn't listening. He swung his rifle around to take a shot at Hawkes. Loud Talker was ready for that. Lunging to his feet, the Osage tossed the dirt in his hands into the eyes of the man's mount. The horse shied violently away, spoiling the Mormon's shot, and before he could line up another shot Loud Talker was dragging him out of his saddle. Stunned by his violent impact with the ground, the man didn't put up much of a struggle, and Loud Talker wrenched the rifle from his grasp and backed up, covering the Mormons from one side while Hawkes had the drop on them from the other.

"Throw all your weapons down," said Hawkes. When the Saints hesitated he added, "Don't make me tell you twice."

They complied. Only then did Hawkes take his knife away from Layton's throat. Sheathing the blade, he relieved Layton of his pistol and stepped away.

"You made a mistake," said Hawkes. "I'm no scout for the army. My name is Gordon Hawkes. And he's Loud Talker. We both rode with Brigham Young and the Pioneer Camp back in '47."

The leader of the group was startled. "Gordon Hawkes? I've heard of you. I was at Winter Quarters. But what are you doing here?"

"I've come to talk to Brigham Young. I'm here to stop a war."

"You're too late to do that."

"Maybe you're right. But I'm still going to try."

The man thought it over. "I'll take you to our camp. You can tell your story to my commander."

"And who might that be?"

"Simon Parker."

Hawkes smiled tautly. "I wish I knew if that was lucky—or not."

* * *

Sitting across a night camp's fire from Simon Parker, Hawkes decided that the whittling deacon he'd first met eleven years ago in John Bonham's hut at Winter Quarters hadn't changed much at all. He still looked like a kid—a slender and soft-spoken kid who was also as dangerous as a nest of rattlesnakes. And he still sported a brace of pistols in cross-draw holsters, only he had traded in his old Colt Patersons for newer models.

There were about twenty-five men in the company under Parker's command. They called themselves Irregulars, as distinguished from the uniformed Nauvoo Legion which, Hawkes learned, had been reorganized and expanded on Brigham Young's orders, and now numbered nearly four thousand men, well armed and well trained. That meant, mused Hawkes, that the Legion actually outnumbered Albert Sidney Johnston's army.

"The Legion is camped about thirty miles west, between here and Salt Lake City," said Parker. "I'd say there are probably twenty companies like this one in the field. Our orders are to harass the Federals. Slow them down."

"The weather has done that for you," replied Hawkes, warming his hands near the fire.

"Yes, I know." Parker smiled one of those wry, crooked smiles that Hawkes remembered so well. "I know a lot about that army." He glanced at Loud Talker. "For example, I know you've been scouting for them."

Loud Talker sat huddled in a blanket, gazing into the fire. "I'm not today," he said.

"He's with me now," said Hawkes, "and, as you must know since you know everything, I'm *not* with the Federals."

Parker didn't say anything. He picked up a stick

and drew a knife from under his longcoat and started whittling. Hawkes took the opportunity to survey the encampment. Parker's men were gathered around several other fires in a hollow encompassed by scrub-covered hills. It did not escape his notice that he and Loud Talker were the focus of attention, and he had to wonder just how badly these men wanted peace. He understood how that might ultimately determine whether he got to see Brigham Young—or even whether he and Loud Talker survived.

Finally Parker looked up from his whittling. "There are a lot of people in Deseret who want to see the Legion march on the army and destroy it."

"Does that include you?"

Parker still wore that infuriating smile, the one Hawkes had never been able to figure out. The whittling deacon was just as hard to read as he had been ten years ago. You just couldn't tell where he stood. Never knew if he was going to offer you his hand in friendship or draw his pistols and fill you full of lead.

"I just follow orders."

"Whose orders? Hosea Stout's? I have a pretty good idea where he stands."

"The question here and now is where *you* stand."

"I'd say enough people have already lost their lives. You're smart enough to know that destroying that army won't do Deseret any good in the long run. Next year they'll just send a bigger army. You might win a battle or two, but this is a war you can't win."

"Maybe you're underestimating us."

"I've never done that."

"We just want to be left alone."

"I know how you feel. But it isn't going to happen."

Parker tossed the stick into the fire. He seemed a little angry. It was the first time Hawkes could recall seeing any emotion from him. "I won't take you to Salt Lake City. You could be a spy. And you might not live long enough to see Brigham Young. You'll wait here while I send a messenger. If he wants to see you, then you'll see him."

Hawkes nodded. Parker's plan meant that he and Loud Talker would have to wait here for at least a couple of days, and this wasn't exactly the friendliest bunch to share a camp with. But there wasn't any point in arguing about it. Parker had made up his mind and that was that.

Parker left them, moving to another fire. Hawkes glanced at Loud Talker. "Well, I guess we better take turns getting some sleep."

The Osage concurred. "If we don't we might wake up as ghosts."

Using his knife, Hawkes dug a deep hole in the snow down to the frozen ground, and then built a small fire. He let it burn down to embers, chewing on a strip of jerky while he waited. Covering the embers with a layer of dirt, he sat on top of it and covered himself with his blankets. Loud Talker did likewise. In this way some of the heat from the embers seeped up through the ground to warm them. Hawkes took the first watch, keeping an eye on the Irregulars. But his thoughts were of Eliza, and how much nicer it would be to be sleeping in his own bed tonight, warmed by her body pressed close to his. Such thoughts seemed to ward off the bitter cold.

The next morning Parker sent a rider back to Salt Lake City. Later, he rode out himself with a dozen men. Hawkes assumed they were going to scout out Johnston's army and possibly make more mischief for the Federals. That left about ten men in camp, and they set about building lean-tos while keeping a watch on Hawkes and Loud Talker. Hawkes had never liked being idle, and he decided their stay here could drag on for at least two or three more days, so he and the Osage agreed that it would be better to be doing something, and set about erecting a lean-to of their own. All they had were their knives and a hatchet that Loud Talker carried, but that was sufficient, and by the end of that first day they had a shelter to protect them from the snow that had begun to fall from an ominous sky.

On the second day they put the finishing touches on the lean-to, clearing out the snow from beneath it and putting down a floor of twigs and cedar cuttings, as well as a fire hole encircled with stones. That left just about enough room for both of them to lie down—not that they ever slept at the same time. Hawkes had a sneaking suspicion that some of the Irregulars would just as soon see them dead. He had no way of knowing just how much Parker had told his men about their mission—the Mormons kept their distance and clearly had no desire to engage their unwanted guests in idle chatter. But no doubt some if not all of them wanted war, and if that was the case then they had no interest in seeing that Hawkes got his meeting with Brigham Young. Hawkes and Loud Talker agreed that their role in helping the Mormons during their westward exodus from Winter Quarters would probably garner them little consideration from the Saints these days. Too much bad water had passed under the bridge. So they took turns standing watch. At least Parker had allowed them to keep their weapons—not that either of them thought they could prevail against twenty well-armed men if a fight got started.

To their surprise, the messenger Parker had sent west returned at the close of the second day. Forty miles there and forty miles back in two days in these weather conditions was no small feat. Even more surprising, he wasn't alone—Brigham Young had accompanied him on the return trip. And Young was himself accompanied by a man Hawkes knew all too well—John Bonham, the Danite avenger.

When he saw Bonham, Hawkes thought immediately of Dane Gilmartin. He hadn't seen or heard from Gil personally since that day long ago in Echo Canyon when Gilmartin and Patience Bonham were leaving the Pioneer Camp. Gil had told him then that they would probably go to California after wintering in New Mexico, and a few years ago Jim Bridger had mentioned hearing that indeed, Gil was living in San Francisco and by all accounts doing quite well for himself. But those rumors had not included any mention of how Patience fared. Seeing Bonham, Hawkes wondered if the holy killer had any news of his errant wife or the man who had stolen her away. What were Bonham's feelings about all that now, ten years after the fact? And what would be his attitude toward Gilmartin's erstwhile friend and companion?

Unlike Simon Parker, Brigham Young had aged considerably since last Hawkes had seen him. The Mormon leader had a lot more gray in his hair, and a lot more lines on his face. He no longer looked quite so robust and resilient as Hawkes remembered him. Was that indomitable will and force of character still intact? Hawkes fervently hoped so. Any and all hopes for peace hinged on this one man and the extent of his power over the Mormon people.

Brigham Young greeted Hawkes and Loud Talker warmly, clasping their hands in his and shaking them vigorously. "When I heard you were here I decided to come straightaway," he said. "It's probably best that we didn't meet in the city, anyway. It's good to see the both of you again, my friends, even under these trying circumstances."

They sat on their saddles around an open fire, and someone brewed some coffee and brought a cup of it to Brigham Young, offering none to Hawkes or Loud

Talker—until the Mormon leader gave Loud Talker his cup and demanded two more. Hawkes glanced at John Bonham—and then remembered that he did not indulge in coffee or tea, being a Danite. There were the five of them—Hawkes, the Osage, Young, Bonham, and Simon Parker, who sat whittling a stick. The rest of the Irregulars kept their distance. When one of the men brought two more cups of coffee, Loud Talker asked if he had any sugar. The man gave him a scornful glance and walked away. Loud Talker shrugged and drank his coffee black.

"I'm certain the first thing you want to know," said Brigham, "is whether the stories about what happened at Mountain Meadows are true." He paused, heaved a sigh, and nodded. "I regret to say that apparently they are."

"You didn't know anything about it," said Hawkes. "You couldn't have." He refused to believe otherwise.

"No, I was not aware of it until too late. Brother Bonham killed two horses bringing the word to me as quickly as he could. But by the time I had sent word to Colonel Hale it was too late. The deed was done."

"Colonel Hale?"

"Commanding officer of the Iron County militia. It was he who gave the orders that none of the people in that wagon train be spared."

"None? Not even the women and children?"

Brigham Young turned pale, so strong was the emotion coursing through him. "I believe that a few of the children were spared. I'm trying to find out what became of them. But our people in the southern counties are very close-mouthed about the whole thing. I suppose that's to be expected."

"What have you done to this man Hale?" asked Hawkes.

"As of yet, nothing."

"But I would have thought—"

Brigham Young held up a hand. "You must try to understand the situation in Deseret before you pass judgment on me, my friend. Under the circumstances, with war on the horizon I need all the cooperation I can get. Were I to punish Isaac Hale now, I'm not certain that I could rely any longer on the militia of Iron County—or the rest of the people in the South, for that matter. Besides, Hale was not alone in committing this crime." He noticed that Simon Parker looked up sharply when he said that, and added, "Yes, a crime, Brother Parker. That's what it was. I realize there are many who do not agree. We've fought Gentiles before, but never have we slaughtered innocent women and children. And I pray to God it never happens again." Brigham turned back to Hawkes. "Others were involved. Haldman, the Indian agent, and several of the leading citizens of Cedar City. Also . . . also, my adopted son, John Lee."

Hawkes could hear the agony within the man emerging through his words. "I'm sorry to hear that."

"As for justice, all things in their own time. First I must deal with the United States of America."

"That's why I'm here," said Hawkes. "Colonel Johnston wants peace, too."

"I find that hard to believe," said Parker. "If he does, it's because he knows his army is in a desperate situation, and outnumbered two or three to one."

"Let's hear what the man has to say, Brother Parker," said Brigham tolerantly.

"What for? A peace with the United States government isn't worth the paper it's written on. Ask the Indians. Ask that one there how many times the United States has failed to keep the promises it has made to his tribe."

"They'll keep this peace," said Hawkes, "because the terms are all in their favor."

Brigham gave him a long, anguished look. "I see,"

he said. "You had better go ahead and tell me about those terms."

Hawkes told him of Johnston's conditions and didn't put any varnish on it. As he went through them, one by one, he realized that Brigham Young, for all his fairness of mind and his fervor for peace, was a proud man, and the government's terms were a bitter pill to swallow. When he was done he was pretty well convinced that the Mormon leader would refuse to cooperate.

Brigham Young gazed into the fire for a moment. The bitter night was closing in and he shuddered—though Hawkes wasn't sure it was the cold that made him do so. Then the Mormon leader stood up stiffly. *Here it comes,* thought Hawkes. *He's going to say no. And the war will be on. A lot of people will die, and I will have to go home and tell Eliza that I've failed.*

"There's one other thing," he said quickly. "I've been told there are companies of men—not soldiers, more like vigilantes—headed this way from California and Missouri. That's what worries Colonel Johnston. He's not sure he can stop them from attacking Deseret."

"He doesn't need to worry about that," said Parker, smiling coldly. "We can take care of mobbers."

"At least now I know where you stand," said Hawkes dryly. "Mormon women and children will suffer. Some will almost certainly lose their lives. Then you'll have more blood to avenge. So where will it stop? You can't stand against the United States. You just don't have the numbers, even if you *do* have the will. Ask Loud Talker how many tribes have tried to resist the United States. And then ask him how many have succeeded. It will be the same with you."

"You're right," said Brigham Young firmly. "We

will have peace. Go back and tell Colonel Johnston that I accept his conditions. With one small change in them. The men responsible for the massacre at Mountain Meadows *will* be brought to justice. But it will be Mormon justice."

John Bonham stood up. His dark eyes seemed to blaze with their own lurid light. "Does that mean you will finally let me go after those men?"

Brigham Young smiled wanly. "Yes. But I have one condition for *you,* Brother Bonham. You must make every effort to bring them in alive."

"Those men would rather die fighting than stand before you in a court of law," said Bonham confidently.

"You must try!" said Young urgently. "Or we might have a civil war in our hands. Imagine, Mormon killing Mormon. I could not bear for that to happen."

Bonham's face was an impassive mask. "If that's how you want it," he replied, without much enthusiasm.

"It's how it must be. Take as many men as you need."

"I don't need any." Bonham glanced at Parker. "And I'm not sure I could *trust* any."

Parker kept whittling on his stick. But that enigmatic smile of his was absent from his face.

Hawkes stood up. "I'll ride with you."

"So will I," said Loud Talker. "This is surely something I must see with my own eyes."

Bonham was staring at Hawkes, and Hawkes couldn't tell what he was thinking, but he was fairly certain that the holy killer would object to his company.

Brigham Young was pretty certain of it, too, so he said, "I think that's a good idea. Here are two men you know you can rely on. And I rely on them, as well."

Bonham got the message. This wasn't really a request on Brigham Young's part.

"I'll wait two days," he told Hawkes, "for you to ride to Johnston and get back here."

Hawkes nodded. "We won't keep you waiting."

Chapter 29

Gilmartin had known almost from the start that his decision to enlist in the company of San Francisco volunteers bound for the Utah Territory was a mistake.

For one thing, many of the men who signed up so enthusiastically to teach those treasonous murderers, the Mormons, a lesson they wouldn't forget were members of the Vigilance Committee. That group had been organized several years earlier for the purpose of fighting crime, which had been running rampant in the city. The leaders of the committee were merchants like James Dows and William David Howard, bankers including Eugene Delesert and James King, and shipmasters such as Ned Wakeman. The city had its own police force, but it was both corrupt and incompetent. In fact, members of the committee suspected some of the constables of being leaders in a criminal gang that preyed on San Francisco's law-abiding citizens. After the vigilantes had dispensed rough justice at the end of a rope to several outlaws, the ranks of the local criminal element were shrinking fast, as burglars and cutthroats hopped aboard outbound steamers in search of easier pickings in some other town.

Gilmartin didn't deny that the vigilantes had a salutary effect on the crime problem. Before, the city court had been overwhelmed with cases. A year after the committee swung into action, the court was able to deal with its docket in an hour or two, and most of the cases involved nothing more severe than drunk and disorderly behavior on the part of a sailor or miner. But when the volunteer company was organized it became immediately clear to Gilmartin that these men, while capable of handling a campaign against the local criminal element, were woefully ill-suited to launching an expedition of the sort contemplated against the Mormons. Few of the leaders of the committee had any military experience whatsoever, and those who did were promptly passed over by the rank-and-file when they voted for their commanding officers. The men weren't interested in subordinating themselves to men who might enforce discipline. The expedition was supposed to be a lark. A good time was to be had for all. The men didn't want to take orders. They wanted free rein—and they got it.

In spite of his misgivings, Gilmartin signed on. He even paid for a wagonload of provisions out of his pocket so that the fools wouldn't starve the first week out. He bought two of the best horses he could find, one for himself and one for Patience. Try as he might, he couldn't dissuade her from coming along. She wasn't the only woman in the expedition—several others tagged along with the wagons to serve as cooks and laundresses. Still, Patience stood out like a sore thumb. It was obvious that she was no ordinary camp follower, and speculation grew concerning her presence. Why was she going off to war? Gilmartin couldn't very well answer with the truth—that Patience was a Mormon herself, and that he was taking her back to her own people. The volunteers wouldn't tolerate her presence, or Gilmartin's. So he lied. He told the others that Patience had had relatives in the wagon train attacked by the Mormons and their Indian allies at Mountain Meadows, and that she insisted on finding out firsthand if any of her people had survived. That seemed to satisfy the curious for the time being, and even garnered some sympathy.

The company marched out of San Francisco with great fanfare in mid-September, a fortnight after Gilmartin had made his decision to get involved in the Mormon Rebellion. By the time they'd crossed the mountains at Truckee Pass, the expedition's mood had changed. Even then there were desertions. The problem, decided Gilmartin, was that most of the men had no idea just how far away the Utah Territory really was from San Francisco. Beyond the mountains lay a couple of hundred miles of unpleasant desert. Thanks to Gilmartin's guidance, the expedition found the Humboldt River, which Gil knew would lead them straight to Deseret. But they were just a few miles east of the mountains when the first snows came. Most of the men were ill-prepared for cold weather. Foolishly, they'd assumed they could get their licks in against the Mormons and be safely back in the sunshine of the California coast before winter struck. Gilmartin had known better, and he and Patience had warm coats and gloves to ward off the bitter cold. There weren't many in the expedition who could say the same, and the snow discouraged them, resulting in more desertions.

Too late, the inexperienced officers tried to exert some discipline. Virtually the whole company rebelled. It became a case of every man for himself. These vigilantes, accustomed to taking the law into their own hands, became a lawless mob. When several of the men began paying Patience too much of the wrong kind of attention, Gilmartin decided it was time to leave. They slipped out of a night camp at the headwaters of the Humboldt's north fork and struck out on their own. Neither one of them had any intention of giving up on the idea of reaching Deseret. For his part, Gilmartin reasoned that he would find another company of volunteers to join up with. Failing that, he would offer his services to the federal army. They'd be glad to have him, he thought, when they found out he had acted as guide for the Mormons during his trek westward. He knew the country—and he knew the enemy.

Later that day he spotted three riders trailing them.

Gilmartin had a pretty good idea who they were—the ones who had been eyeing Patience. They'd deserted what was left of the company and were now, he was sure, up to no good. He didn't know much about them, except that they weren't members of San Francisco's business community. They weren't merchants or shipmasters or lawyers. Just riffraff. Gilmartin expected the worst from them. He figured they were bent on robbery and murder. And in all likelihood they intended to have their way with Patience.

He made a quick decision. Alone, he might have tried to outrun or throw off his pursuers. But there was Patience to think about. She hadn't once complained, but he could tell she was nearing exhaustion. The long days of arduous travel and the terrible cold were taking a toll on her. For a moment Gil felt sympathy for her plight, and was impressed with her gumption. Then he came to his senses and remembered why he was here in the first place. Why should *he* feel sorry for *her*?

Nearby stood a knoll covered with scrub and boulders—a perfect place to make a stand. Leaving their horses securely tethered at the base, they climbed to the top of the high ground. At the top, Gil found a vantage point among the big rocks, where he could see for miles in every direction. The riders were three dark specks on the snow-covered flats below. Gil checked his rifle. He had bought a Sharps Model 1852 Slanting Breech carbine before leaving San Francisco. He also carried an English-made Adams army revolver, a five-shot .44 caliber pistol. His saddlebags bulged with plenty of ammunition for both weapons. He had a canteen of good water, a flask of whiskey, and a small bag filled with hard biscuits and some jerked venison. He was well provisioned to make a stand, and this was a good place to do it. An odd exhilaration filled him. It was strange, but after all those years of town living, the old survival instincts were still there, quick to surface, ready for action. He hadn't seen any action since that trip to Independence, Missouri, the one he'd taken with Gordon Hawkes. It would be nice, he thought, to have Gordon here with him now. Hawkes was a good man to have siding with you. Of course, they hadn't parted company on the best terms. . . .

The three riders checked their horses beyond rifle range. They weren't fools, mused Gil. They weren't going to make it easy for him. The problem for them was that they had no cover in approaching the knoll. It just depended on how desperate they were.

As it turned out, they were desperate enough to make a try. There was no other possible explanation for their decision to mount a three-man charge on the rocky knoll. They were betting Gilmartin couldn't knock but one, maybe two of them down before they reached the big rocks.

Gil put the carbine to his shoulder, drew a bead on the man in the middle, and squeezed the trigger.

The bullet hit him high in the shoulder, but he managed to stay in the saddle. Adjusting his aim, Gil fired again. This time he plugged the man square in the chest and he rolled off the back of the galloping horse, sprawling lifelessly in the snow. The other two spread out and kept coming, firing their pistols now. Gil didn't think they could hit anything at this range. He heard their bullets singing off the rocks below him as he reloaded. But killing the first man had taken twice as long as it should have, so he rushed his third shot, and missed entirely. Cursing, he reloaded again and took another shot. He dropped the second man's horse. The dying animal nose-dived into the snow, hurling its rider a good twenty feet. The man was stunned, and slow to get up, giving Gil the time he needed to plug another round into the carbine's breech and take a shot. He hit what he was aiming at this time, and the man went down hard. Gil knew he wouldn't get up.

Whirling, he looked for the third and last man, but this one had made it into the rocks at the base of the knoll, leaving his horse and proceeding on foot. Reloading the Sharps, Gilmartin searched the slope below for any sign of his adversary. Where the hell was he?

Drawing the Adams revolver, he turned and offered it butt-first to Patience, who was sitting quietly in the snow, backed up against a boulder, her knees drawn tightly against her body. She looked blankly at the pistol as though she had never seen one before and had no idea what it was.

"Here," he said brusquely. "Take this. There's one man left. I've got to go down there and flush him out. But you'd better hold on to this, just in case."

She took the revolver.

Gilmartin hesitated. He wanted to say more, wanted to apologize for treating her so badly these last few years. Just in case something went wrong and he didn't come back. But another part of him angrily denied that he had anything to apologize for. Shaking his head, annoyed with himself for being so uncertain of himself and of his feelings for Patience, he kept his mouth shut and started down the slope. He knew that a wiser course would be to stay put and let the man come to him. But that would endanger Patience, and might place her in the line of fire.

He was a third of the way down the slope, clambering quickly over a boulder, when the last man popped up out of hiding about fifty feet below and to the left. Gilmartin saw movement out of the corner of his eye and spun around, trying to bring the Sharps carbine to bear, but he didn't quite have his footing and slipped as he fired, which spoiled his aim. His adversary's aim was only a little better. The bullet struck the boulder at Gil's feet and glanced upward, hitting him in the thigh, knocking him off balance. He fell into the rocks below.

He knew immediately that he had broken his leg in the fall. He'd also lost his grip on the carbine. It lay a few feet away, and as he dragged himself toward it, gritting his teeth to keep from crying out at the pain, he prayed the Sharps hadn't been damaged. Taking another cartridge from his shot pouch, he reloaded, and just as he finished a shadow passed over him. Gil rolled, wincing as a bullet kicked rock dust in his face, and he glimpsed the man, silhouetted against the pallid winter sun on the rocks above him, lining up another shot. Gilmartin fired the Sharps, and the man dropped his pistol, clutched his belly, and then toppled forward, landing a few feet away. Reloading the carbine, Gilmartin put another round into him at point-blank range, and the man stopped moving.

Laying the Sharps down, Gilmartin lay there a moment, waiting for a bad case of the shakes to subside, watching a thin film of cloud cover drift across the face of the sun, and feeling the pain from his leg seep like liquid fire through the rest of his body. He was suddenly very cold, and feeling very weak. Afraid, too. Because he knew he was badly hurt, out in the middle of nowhere, and there was only one person who could help him.

He called her name.

At first he thought she wasn't going to come to him,

that maybe she had run away, had seen a chance to be rid of him and taken off alone for Deseret. Or maybe she just couldn't hear him. He called out again, louder this time. Still there was no response. Panic started to creep into his soul but he fought against it. He was too proud to keep crying out for her. So he lay there and tried to conserve his strength.

Then he heard her, picking her way down through the rocks. He called out a third time and she was there, kneeling next to him. To her credit, she kept her composure, ignoring the bloody corpse that lay nearby.

"Leg's broken," he said.

She took the knife from his belt and cut the leg of his trouser. The bullet and the break were in the same leg, soaking his trouser leg with blood, but she didn't let that deter her. When he heard her gasp he raised his head and looked at his exposed leg and saw that the fractured bone was protruding from his flesh.

He knew that he was done for.

"I can't set this," she said, distraught.

"That's okay." And then he laughed.

"Why are you laughing?" she asked, shocked, looking at him warily, as though he had lost his mind.

"Your husband was in the same sort of fix when I first met him," said Gilmartin.

"What are you going to do?" she asked. "Can you ride?"

He shook his head. "Not a chance of that. Make me a tourniquet, will you?"

"Of course." She took a woolen scarf from around her neck, and ripped it into two halves, longways. She found a stout stick about eighteen inches long in the rocks nearby. Tying half of the scarf around his leg above the bullet wound, she made another knot in it above the first, slipped the stick in between, and tightened the second knot. Slowly, she turned the stick, drawing the tourniquet tighter until Gilmartin's body arched rigidly.

"That's enough," he gasped. "Now, if you'll just bring me a blanket and some of the food you can be on your way."

"Yes," she said softly. "I'll get some help."

"Yeah, sure."

She climbed back to the top of the knoll and down the other side to the horses, leading them around the base of the rise to a point not far below where Gilmartin lay. Carrying two blankets and the sack of food, she returned to him.

Gilmartin had been thinking about what he wanted to say to her. It might be his last chance, so he wanted to get the words right. He watched her as she spread the blankets over him, and strong emotion nearly choked him.

"It's time for you to go, Patience," he said. "Head due east and in a day or two you'll be in Deseret. Back with your people, where you belong."

"Can you hold on for a few days, Gil? I'll come back with help. I promise I will."

"Take both of the horses."

"No. I'll leave yours here."

"No point in that. Take them both."

She suddenly began to cry, kneeling beside him with her hands over his face.

Gilmartin reached up and touched her chestnut brown hair. "I'm so sorry," he said thickly. "For everything. I just wanted you to be happy. And I want you to know that I always loved you, Patience. No one else but you."

She took his hand in both of hers and gave it a squeeze, attempting a brave but faltering smile.

Gilmartin felt his own eyes burning with tears, but he refused to let them fall. "I don't know how something that felt so right could have turned out so wrong.

Didn't you love me, Patience? I know I loved you. More than anything in the world. Didn't you love me like that, even at the beginning?"

"I did. And I still do, Gil. But that doesn't change anything. We didn't belong together."

He nodded, even though he didn't agree, feeling emptier inside than he had ever felt before. "You'd better get going. Keep that pistol handy. And keep your eyes open for trouble."

Patience leaned over and kissed the corner of his mouth.

"Go on," he said gruffly, squeezing his eyes shut.

She stood up. "I'm coming back for you, Gil. You just hold on."

"Yeah. I'll hold on. Now go."

Still, she hesitated. But he didn't open his eyes. He didn't want to watch her leave. He had a vision of her in his mind's eye, of the radiant beauty of her face as they danced and danced that night at Council Bluffs, before the Pioneer Camp headed west. It was on that night that he had decided he could not live without her. And that was still true.

Then she was gone.

Chapter 30

John Lee was sitting in his wing chair near the hearth of his home on the outskirts of a small town called Harmony, gazing absently into the roaring fire he had just stoked, when he heard the faint tattoo of horse's hooves in the night. Fear shot through him like a bolt of lightning, causing him to sit up suddenly. Sitting opposite him was his wife Rachel, gently rocking in her chair, her knitting in hand. She didn't hear the horse at first, but John Lee's abrupt reaction to what he had heard alarmed her. Their eyes met—and both knew what the other was thinking.

Her husband had never provided Rachel with the full details of what had transpired at Mountain Meadows. She could tell that the mere mention of those events caused him great distress, so she never mentioned them. But she had heard all the rumors, and she knew that John Lee had been active in trying to find homes for the sixteen little children he had managed to save. She was also aware that he had become very fatalistic of late. He refused to speak of the future, or make any sort of definite, long-term plans. He was, she feared, like a man awaiting a preordained visit to the gallows. John Lee knew that retribution in some form or another would eventually come. But, unlike some of the other men involved in the massacre, he had refused to go into hiding. While Rachel, who loved her husband with her whole heart and wanted to see him safe, inwardly wished he *would* go away, at least for a while, just as a precaution, she would not plead with him in that regard, or even speak of her true feelings. She didn't really need to—John Lee could read them in her eyes.

Lee could tell that the horse was being ridden hard. He heard it come to a sliding stop in front of his house, and he swallowed down the lump in his throat, trying to smile reassuringly at his wife, who was frozen, with knitting needles poised, her dark eyes glistening in the pale oval of her frightened face.

"I'll see who it is," he said, pleased that his delivery was so calm.

He got up, sparing a glance for the rifle in the corner of the room—and decided to leave the weapon where it was. Not just for Rachel's sake, although that was an important consideration. But also because there had been enough bloodshed, and he was not about to take up arms to protect himself from the justice he was convinced he so richly deserved.

Even as he reached for the door latch he heard a soft thud against the portal, and when he threw back the latch the door flew open so suddenly that Rachel cried out in alarm and Lee jumped back—only to lunge forward in order to catch the person who, having been leaning heavily against the door, slumped to the floor. Lee laid the stranger gently down, removed the snow-covered blanket that covered his head and shoulders, and realized then that it wasn't a *he* at all. It was a woman, a young woman with chestnut brown hair and a dusting of freckles on her cheeks and dark hazel eyes that fluttered open and focused on his face.

"Dear Lord," breathed Rachel, standing beside her husband. "Is she hurt, John?"

"I'm not sure." Lee glanced out the open door into the night. A light but persistent snow was falling in the blackness. A horse stood just beyond the porch, its head down, forelegs splayed, clearly bottomed out.

"Quickly, bring her to the bed," said Rachel. "I'll heat some water."

Lee did as he was told, scooping the woman up in his arms and carrying her into the bedroom to lay her on the four-poster which he shared with Rachel. He hoped the children were still sound asleep in their room on the other side of the house. He had enough to worry about without having to try and explain these strange goings-on to the youngsters.

As he began to back away from the bed, the woman reached out to clutch his arm.

"Help me," she whispered, trying to sit up.

"Now, now," said Lee. "You just lie back and rest yourself. Whatever you have to tell me can wait until you are stronger. Poor child, you're frozen clear through."

"No, this won't wait. A man is badly hurt. He's alone out there . . ."

"Out in this weather? Badly hurt? Who is this man? Is he your husband?"

"He is my . . ." She shook her head. "Not my husband. You know my husband. My name is Patience Bonham."

"Bonham!" Lee was shocked. "John Bonham's wife? The one who . . ."

Patience nodded. "Yes. The one who ran away."

"This man who's hurt. It isn't—"

"It doesn't matter who he is, does it? All that matters is that he's been shot, and his leg is broken, and I had to leave him two days ago—or was it three days ago? I can't remember. And I promised him that I would bring help, and told him to hold on. Please, please, you must try to save him."

Lee glanced at Rachel, who stood just inside the bedroom door.

"The water is heating," she said. "What did she say, John? Is there someone out there, suffering in this horrible weather? Someone who is injured?"

Lee nodded. "Yes, dear. Apparently so."

"Save him," murmured Patience, her eyelids fluttering as exhaustion overcame her, and the warmth of the house and the quilt Lee had covered her with insinuated itself into her numbed limbs and made her drowsy. "Save him, please."

"We will do all that can be done to save him," promised Lee. "But there is nothing we can do tonight. In the morning we shall set out to find your friend."

"Yes," whispered Patience, and her eyes flickered closed.

Lee gently pried her hand from his sleeve and stepped away from the bed.

"Whoever she is talking about must be in an awful way," worried Rachel. "Didn't I hear her say she'd left him two or three days ago?"

"Yes. And quite some distance away, by the looks of her and of her horse. Well, if he is still alive, he'll just have to hold out a little longer. I'll go see to the horse."

"I will bathe her," said Rachel, "and warm her hands and feet. She might have frostbite."

Shrugging on his heavy coat, Lee went outside. As he led Patience Bonham's horse to the barn, he was startled by the sudden appearance of a second horse, riderless, reins dragging, emerging from the snowy darkness. The second horse followed them right into the barn, and it was obvious to Lee that these two animals had traveled a long distance together and derived comfort from each other's company. He put them both up, gave them some grain, and unsaddled them. He found no saddlebags or blankets on either saddle, and nothing that might have helped him discern the identity of the man Patience was so desperate to rescue.

As he trudged back to the house, Lee shuddered as the cold lanced into his joints. He didn't see how an injured man could survive several nights of exposure to this kind of weather. But he intended to keep his promise to Patience Bonham, to help her find her companion. He wondered if it was the man for whom she had forsaken John Bonham. He had started to ask her that.

Of course, he couldn't help but think about her husband, the holy killer. In fact, John Bonham had been on his mind a lot these past months. The man, after all, was Brigham Young's terrible swift sword of vengeance. Brigham had been ominously silent on the subject of the Mountain Meadows massacre and his opinion of the men who had committed the crime. And a crime it was—Lee harbored no illusions on that score. If Brigham decided to punish him and Rigby and Haldman and the others, he would probably send John Bonham to see it done.

A few hours later, John Lee had ample cause to pause and reflect on the irony of those thoughts about Bonham, and of the strange way life's seemingly random coincidences had a habit of coalescing into a monumental moment of truth.

He was dozing off in his chair beside the hearth when they came calling. His wife was sitting up in the bedroom, just in case Patience Bonham awoke and needed something. With nowhere to sleep, Lee had resumed his place by the fire. He hadn't expected to get much sleep anyway, so when he awakened he was a little surprised to see that he had been out for so long, the fire having already died down to glowing orange embers in a heap of gray ash, smoky threads of dawn light now seeping through the window curtains. The first birds of morning were singing in the black cottonwoods outside, trying to stir the sleeping world. This time he was sure there were several horses, on the run. Rising, he moved swiftly to the window and peered out. As the riders checked their weary mounts, he identified them, even in this poor light, because he knew them all.

Haldman, the Indian agent. Griffin Ward, the shopkeeper from Cedar City. Major Rigby of the Iron County militia. And a slender young man Lee had met several times before, one of Hosea Stout's famous whittling deacons, whose name was Simon Parker.

Before they could hammer on the door, Lee opened it.

"Come in, gentlemen," he said with quiet resignation, for he felt he knew why they were here. "Please bear in mind that my family is still asleep."

"Better wake them up and get them out of here," said Haldman gruffly, brushing by Lee and heading for the fireplace to see if he could coax some heat out of the embers.

"Why would I want to do that?" asked Lee.

"Because hell is on its way here," said Griffin Ward, his voice hollow, and Lee could clearly see the fear reflected in the man's eyes. "John Bonham is coming for us all."

"Brother Parker came to give us warning," explained Major Rigby, stamping the snow off his boots before crossing the threshold into John Lee's home—a small courtesy none of the others had shown. Not that Lee could really blame them, under the circumstances. "He arrived in Cedar City yesterday morning. No, I suppose that would be the morning of the day before yesterday, now. Brother Ward and Brother Haldman and I discussed the matter and deemed it wise for all of us to go into hiding."

"I was lucky to be in town at the time," said Haldman. "If Bonham had caught me alone out at the mission . . ." He didn't need to finish.

"Into hiding?" echoed Lee. "Where do you propose to hide that John Bonham cannot find you?"

"Among the Utes," replied Haldman. "They'll take us in. None of them will talk to Bonham if I tell them not to."

"You have inordinate faith in the sway you hold over those people," remarked Lee, skeptically.

"They know who their friends are. And if I tell them to kill the Danite they'll do that, too."

John Lee glanced at the door to the bedroom. He couldn't be sure what an unprincipled man like Haldman would do in such desperate circumstances if he found out that John Bonham's wife lay just beyond that door. In fact, he wasn't sure of Ward, either, or that silent, watchful, deadly young man, Simon Parker. Only Rigby, Lee surmised, was too much the gentleman, too hidebound in his adherence to a quirky code of honor, to abuse Patience Bonham by using her in some fashion to shield himself from her husband. Not that anything on earth would suffice to stop the holy killer from following Brigham Young's orders. And it wouldn't occur to desperate men to question whether this woman, who had abandoned Bonham ten years ago, mattered enough to the Danite that he would be deterred from his task if she were placed in harm's way.

"Unfortunately," said Rigby, "Isaac Hale refused to flee Cedar City."

"I wonder what has happened to him?" muttered Ward. "He also refused to call out the militia to protect himself from Bonham. I don't know that all of them would have answered his call, but enough would have done it. Yet he said he would not instigate a civil war in Deseret just to save his own neck."

"Brother Parker tells us that Bonham is only a day

behind him," said Rigby, nervously pacing the room, constantly glancing through the window. "So, whether he killed Isaac or took him into custody, what's done is done by now."

"Bonham's not alone, either," said Parker. "He's got two men with him."

"An Indian named Loud Talker," added Haldman, "and a mountain man called Gordon Hawkes. They both served the Pioneer Camp as guides. And it was Hawkes, or so Brother Parker tells us, who brought Brigham the terms of surrender."

"Surrender?" asked Lee. "Did he accept them?"

Ward nodded glumly. "There will be no war, I'm afraid. Brother Brigham will step down from power. We will have a Gentile governor. And an army of occupation in Deseret."

It took John Lee a moment to digest this stunning news. Then he smiled—a slow grin of pure relief.

"I'm glad of that," he said.

Haldman rocked back on his heels, as though Lee had physically assaulted him. "You're glad, you say? The state of Deseret will cease to exist. The Gentile emigrants will be allowed to settle among us. Then eventually, they will be strong enough to drive us out of our homes, just like before. And the United States government, as usual, won't lift a hand to help us when that happens."

"It could be different this time."

"You're overlooking something, Brother Lee," said Ward. "A war with the Gentiles would have made us heroes for what we did at Mountain Meadows."

"I doubt that," snapped Lee. "I doubt anything could exonerate us."

Haldman glanced at him as though he were beneath contempt, then turned to Rigby. "We shouldn't have wasted our time coming here to warn him."

"I agree," said Lee coldly. "Because I'm not going anywhere."

"Come on," said Haldman to the others, making for the door.

That was the moment that Rachel emerged from the bedroom, sleepy-eyed. "Please, gentlemen! You'll wake the poor girl, and she needs her rest."

Lee winced. If only Rachel had waited another minute or two before coming out.

The other men exchanged puzzled glances.

"Oh," said Rachel, "are they going to help you search for that man, John?"

"Be quiet, Rachel."

"What's going on?" asked Haldman, suspicious. "What man? What poor girl?"

Simon Parker didn't waste time with words—he moved to the bedroom door with such grim purpose that Rachel shrank away as he approached. Lee started for him, but Parker stopped just inside the bedroom, gazing at the face of the woman sleeping fitfully in the bed. Then he turned with a wry smile on his face.

"Well, what do you know," he drawled. "That looks like Patience Bonham."

"What?" exclaimed Rigby. "Surely you are mistaken."

He and Haldman started for the bedroom together, but Lee placed himself firmly in their path, trying to block the door.

"You'll leave her alone," he said sternly. "She's not well."

"How the hell did she get here?" asked Haldman.

"What does it matter?" asked Ward, who had positioned himself across the room, at a window. "Let's just get out of here."

"No, wait a minute," said Haldman, brows knit in

thought. "Why should we look a gift horse in the mouth? She might be of some use to us."

"I knew you would be the first to think of that," sneered Lee.

Haldman ignored him. "Listen. We'll take her with us and—"

"Are you mad?" asked Rigby. "Bonham would hunt us to the ends of the earth. He would kill us all."

"He's going to try to kill us anyway. But he might think twice if—"

"I won't allow it," said Lee.

At the window, Ward muttered a vivid curse.

"It's them," he said, his voice pitched high with panic. "God in heaven, it's John Bonham and those other two!"

When Hawkes saw the saddle horses tethered out in front of the house that Bonham said belonged to John Lee, he knew the chase was finally over.

He was glad of that. Because ever since Isaac Hale had decided to kill himself, Hawkes had lost any enthusiasm he might have had for helping Brigham Young resolve the one problem that could destroy the peace between the Mormons and the United States that he'd helped arrange.

Yesterday they'd arrived at Cedar City—he and Loud Talker and the holy killer—and Bonham had barged right into Hale's house with pistol drawn and sudden death on his mind, and the rather portly, ruddy-faced colonel was seated in a chair, smoking a pipe and not looking at all alarmed or surprised by the avenger's appearance. In fact, he said he'd been expecting them. The others—Ward, Haldman, Rigby—were gone. They'd been forewarned. But Hale refused to disclose the identity of the person who had given them that warning.

Bonham was expecting trouble in Cedar City. He

had advised Hawkes and Loud Talker to be prepared to tangle with the whole Iron County militia. But Hale hadn't summoned his men to his defense. In fact, he'd forbidden them to lift a hand to protect him. He was willing, he said, to answer for his deeds before a higher authority. He seemed so calm and resigned to his fate that for once, Bonham dropped his guard.

Hale was a widower, having lost one family to mobber violence in Missouri and another to disease during the exodus. He lived alone in a small, two-room, shotgun house. When he went into the back room to get his coat, Hawkes and Bonham could watch him through the connecting doorway. Loud Talker was waiting outside, keeping an eye on the quiet street. Hale shrugged the coat on, then drew a five-shot revolver from a pocket, put the barrel in his mouth, and pulled the trigger before Hawkes could reach him.

Bonham didn't move. The only emotion he betrayed was disappointment.

They rode on, hot on the trail of the other ringleaders of the Mountain Meadows massacre. Disturbed by Hale's suicide, Hawkes questioned his participation in the manhunt. The only thing that kept him in harness was the knowledge that Brigham Young depended on him to see it through. More men were going to have to die, Hawkes told himself, to secure the peace. That was the bitter irony of the whole business.

Much to Gordon's relief, John Bonham made no mention of Patience or Dane Gilmartin during their journey. He didn't say much of anything at all. The gaunt, bearded holy killer was completely focused on the task at hand. He hardly slept, ate very little, and did not drink anything but water, refusing the coffee that Loud Talker insisted on making every morning. Hawkes remembered wondering years ago, back when he had first met Bonham, when he'd transported the wounded Danite to Winter Quarters, if the man was quite human. He seemed utterly impervious to hunger, thirst, pain, and fatigue. Impervious, too, to ordinary human emotions. Maybe, Hawkes mused, he'd felt nothing when his wife ran away with Gilmartin. Maybe that was why he didn't talk about it—because he could not care less.

Hawkes decided he'd never before met a man like John Bonham. And he fervently hoped never to meet another.

As they checked their horses about a hundred yards from the Lee house, Hawkes surveyed his surroundings. To the right of the house stood a barn and corral. To the left, a stone smokehouse or springhouse and a privy. A few cottonwoods were scattered about the property. Two hundred yards beyond the house, more trees, stripped of all their foliage by winter's cruel embrace, marked the course of a rocky creek. An irrigation ditch connected the stream to a field off to the right, beyond the barn. And beyond the creek stood a cluster of houses, the town of Harmony, just awakening to a new day, with ribbons of smoke rising from some chimneys, rising into a low gray sky that, for the moment at least, had ceased dispensing snow.

Bonham drew his Colt revolving rifle from its saddle scabbard. Like Hawkes and Loud Talker, he saw movement at one of the front windows of the Lee house.

"We should give them a chance to surrender," said Hawkes.

Bonham didn't even look at him. "Why bother? They're going to put up a fight."

"I wish I had known this was going to happen today," said Loud Talker morosely. "I would have put on some war paint. White people do not understand why Indians do that kind of thing. But it is important to us. War paint is a prayer to the Great Spirit for protection and success in battle. I would get the Great

Spirit's attention if I had time to put on the war paint. Now, though, He will not have time to prepare a home for me in the Other Side Land. If I die today, there will be no one waiting to greet me."

"You're not going to die today," said Hawkes. "No one has to die here. I'm going to try to talk to them."

"You're the one's going to get killed," remarked Bonham.

Hawkes kicked his horse into a slow walk. He kept the Plains rifle in its sheath, tied to the saddle, wanting to make it obvious to the men in the house that he had come to palaver, not shoot. He was confident that the fugitives would give themselves up without a struggle, if they were convinced that John Bonham wouldn't execute them on the spot.

But he was wrong.

The front door flew open, someone stuck a pistol out, and fired at him when he was about thirty yards away from the house.

His horse staggered, and Hawkes kicked his feet out of the stirrups and jumped clear as the animal went down. The pistol spoke again, and again, and he heard the whine of bullets too close for comfort. The only available cover was the downed horse, so Hawkes dove behind it. Another bullet struck the animal, and it made a grunting noise, its legs thrashing. Hawkes didn't hesitate. He drew his knife and cut the animal's throat, ending its misery. Then he slipped the Plains rifle out of its sheath, thanking Lady Luck for looking out for him—his mount had fallen on its left side and not the right.

Behind him, Bonham and Loud Talker were charging forward. The holy killer rode with reins in teeth, firing the Colt rifle from his shoulder as fast as he could, and the Osage uttered a piercing war whoop that surprised the hell out of Hawkes. Several guns were being fired from Lee's house now, and the hot lead being exchanged burned the air overhead. He laid the rifle across the dead horse and took steady aim at one of the windows. When he saw the barrel of a pistol protrude, he squeezed the trigger. The gun disappeared. Hawkes fished cartridge and percussion cap out of his shot pouch. By this time Loud Talker had reached him, dismounting on the run. But John Bonham galloped right past, straight into the hail of lead being thrown at him, and Hawkes thought it must be one of those Mormon miracles that he wasn't hit. The holy killer urged his horse right up onto Lee's porch and fired a round through the partially open door at point-blank range. The rifle empty, he cast it aside and drew his pistol, swinging out of the saddle and going straight into the house.

"Christ," muttered Hawkes. "Get around back," he told Loud Talker, and as the Osage broke for the corner of the house in a crouching run, Hawkes fired into one of the windows again to cover him, then got up and went after Bonham, reloading as he ran.

The first thing he saw when he went through the door was a man whose description, provided to him by Bonham, fit that of Major Rigby. Hale's second in command was sprawled on the floor behind the door, shot through the chest, eyes filled with surprise and staring lifelessly at the ceiling. The second thing he noticed was a man down on one knee over by the window, blood staining a sleeve of his coat and dripping from his fingertips. He fit Bonham's description of the Indian agent, Haldman, and he was taking aim at the Danite, whose back was turned to him. Hawkes didn't have time to find out what Bonham was so interested in on the opposite side of the room. He didn't even have time to shout a warning. He just brought the Plains rifle around and fired at hip level. The big-caliber bullet hurled Haldman backward. Haldman's pistol discharged, the slug tunneling harmlessly into the floor.

Hawkes spun around—and froze at the scene that greeted him.

Simon Parker stood in a doorway to another room, holding Patience Bonham in front of him as a human shield, a pistol to her head. They were both staring at Bonham, and the holy killer was staring back like he couldn't believe his own eyes. John Lee stood in a corner of the room, his arms around his wife.

"Surprised to see her?" Parker asked Bonham. "So was I."

"Let her go," said Bonham flatly.

"I don't think so. Drop that pistol, and step away from the door."

"So you're the one who warned these traitors."

"You've got it all wrong, John. They're not the traitors. Brigham Young is the one who betrayed our people. Now get back."

"You're not leaving here alive, Simon."

Parker's crooked smile was taut. "You won't shoot. You still love her. I've known that all along. I didn't think you had a weakness. But you do. Her."

A gunshot rang out behind the house, then another, and Hawkes realized there was one man missing, the one named Ward—but he couldn't worry about that, or Loud Talker, just now.

Parker was edging toward the door, keeping Patience between himself and Bonham—and to Gordon's surprise Bonham lowered his pistol and took a step back to give the whittling deacon some room to maneuver.

"Brother Parker."

This was John Lee. He was standing with his wife behind him, a rifle in his hands, and the gun was aimed at Parker.

"You're not going to take—"

It was all Lee had a chance to say.

Lightning quick, Parker fired. The bullet spun Lee around, and Rachel cried out in horror as she watched her husband go down.

Hawkes was closest to Parker and he acted, lunging forward, grabbing Parker's gun arm, driving him backward, away from Patience. They caromed off the door and plummeted over the threshold, sprawling across the weathered boards of the porch. Hawkes was surprised by the wiry strength in Parker's body as he strained to keep the pistol in the man's grasp pointed somewhere else besides at him. Parker was trying to get to his other pistol, and Hawkes grabbed it by the barrel as it cleared the holster. They rolled across the porch and off the edge, and Hawkes hit the ground on his back with Parker's weight coming down painfully on top of him. He felt Parker turn the second pistol, the barrel sliding across Gordon's chest, and Hawkes saw that cold smile curl a little wider because Parker knew he was going to win. . . .

Then Bonham loomed over them. His pistol came down on Parker's skull with such force that Hawkes thought he heard bone crack. The whittling deacon slumped sideways, leaving one of his pistols in Gordon's grasp and dropping the other. Half-conscious, Parker managed to get up on his hands and knees, head lolling, blood from the gaping gash above his temple staining the snow.

Bonham cocked the Colt revolver.

"Don't do it," said Hawkes, getting to his feet. "He's finished."

Bonham glanced at him. Hawkes saw more pure anguish on the holy killer's face than he had thought any person could experience and survive.

Hawkes walked by him and took the second pistol from Parker, who slumped facedown in the snow, unconscious.

Then he went around back and found Loud Talker, sitting on his heels near the body of Griffin Ward. The Osage was gazing bleakly across the snow-covered valley at the town of Harmony and the distant mountain range beyond.

"I have set loose another ghost," said Loud Talker gravely. "There are too many of them in this place already."

"You can say that again," said Hawkes.

Epilogue

They did not linger to bury the dead. John Lee said he would see to that. Of course, with Parker's bullet lodged in his shoulder, he was in no condition to dig the graves himself, but he would enlist some of his neighbors from town. As for Parker, Lee assured John Bonham that the whittling deacon would be held in Harmony until the holy killer returned for him. Hawkes was surprised that Bonham accepted Lee's assurances without reservation. He was even more surprised that the Danite didn't seem at all concerned about what John Lee would do once he was gone. Lee was, after all, one of the men he had been sent to bring in. Hawkes had a sense that Bonham was giving Lee room to run if the man wanted to, a concession that was completely out of character. As far as Hawkes knew, Bonham had never given anybody an inch his whole life. But Lee wasn't going to run.

What didn't surprise Hawkes was Bonham's determination to come with them as they set out that same day to find Dane Gilmartin. He figured the Mormon avenger wanted a reckoning with Gil. But Hawkes couldn't worry about that now. All he worried about was whether Gil was still alive.

Patience was still weak from her ordeal, yet she insisted on coming along. She could tell Hawkes roughly how far it was to that rocky knoll where she'd left Gilmartin, and she could accurately describe the immediate area, but she wasn't about to stay behind, and Hawkes didn't argue. He had never been through the country west of here, and she had, so there was a good chance that her presence would facilitate finding Gil.

They pushed hard on the fresh horses John Lee provided, and as the second day out of Harmony began to wane, they found the knoll.

The first thing that greeted them were the bodies of the two men and the horse that Gilmartin had shot out on the flats near the base of the knoll. The corpses of the men had been horribly mutilated, and a half dozen vultures were feasting on the frozen flesh of the horse, so engorged that they could not fly away as the riders approached.

When they reached the foot of the knoll Patience was first out of the saddle, but Hawkes jumped down and stopped her before she could begin her climb.

"You'd better let me go," he said.

She started to protest, and then, trembling slightly, she pointed. "I think he's right up there."

Hawkes nodded. As he and Loud Talker began their ascent, Patience turned to find Bonham standing behind her, watching her intently, his face an inscrutable mask. They had not spoken since leaving John Lee's place. But now she summoned the courage.

"I'm sorry if I caused you pain. I should never have gone away. I know that now. Actually, I knew it even then."

"You were coming back?"

She nodded. "Yes, I was."

"And he was bringing you?"

She nodded again, looking down at the ground, unable to look her husband in the eye.

It was Loud Talker who found Gilmartin. He and the dead man who lay near him were nearly buried by the snow that had accumulated among the big rocks.

Hawkes gently scooped away some of the snow, until he could be sure that the scavengers had not disturbed Gil's body. Taking a deep breath, he reached out and closed his friend's eyes.

"I think he bled to death," he said.

Loud Talker was looking around. And just as Hawkes began to dwell on how Gilmartin must have felt in those final hours, dying by inches in this lonely place, the Osage said, "It is good that a man dies alone, I think. It is easier that way. Sick animals do that. They go off to die alone. And Indians do, too, sometimes. One's death should be a private thing."

"Yeah."

"We will meet him again," said Loud Talker confidently, "in the Other Side Land."

"I'd better go tell Patience."

"We should bury him at the top of this hill," said the Indian. "Then I will go back to my people, for I have much to tell them."

"And I'll go back to mine."

Patience knew the truth long before Hawkes reached her. She could tell by the way the mountain man moved as he came down through the rocks. She thought that maybe she'd known the moment she left this place.

"I was hoping you'd give me one more chance," said John Bonham. His voice was softer than she had ever heard it. "And maybe someday you'll love me the way you loved him?"

Patience reached out, and he took her hand.